A HISTORY OF
GLITTER AND BLOOD

A HISTORY OF GLITTER AND BLOOD

HANNAH MOSKOWITZ

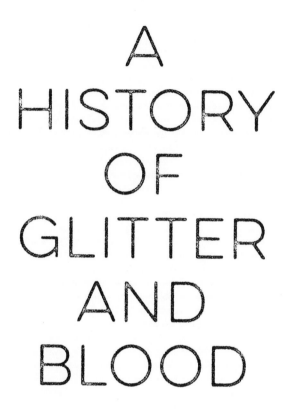

CHRONICLE BOOKS

SAN FRANCISCO

To Leah G. and John C.
Who always, always, always believed in fairies.

Library of Congress Cataloging-in-Publication Data:

Moskowitz, Hannah, author.
A History of Glitter and Blood / by Hannah Moskowitz
pages cm
Summary: Beckan, an immortal teenage fairy, and Tier, a young activist, are on opposite sides of a war, but strike up an unlikely friendship anyway.
ISBN 978-1-4521-2942-6
1. Fairies—Juvenile fiction. 2. Gnomes—Juvenile fiction. 3. Friendship—Juvenile fiction. 4. War stories. [1. Fairies—Fiction. 2. Gnomes—Fiction. 3. Friendship—Fiction. 4. War—Fiction. 5. Fantasy.] I. Title.

PZ7.M84947Sc2015
[Fic]—dc23

Manufactured in China.

MIX
Paper from responsible sources
FSC
www.fsc.org
FSC™ C101537

Design by Kelsey Premo Jones.
Typeset in Bulmer MT, Eveleth, 1820 Modern, Formosa, Rougfhouse, Times New Roman, FF Justlefthand, Bulletin Typewriter, and Quickpen.
The illustration in this book by Sam Weber was rendered digitally.
The illustrations in this book by Cathy G. Johnson were rendered in graphite.

Quotations on pages v and 200 are from "somewhere I have never travelled, gladly beyond" by E.E. Cummings.

10 9 8 7 6 5 4 3 2 1

Chronicle Books LLC
680 Second Street
San Francisco, CA 94107

Chronicle Books—we see things differently. Become part of our community at www.chroniclebooks.com/teen.

i do not know what it is about you that closes
and opens

—E.E. Cummings

1

ONCE UPON A TIME there were four fairies in the city who
hadn't been maimed.

The second youngest, the only girl, was Beckan Moloy.

She was sixteen, and there were fifteen fairy children her junior
in the city, but most of them had been in a day care a few years ago
that was attacked by a gnome custodian, and others had lost eyes
and tongues and fingers in various other incidents. Another handful
around her age lost feet when they were ten and had gone down to
the mines on a dare at a birthday party. Beckan hadn't been invited.

Missing body parts were nothing to cry about and nothing to take
too seriously. Ferrum (the oldest fairy city, the living, gasping legend)
was nine square miles of cracked cobblestone and iron scaffolding
and playgrounds and libraries and was hardly a hazardous space,
all in all, so the chunks of fairy that ended up in gnome stomachs
were reasonable collateral damage. They were conveniently located
around the waterways and farmlands, and they had gnomes to drive
their buses and sweep their streets. Sometimes some fairy limbs had
to be sacrificed to keep all of that. Call it a tax.

It was only an interesting coincidence that had Beckan make it
to this age unscathed, and to have Josha, her best friend, tall, happy,

several years older; Scrap, two months and two centimeters below her, eyes like something burned; Cricket, Scrap's cousin, music in his ears, eyes on Josha—somehow slip through as well. Somehow the four of them came to feel like their own generation, as if they were the last vestiges from an old world where things didn't eat each other. But if a world like that had ever existed, these fairies wouldn't know. These fairies had never been outside Ferrum.

So if someone could have predicted the start of the war, which to this historian's approximation was three hundred and forty days ago, it would not have been Beckan. She didn't need a job, as she lived comfortably off her father's money, and he, with only a tooth left by way of a mouth (and only an eye and an ear besides), could protest very little. She stayed home and worked on her welding and thought about skirting around the city on roller skates delivering newspapers, like Josha, or doing whoknewwhat with Scrap and his cousin, Cricket, who somehow afforded to keep one of the cottages dotting the hills on the rims of the city that otherwise housed the richest and oldest and most exhausted with city life. But for Beckan, usually, her father was her only company. The gnome king, Crate, ate most of him when she was ten. A boy gnome—one she didn't realize until much later was Tier—respectfully delivered his remains. She didn't cry. She knew her world. She made hot-glue flowers and stuck them to the lid of a jar and tossed her father inside. Like most of the fairies, all of whom came from non-fairy mothers (due to every lady-fairy's lack of uterus, a condition that sometimes left Beckan in front of her mirror for long periods, smoothing imaginary lumps on her belly), Beckan never knew her mother. Beckan was half gnome, and that was the only real burden she carried—that and her father in his jam jar, usually stuffed in the bottom of her bag.

Beckan was invincible.

Now, it's a year later—a year into the war—and Beckan stands in front of the mirror thinking about getting dolled up in heels and hair spray (and she thinks about back when she used to wear whatever she wanted).

She touches her hair and immediately wishes she hadn't, because now she can't avoid thinking about how long it has been since she's showered. But the dirtier her skin gets, the less the glitter shows, and the less the gnomes glare and complain and gnash their teeth when she goes down to the mines. She figured that trick out on her own.

She shoves her hair under a black cap. Her sleeves are long enough to cover her hands.

She knocks on Josha's door and says, "Sure you're not coming?"

He doesn't even grunt.

She says, "We'll let you know if we find him. Try to eat something?"

She is almost seventeen, and now she and Josha are the only fairies in Ferrum (in their whole world) who haven't been maimed (and she is the youngest).

Scrap and Cricket's cottage is home now, with its uneven maple floors and squeaky faucet knobs and peacefully necrotic bathroom ceiling. Even after everything, Beckan is still living in a dollhouse, where every chipped dish and mismatched mug and unread newspaper feels perfectly and cleanly placed.

The moonlight's hitting Scrap hard through the glass-paned kitchen ceiling. Beckan has to rub her eyes for a minute after stepping in before she's sure he's really there.

Her sneakers are so thin that she feels the chill of the tile.

"Scrap."

He looks up.

She stands in the doorway, her hand on the frame, her fingernails scraping up a few splinters.

She says, "You okay?"

He smiles at her and nods with just his eyes, a bit of paper still clamped between his lips, another bit torn and captured between sticky fingertips.

The rain outside sounds like someone running.

"You ready to go?"

He looks down at his manuscript. "Yeah. When I finish this page."

"Soon?"

"Wouldn't that be nice."

"What are you even writing about? Hardly much happening."

Throughout the war, Scrap has written dry diaries of the days. A few lines only, descriptions of the weather and body counts and what there was to eat.

The war has been so quiet these past few weeks, which doesn't explain why he's been writing more.

"Just transcribing," he says. "Cross-referencing. Moving things"— he gestures to a torn-out page, then to a different book—"to other things. You know."

She's confused and crosses to the table to take his coffee cup so he can tug on his boots. His right arm is gone now, from just below the elbow, and they're learning to make allowances for that, because there are things to do and pieces to find. (Not Scrap's pieces. Something more important.)

At night, in the rain, their city is more alive than it has been since the start of the war. Beckan watches glitter drip from her fingers onto the ground.

Above them, they hear whispers, giggles, a fire crackling.

They don't look up.

The immortality of fairies is a strange one; while it is true that no fairy can ever be truly without consciousness, the immortality is in no way protective. Documents of fairy lives invariably end in torture, dismemberment, or, unfortunately, consumption. It cannot be said that these fairies are truly dead, but the fate of the miniscule remaining pieces is likely neither hopeful nor noteworthy. As early as 30 years After Ferrum, there are accounts of the word 'dead' used to refer to fairy states of being, likely appropriated from the rather ill-fated NewtCreachers during the drought of 28. Famed fairies such as Sir Cornela de Frank, one of the founding fathers of Ferrum, have been shredded and lost entirely. Searches for lost fairy pieces rarely continue past a cursory look; a bit of a nose and a few specks of glitter cannot truly contribute to society.

The species of a fairy's mother seems to have no effect on his longevity, and indeed nearly all the traits of this other half are concealed or lost. This is merely an example of what makes the fairies the superior race; even the current generation, diluted at least to an eighth of pure fairy blood, remains, inexorably, fairy. It is a name that cannot be stolen, an immortality that cannot be faked.

The oldest fairy is Lima Yon, a former glassblower currently residing just outside the Ferrum limits. As she is missing large sections of her mouth and hands, her methods of communication are as limited as her significantly dwindled memory, and, as she is at most only four generations above every currently documented fairy, she offers few answers to questions of fairy evolution, creation, and history, and no definitive evidence as to whether or not fairies ever had wings.

It still seems so quiet, compared to when Ferrum was a real city (when there were more fairies than just their lost little generation, when there was life) and when Ferrum was in the heyday of war (when there was only smoke and noise). Now everything is petered out, quiet. It's not in a fairy's nature to know what it means to sit still.

But it's been a year since the city was really theirs. The fairies used to rule this place, above the ground, with their steel apartments, their manufacturing plants, their white-collar jobs in their industrial city, while the gnomes handled their dirty work in exchange for scraps of meat and the promise of a future immortal baby with a fairy boy. They played nice for their future generations. They loved the hope of having immortal children more than they loved your bones between their teeth. That was the reassurance fairy fathers whispered in gnome-nibbled fairy-children ears.

But gnomes were unpredictable and irresponsible, and a few fairies would always lose a few bits, a few fairies would sometimes lose a lot of bits, but every other fairy threw an extra bit of lamb meat (there was always extra, back then; this was never a thought) down the manholes every once in a while and in return got their trash taken and their jewels dug and their money minted and their roads paved, so who would complain? (They hadn't.)

And then the tightropers came and brought the war and the fairies were caught, quite literally, in the middle of it all. The tightroper radio announcements and fliers used to call it a *fairy liberation*.

And maybe that was why, for the first time in decades, the fairies counted maimed family members on the remains of their fingers and decided they needed to be liberated from a city they'd built and a city they loved.

Anyway, those radio announcements and those fliers had petered out too.

"Fucking freezing," Scrap mumbles.

"I'm hot."

The words *you're always hot* and *you're always cold* hang in the air between them, and Beckan scrapes her shoe against the pavement to block out the silence.

"Meet back here in an hour," she says. "Don't wait past an hour and a half."

Scrap swipes his hand under his nose. He's in all black, like she is, but he's wearing one of the lockets Beckan made, the heavy brass one he and Josha share. It's empty. "Okay."

Scrap heads north and she heads roughly west, tracing the streets of the city she used to draw from memory when she was bored. Now, without the storefronts and street signs, she's embarrassed to say (she would never admit) that she gets lost. This is where the cheap apartments were, she thinks, where the newer immigrants, fairy families from other cities or visiting races foolishly trying to stay, usually ended up settling. There was a playground here once but it was gone long before the war, turned into a tiny restaurant with vats of vegetable soup served up by sweaty fairy teenagers. Josha worked there for a time. There were fairy protesters out front the year it was built with signs petitioning to get the elders to rebuild the playground. *Do we really need more food?* their signs said.

But they've already searched the square where Cricket died (was swallowed), and there isn't a trace of him there. The gnomes cleaned up and they cleaned up well, but he has to be somewhere. They only need a bit. Something to talk to and pet and give to Josha. Cricket could be a jar fairy like her father.

(And parts of Cricket have to be out there. Every time Beckan eats now, she counts crumbs that fall onto her shirt or onto the table. There are always a few. It's impossible to eat every single bit of bread. It's impossible to eat every single bit of fairy.)

Beckan feels her own glitter as it falls to the ground and crunches beneath her feet. She's used to it. She's used to feeling the ground and the bottoms of shoes and the grout in the bathroom tiles with the bits of her that slough off and stay sentient. She never used to think about these wimpy bits of pain until Scrap's stupid books about fairy anatomy started showing up everywhere in the house, stacked up on the floor just like their swept-up glitter, and no, she does not want to know about the complex sensory capabilities of every speck of her— she spends her time welding things together and laughing at stupid jokes and trying to feel *very, very whole*—but now she thinks about losing parts, and she fucking has to find some of Cricket.

A voice above her head says, "What are you looking for, empty girl?" The tightropers are civil during the day—they need the fairies; who else is going to justify their war—but there are no rules at night.

"Bite me," Beckan says.

"So bitchy tonight, Beckan," the voice growls back, because of course they know it's her. They're just trying on gnome insults— *empty-girl, empty-girl*—for fun.

She does not look up. They can't hurt her.

They won't hurt her.

She's restless tonight. She can only dig through so many dumpsters and so many piles of rubble and dodge so many long, thin ropes hanging above her head before she has to be somewhere else. She's at the laundromat now, close to the west edge of the city, and the walls seem like her best choice.

She thinks she remembers Scrap telling her once that Ferrum used to be a fortress. Or maybe she wants to believe there's something other than racism that made a modestly sized fairy city surround itself with walls too high for anyone to climb. For as long as she's known them, the gates have been unguarded and openable, and before the war, Beckan used to bring her father to the groves outside the city and keep her distance and avert her eyes from the gnomes tilling soil and scooping animal shit to stand on her tiptoes and pluck peaches from her trees. Now the gates are rusted over and some of the latches have been blown up and broken, so it's hard for a fairy to leave. But the tightropers swing over the walls and the gnome tunnels extend underneath them and out to the farmlands, and sometimes when she is close to the wall she can hear voices on the other side, gnomes or tightropers strategizing or yelling or crying.

Like tonight, for instance, there are voices. Quiet.

She finds a thinner bit of mortar and presses her ear against it. Two voices: one high and one low. A tightroper and a gnome.

Then soft footsteps come up behind her, and she startles so hard her cheek scrapes against the stone. She bleeds thick and dirty.

"Just me," Scrap whispers.

She nods and tugs him to the wall.

They hear words—*treaty, peace, long enough.*

They hear them over and over.

Treaty, peace, long enough.

Scrap picks her up with one arm and wraps her legs around his waist and spins her in Northwest Park Square and then they're running home, breathless and incredible and *childish,* and Scrap says, "You should tell Josha. You should be the one."

"This isn't the news he's waiting up for. I'm going to tell him"— she can't say it, can't say *the war's over* because she's afraid the words will fall off her lips and get lost—"and he'll just be sitting there staring at me with that *look* until he figures out that I'm happy because of this and not because we found some of Cricket."

"You're better with him," Scrap says. He and Josha hardly talk anymore, ever since Cricket died a few weeks ago. Ever since the world got so quiet.

They slow down, panting, blocks before they reach their house (which is just against the South gate, all the way on the other edge of the city, but Ferrum is small and they like to run). She presses her nose into the back of his neck when she smiles and smells sweat and glitter on his skin. Scrap's glitter is blue and pink while hers is blue and black, but it somehow always surprises her to find a bit of Scrap's glitter that matches hers. She's always been used to looking like Josha, who is so close to her color that it would be hard for her to believe they weren't related if she hadn't spent her whole childhood filled with very unsiblinglike feelings for the boy (feelings that are, for better or worse, very, very over). Her feelings for Scrap aren't nearly as complicated. Not for a while now, anyway. He's the boy with the room next door. He's the boy she leans into when she's happy without any hesitation because she is just happy and he is just nearby. But it's still hard to reconcile, sometimes, looking like Scrap.

They hike up their hill and Beckan walks backward for a few steps, like always. From the peak of their hill, the city is a blur of gray, useless, half-bombed buildings. If there was anyone on the streets, they would be too small for her to see, but when she looks up and focuses very, very hard, she can still find a few tightropers skittering from rope to rope like spiders on a web. The tightropers are bigger than the fairies, really, but from this cabin on the hill, everything looks very small but the sky looks a little nearer.

Then she smiles and says, "Hey, Scrap. We're liberated."

He wrestles his way out of his jacket. "Liberated!"

"Look at us!"

"Hug again," he says, and wraps her up.

Then they're unlocking the front door and racing down the hall to Josha's room. They pound on it together, Scrap's one hand and

Beckan's two, until they finally stop so they can hear him answer, yell at them, tell them they can fuck off or come in. But he says nothing.

"Josha," Beckan says. "We're coming in."

Still no answer. Scrap tries the knob. Not locked.

Josha is only a lump in the bed and a bit of black hair sticking out from the top of the comforter.

"Josha, the fucking war's ending. Scrap and I heard."

She is still excited, but it feels so different now, as if it has solidified and sunk to her feet. It is so hard to be happy in front of Josha now. Hard to be anything but guilty.

"Josha," Scrap says. "Get up. Did you hear her?"

"Yeah," Josha says.

Late at night, alone in her room, desperate, she would tell herself that the end of the war would be the thing to fix Josha. Since nothing else has worked.

Since they can't find Cricket.

"Get up," Scrap says. Harshly. Cruelly. Finally.

"I'll make waffles," Beckan says. "Do you want waffles? You'll feel better."

Josha sits up a little and says, "It's the middle of the night."

"I'm making waffles. I'll waste flour. We can have so much flour now, y'know? We can have anything. Everyone's going to come back and the shops are going to open and so much fucking flour, kid."

"I'm not hungry," Josha says, but he does raise his eyes to Beckan and give her the smallest smile she can imagine. "I love when you're happy," he says.

"We're all happy. You had to do this war too," she says, even while she's realizing that maybe the problem is that it isn't Josha's war anymore. That Josha's war, somewhere along the line, became something very different.

"You should write a story about Josha and Cricket," she'd said, months ago to Scrap, while they were laughing their way through scrubbing the kitchen floor and Josha and Cricket were drunk in the living room.

Scrap threw up his hands and said, "I don't write love stories! I write epics and historical accounts and dry nonfiction!" and then grabbed a long, stale stick of bread with one hand and snapped it in half with the other, threw her the larger bit, and announced that they were now sword fighting.

Now Scrap pulls Beckan outside Josha's room, closes the door on him. "He's getting better," he says. "He is. Talking and everything."

"Yeah. Definitely. Definitely, he'll be fine."

Scrap nods.

A pause hangs between them.

Recently Beckan has developed a habit of trying to catch the moments on Scrap's face when one thought chances to another.

When he starts to chew his cheek, she interrupts. "What do we do now?"

"Waffles."

"After that."

"I . . ."

She feels triumphant for stumping him.

Lately, she tests Scrap like you'd check a limb after a fall. Looking for a break.

It's a hideous metaphor, considering the missing arm.

"I guess we wait for the cease-fire and go to work?" he says.

It feels wrong to go to work this morning, but at the same time, she doesn't know what else to do, and she has no idea if the cease-fire has really changed anything. Probably, the gnomes still need them. Who knows if the gnome women are back yet, and if they aren't, Scrap and Beckan should trick as much as they can before they are.

There's no point in a real cease-fire without even a little bit of Cricket, anyway.

And without any of the other fairies home.

And without Josha out of bed.

And without Scrap smiling like he used to.

She heads to the kitchen, but she stops halfway to watch Scrap leaning against the archway to the hall, writing in his notebook. He balances it against his half arm and the wall while he writes.

"Midnight, 5/9/546." he says. "The end."

"You'll have to find something else to write now."

Scrap's expression stays the same, but Beckan is good enough now at scanning his face to know that she has just terrified him.

A part of her likes that, and she doesn't want to know why.

Enough. She shakes her head, remembers what is important, and goes back to her room and wakes up her father to tell him the news. She smiles with all her might.

An hour later, there's cease-fire.

The thing is that (historically speaking) fairies are very, very bad at keeping histories. The thing is that they tend to give up.

In the morning, Scrap and Beckan take their usual route down to the mines. And shit, okay, a better author would insert a map right here. Remember that for the next draft.

Shit, what the fuck am I even doing? What kind of history book doesn't have a map?

Once upon a time there was a writer who couldn't write a fucking book.

I don't know what comes next. That whole chapter's going to need to get thrown out anyway. You completely forgot halfway through that you'd said it was raining at the beginning.

Was it raining?

No one's ever going to know, and it's all your fault.

Put a fucking map in the next draft.

Chapter two.

2

IN THE MORNING, Scrap and Beckan take their usual route down to the mines. The sun is so bright that her own glitter hurts her eyes. Somewhere above her head, a tightroper is playing a string instrument that doesn't sound quite familiar. It's beautiful. She hears a tightroper yell—maybe something mean, maybe something that has nothing to do with her—but it makes her smile, because *they're not in a war.*

The glass in the abandoned storefront windows on 5th Street glints as she walks by. Her reflection doesn't look as small and solid as it usually does, and the smears of dirt on the windowpane almost, at a certain angle, make it look like she has wings. This was once a jewelry store. She is allowed to feel lovely for a minute.

"Look," she tells Scrap, but he says he doesn't see it. He doesn't much like to look at his reflection. He is small as fairies go and more inky than pretty. A little scrap of a thing.

They take the same route every time. To 6th Street, toward Fremont, cross at the shattered streetlamp, take the manholes to the mines at the intersection of 7th and West Streets. There are dozens of other entrances, but they always take this one, partly because it is the central way station with the manned elevator, but really because this is where they are expected and it is best not to surprise. Last night, they felt like bandits in a dangerous wasteland. Today, with the sun up, Ferrum and its shrapnel and split buildings look as harmless as a broken dollhouse (a broken doll city).

It isn't a big city, not really, but to them it is a whole world. None of them has ever been farther out than the groves right outside the walls. They weren't allowed to visit the houses of the strange children in school who lived in the stilted houses in the orange trees. And they didn't want to. They were in love with their city and anything not their city was wrong. Anyway, those houses are bombed-down now, so it shouldn't matter anymore.

They stop at the tightroper shop, and Beckan digs around her pocket for enough money for some candy. Tightroper candy, she discovered early in the war, is phenomenal. They put sugar in their mouths and spin it like they do their ropes. Scrap gives the man behind the counter a quick nod. Beckan thinks his persistent dislike of the tightropers is very, very tiresome. They might be creepy at night, but they're nothing to really worry about. After all, they're on their side (sort of). They're on their side more than they are not (probably). More than the gnomes, at least (possibly). After all, the tightropers came to help them. (Of course.)

"Thank you," Beckan tells the tightroper soldier behind the counter, shooting him her biggest smile, and he smiles back and tells her, in his scratchy accent, that he likes her eyes.

She hums to herself as she and Scrap keep walking and she saws through the candy with her back teeth.

"C'mere," Scrap says. She stops, and he blows extra glitter off the back of her neck. His breath itches and she squirms.

He says, "I know Tier is uptight about it," and sneezes and waves the glitter away from his face.

A hastily drawn map of Ferrum's steel mills, adjacent farmlands, and access to waterways.

Not pictured: diamond supply in the mines, nice weather.
Pictured: Reasons to invade. Not pictured: Fairy liberation.

I talk about Tier too much, Beckan thinks, since Scrap and Tier have only met a few times and all Scrap really knows about Tier comes from her stories. Then again, it hardly takes much knowledge of Tier to know that he is a gnome, and gnomes hate glitter almost as much as they hate fairies.

"What used to be here?" Scrap says. He points to a bombed-out building ahead of them, down by Gramar Street (it always flooded a little here during big storms, and they would roll their eyes and call it *the river Gramar* and then hide behind this very building to watch the gnomes who lived underneath it come up shivering and half-drowned to gnash their teeth and warm up). "I can't even remember anymore."

"The bakery," she says, and the minute the words are out of her mouth it's filled with the taste of cracked crust, white chocolate cookies, gnome taffy hard as metal.

She so very rarely misses things. It always surprises her.

Scrap says, "I don't think I ever went."

"Missed out."

"My mom and dad used to bake."

Scrap's mother was a backpacker. Their babies grow between the blades of their shoulders and their skin. Most of them die in childbirth, but she survived. Making an immortal baby wasn't enough for her; she wanted to stay and raise it. She was stupid and stuck around the city, and she died mauled so badly that they buried her facedown.

No species any gnome had yet chewed was as sweet or as filling as fairy (once you scraped off that pesky glitter, anyway) but a hungry gnome is a hungry gnome, and generations of new, not-heartless gnomes who were taught it was bad manners to eat a fairy didn't extend the rule to invaders. Everyone's foreign mother either ran away or was eaten, and the fairies threw down lamb meat and closed their eyes.

***

They reach the manhole at 7th and West. Leak, the gnome elevator operator, is there, same as always, standing on the ladder beside his elevator car, halfway between the tunnels and the surface of the ground, the rope of his elevator car in his hands. He stands there every day and hauls gnomes and fairies up and down, and that is his only purpose.

He sees them and begins hauling the elevator up from the ground. "Did you guys win?" Beckan shouts to him.

Because they don't know who won.

But Leak only spits and says, "Nah."

She supposes this means the fairies won. She is still learning how wars keep score.

"Come on," Leak says. "Aren't you late?"

They clamber into the elevator and Leak stays at the manhole and lets them down, grabbing the rope, pulling, letting it slide between his fingers. They sink down into the tunnels, level after level of smooth, frozen mud and granite, all of it dimly lit into a soft brown.

"Be safe today, all right?" Scrap says. He isn't looking at her.

Beckan's throat hurts when she swallows. "Why today?"

"Always."

She nods.

The elevator stops at the third floor and Beckan lifts the cage and steps off. When he pulls the cage back into place, he presses his hand against the steel for a half a second. Smiles at her.

Just this ghost of a smile.

Then he locks the grate in place and he's gone. The elevator always seems so much faster to Beckan when she is alone and watching Scrap go away.

She starts down the tunnel. The gnome guards hiss dirty things at her, but they don't poke her or gnash their teeth today. One of them licks his lips, but he's just eating some sort of meat off a spit.

They're all eating. They have food. Burned bits of tightropers, or something the tightropers gave them, or something they'd been saving. They aren't hoarding it in preparation of the next cave-in. They're celebrating.

The war is over.

She enters the third doorway on the right, like always, and Tier grabs her and hugs her tight, so tight, and then he is laughing and spinning her around and kissing her cheeks, and Beckan has never been more relieved by a smile. This is the smile she wanted from Josha, and this is why she does not hate to be here, even though she is supposed to.

She kisses him, hard, and he remembers to slip money into the pocket of her skirt before he slides it off her. He always does.

Since it's a special day, she lets him chew on her neck a little. The risk tastes amazing to her, too.

He pays extra to fuck her twice, and she forgets for a while that they were never really on the same side.

At home, Josha traces words on his pillow, mouths words to himself, sings words in the back of his throat that he can't force into the air. *The war is over. The war is over.* This is the end of something.

He hugs the pillow to his chest and closes his eyes. He should be used to the empty house by now. Every day, he had stayed here, too afraid or too proud or too spoiled to go down to the mines with Beckan and Scrap and Cricket and strip down and suck up. He'd stayed here and cooked, or read some of the hideously boring history textbooks in the basement, or fussed over the bean sprouts he had taped to the window. He'd listened to gunfire and maybe worried a little, but the sun still shone up here at the edge of the world and he never forgot that in a few hours he would hear that laugh bubbling up the hill like it was a brook and this was a fairy tale.

He can still hear it. He squeezes his eyes into slits.

Beckan and Scrap will be home soon, and maybe he'll find something to say to them, or the strength to scrounge up something for dinner or to check the bean sprouts that are still taped to the window.

I dreamed we were exploring someplace neither of us had ever been. We came to a cliff and you told me to jump. I was too scared. You jumped off and flew away.

Someday I will.

An old note stuck to Tier's wall, from someone else.

Reconstituted.

3

WHILE TIER IS ZIPPING UP, Beckan says, "So I guess this is the last time we're going to be doing this."

Tier clears his throat but doesn't say anything.

She says, "Because Rig is coming back, yeah?"

It's still funny for her to say *yeah* with Tier. With her fairy boys, she is unapologetically casual, but as a diplomat's daughter she was raised to be polite with the gnomes, to be formal, to be so careful, and it's hard to forget that, just because of a job or a friendship or whatever this is.

She touches Tier's drawing. It's the only image she's ever seen of Rig, and it and Tier's stories have made her royalty in Beckan's mind. Rig is a capital-letter Her to Beckan, always, and she knew that even before she was good with letters.

Tier never talks much, but after a pause, he says, "The tightropers are letting the girls go tomorrow. Preparing them today. My uncle said." They've been kidnapped for months.

Whenever Tier mentions his uncle, Beckan hears a roughness in his voice that probably isn't really there. The word *uncle* points to a great glaring hole where Tier does not say the word *father*.

"Scrap came down long before the war," Tier says. "Maybe he still will." He doesn't say *maybe you still will*.

She plays with the quilt.

"Scrap goes up on the ropes sometimes, doesn't he?"

"Just for food."

"He never sees the girls?"

"No. He asked, but they wouldn't tell him where they are." She speaks faster. "He isn't friends with them, you know? He goes up to buy things, that's it. When you guys don't have stuff to sell us. You guys don't usually have stuff. You give us money and we have to buy things. We have to eat. Scrap goes. He goes now. Cricket used to."

"He won't have to go up anymore," Tier says. "Tightropers are on the streets. Setting up shop."

"There's no reason for them not to. It's space no one was using."

"You guys."

"There are three of us. You all should have come up a long time ago. You still just have those two guys up every other day."

Tier says, "We aren't really welcome."

She picks a hole in the quilt. "Because we're afraid you'll eat us."

"I don't eat you, do I?"

"No." Never. Not any of her, and she doesn't fully understand why, and every day when she gets home she sees the fear in Josha's eyes that he might have harmed her, but no. Scrap comes home with nibbles out of him sometimes, deep teeth marks in his shoulders that will never fully fade away. It's not at all the same as the day they came home without half of his arm. (There are no longer four fairies who haven't been maimed.)

"No word on Cricket?" Tier says.

She shakes her head.

"I've been poking around down here. I can't find anything of him. Or Scrap's arm. I'm not giving up, okay?"

"We don't care about the arm." Scrap must be able to feel it, but he never mentions it, doesn't want to talk about it. So they talk about Cricket. They're used to some discomfort of that, after all;

23

as children they learned very quickly not to cry when someone trampled over their glitter. Beckan's currently ignoring the crawling feeling of Tier scraping a speck of glitter off his jeans. It doesn't surprise them, anymore, what they can learn to ignore.

"How's it healing?" Tier says, without any real worry.

So she says, "He's fine."

She looks at his bookshelves, twice as tall as Tier and stacked with books so thick they scare her. At the bottom, level with her chest and below, are the books she's read and the ones Tier has decided she's ready for. She still doesn't read well.

"Anyway," she says. "Who cares if we make you feel welcome? It's not like we have much say." Beckan's inkling that the fairies might somehow be influential has been squeezed out of her. "And it was an amicable ending to the war, yeah?"

"Amicable."

"You taught me that word."

"I may have taught you too many things."

But before the war, the gnomes frequently were aboveground. They were behind the scenes, always—unloading trucks into their stores, digging ditches for their buildings, scraping muck off their streets. She learned from a young age not to look at gnomes.

And then the tightropers came, and they told the fairies that they were there to rescue them from the tyrannical rule of Crate and his hungry gnomes. The fairies in their shiny apartments found out that the rest of the world thought that, metaphorically speaking, the gnomes were on top.

What I'm saying is, before the tightropers came, no one in Ferrum had any idea that the fairies needed to be rescued.

When really, you don't stare at the gnomes because it's rude to stare at the help.

And sure, maybe especially so if the help eats you from time to time. Ferrum is a stupid, beautiful, unsimple city.

Tier helps Beckan into her jacket. "Josha still has one of my books," he says. "Thick brown one. Smear of blood on the cover. Not real blood. It's part of the picture."

"The love story."

"Yeah."

"He's not going to read it. I'll get it from him."

He says, "You can keep it longer if you want."

"Scrap won't read it. He doesn't like fiction, just history. No love stories."

"You?"

"I read it before, remember? It was the first one you gave me."

"Josha *should* read it. Maybe it will help."

She shakes her head. "He shouldn't. Leave it." He's never even met Josha.

Tier leaves it. Beckan feels the coins in her pocket and wonders who is in charge here.

Then Tier says, "What do you think you'll do? When our girls come back."

When we don't need you.

Because the traumatized girls aren't going to be immediately ready to jump into bed with them, presumably, but Beckan doesn't know exactly how that works down here, how much say the girls have.

They might still need Scrap, but they will not need her. They'll have their own girls. Fairy girls are sort of worthless, is the thing.

She says, "The city needs to be rebuilt. I've been welding some again. I could help." This seems unstupid, uncomplicated.

"You could fix some of our tunnels," Tier says. "If you wanted to keep working for us."

She doesn't say anything.

"You've been working for us for a year," he says.

"I've been working for *you*, and I didn't exactly do it out of choice, anyway. If the tightropers had been looking for prostitutes, maybe things would have been different."

"You'd rather have worked for them?"

They've had this conversation a hundred times. "You eat us," she says.

She's said it a hundred times.

It's not that simple, she'd like for Tier to say. Just this once.

But he's just quiet. "Yeah."

"Yeah."

She stands to leave, and he kisses her. He catches her halfway out the door, asks her to wait. For some reason, this is when she realizes that he hasn't complained about the glitter the whole time she's been here. Didn't gripe that he'd have to throw out the sheets.

Didn't worry about what Rig would say when she came home and found glitter all over his floor.

But then he says, "About Rig," and takes a deep breath. "I've changed," he says, very slowly, like he thinks he's speaking a language Beckan won't understand.

She thinks for one terrible moment that he is about to say that he is in love with her.

And then she wonders if that really would be so terrible.

And she thinks about the money in her skirt.

And about how small Scrap's hands are.

When was it that she realized that Scrap had the smallest hands of anyone she's ever seen? There was a moment. She feels the moment, somewhere in the nape of her neck, gnawing on her brain, begging to be remembered.

It was a moment.

But she doesn't know when it was.

Tier says, "I'm not the same," and snaps her back. "I can't . . . how could I even be the same after this? I don't even know how it looked up there."

She nods a little. She tries to pretend a bit of her mind isn't still somewhere else.

"What if I don't know what to say to her?" he says.

"There isn't anything you can say. So say anything."

"I'll say something wrong."

"What if you don't?"

"Will you help me?" he says.

"What?"

"Just help me think of some things to say. How to connect to her. You know what I've been through. You were here. And you're, you know. A girl."

A girl.

He called her a girl.

Not an empty-girl. Not a worthless, infertile, waste of space barren no baby little empty-girl.

Just a girl.

And then he says, "You owe me, you know?"

"What?"

"For looking for Cricket."

Beckan breathes out. "I'm so fucking sick of looking for Cricket. We're not finding anything. How many nights do I have to comb through sidewalk cracks and not find anything?"

"Please?"

"Yeah, I'll help you. But I'm going now." She always tells him. She is always the one to make the decision. To put one foot back into the hall.

Tier's picture of Rig (a re-creation. Sorry.)

"Thanks for coming," Tier says, and he shrugs instead of saying goodbye. As soon as she steps into the hallway, she hears Tier brush glitter off his sheets and blow out the candles he lit for her.

She goes home without waiting for Scrap. Josha is puttering around the kitchen, opening and closing cupboards, boiling water.

At least he's out of bed. "You doing all right?" she says.

He gives her a smile that doesn't part his lips. "Fine. Need tea?"

"I'm fine. It's warm out."

"You're always hot."

You're always cold. It's her default response to both her fairy boys, nowadays.

But the truth is, Josha isn't. There is nothing cold and will never be anything cold about Josha. The entire world can try to trap him and soak him and freeze him solid, and he will stand in the kitchen burning like a lantern.

His eyes rush up and down her body, checking for wounds. She casually covers the bite on her neck and doesn't think he notices.

"Good," he says, and turns back to his cup. As if he needs his full attention, needs the strength of everything in him, to lift that cup and take a sip.

She comes up behind him and holds him for a while. Josha is the simplest part of her world, and has been for so long. He loves her and she loves him back, and it has been a long time since she realized she would never sleep with him, and even longer since she stopped wanting to, and now they are like two very different, very unequal halves of what might have been one very amazing fairy. Maybe even a pretty one.

She clears her throat. "Do you think Scrap would hate me forever if I stole his red notebook?"

"The war chronicle? *Here's what blew up today?*"

"Yeah."

He shrugs. "There's nothing secret in there. He's all about that blue notebook lately anyway. It's in the basement, I think. On the shelf snuggled up with the real books."

She kisses his cheek before she scampers downstairs. He gives her the same smile.

In the basement, she trails her fingers over the spines of Scrap's encyclopedias and history books. The novels they've borrowed from Tier are collapsed on top of themselves on the bottom shelf, because even now that Scrap reads them in guilty binges he later denies (because he is a pretentious fuck), he won't put them up with his *real books*, his *nonfiction* books. She mumbles to herself, maybe just reading the titles, probably something about him being a pretentious fuck.

1/10/546. Snow. Tightroper arm discovered on 11th Street.

1/11/546. More snow.

1/12/546. No longer snowing. Drugged at work.

1/13/546. Snow.

1/14/546. Rain.

Scrap's red notebook, reconstituted

She finds his red notebook and flicks it open. Each day is marked with its date, and each has a few bland sentences spelling out the events of the day. There are no feelings, no opinions. No fictions.

Beckan has seen this notebook a hundred times, and she knows she was stupid to hope that there might be something she hadn't seen. Something secret in here. Something to remind her of his small hands.

But this will do. She brings the notebook up to her room. She begins to read. She waits for something.

There is no narrative.

There is nothing about Scrap.

There is nothing about her.

There is dry, pointless, objective, timeless history. The kind fairies never thought they could write. Maybe she should be impressed that someone finally took the time to sit in one spot, to write, to record. Maybe this should enthrall her.

She falls asleep reading.

In the middle of the night, she wakes up and the notebook is gone. She finds Scrap in the kitchen, bent over it, writing in a blue book, folding over corners in a textbook, a pretentious fucking candle lighting his work. She is embarrassed and angry.

"I can't look at it?" she says.

"I need it right now. Reference." He glances at the red notebook, moves his pen back to the blue, writes faster. He looks up at her face like he doesn't recognize her.

She says, "Scrap, what the fuck."

She can hear Josha somewhere behind her in the hallway, pacing.

"You can have it back later," Scrap says.

Something is very wrong about the way she feels, and about Scrap, and about everything, so she shakes her head a little and leaves before it can scare her. She goes back to her room and digs under her bed until she finds Tier's book of poetry, the one with the very long poems, the very romantic ones, and she brings it out to the kitchen and throws it on the table. Scrap flinches.

"Read something not as fucking boring," she says. She doesn't know why she's so angry.

Look at me, she thinks.

Scrap picks it up.

"I have to write mine," he says.

"Your new book's probably boring too. Read this. Maybe you'll learn something," she says, and she leaves. *You're always cold* echoes in her head. He is always so cold, in the hot kitchen with his cold histories.

4

(Throw away all of that. Start the book here.)

THE DAY THE TIGHTROPERS came, Beckan and Josha, who was avoiding his lonely high-rise apartment in center city and drinking Beckan's coffee, watched from the window of her father's apartment as the tightropers spit their ropes out and slung them across the tops of their buildings, creating lines and knots and nets up in the sky. They talked about how rude it was for a new race to come by without any notice.

"I wonder how they taste," Beckan said, which was a little cruel of her. But all she could do when a new race came by was watch the fairy men sleep with them and the gnomes lick their teeth, and make a friend who would, one way or another, be gone in a few months. The last ones were the pixies, years ago, and they left Ferrum three fairy babies. By now, one of those babies was destroyed and lost (dead) and the other two were missing three limbs between them.

She took her father off the counter and held his jar to the window so he could see the threads rapidly expanding across the sky.

Had he lips and a tongue left, she knew he would have clucked the predictable notes about foreigners and peculiar habits and that this had never happened back when he had a body.

"I know about these guys," she said. "They spit up ropes. Scrap writes about them. They were here a few hundred years ago. They die young."

"When have you been talking to Scrap?"

"Just sometimes."

Josha didn't know Scrap well, but he resented him for knowing Beckan first and judged him for having a short name that sounded suspiciously gnome-like (but there was never anything else to call a little dark bit of a thing, with rumpled hair and a lopsided smile). Josha was a boy full of prejudices. It was something Beckan loved. She needed someone to weigh her down, and she needed tall, dashing Josha to have a very obvious flaw.

"So who are they?" Josha said.

"They're tightropers," Beckan said. "They . . ." She let her voice die out while she watched the tightropers haul armfuls of explosives over their ropes, from one rooftop to another. To hers. "They build tightropes," she said, quietly.

"So," Josha said, later that same morning, his feet up on the railing of Beckan's balcony, his ass on the porch swing. They were watching the tightropers continue to string their lines and the fairies on the streets rushing around with their heads covered, like they were expecting rain. "So. Scrap?"

"He's teaching me to read." She could read, a little, but her letters were always jumbled and backward and she gave up at a young age. Her father complained about it sometimes, but fairies were lax about school. Beckan could learn whenever.

She had plenty of time.

A photograph of Beckan and her father, taken by Josha (thumb visible on the bottom left corner), 3/13/545. Before.

"How charitable," Josha said.

"Not really. He wants someone to read his stupid stories. So boring. All of them true. He's desperate for a reader."

"Cricket won't read them?"

"You know Cricket?"

"I know of him," Josha said. "Don't they live together?"

"Yeah. I barely see him, though." He was usually walking from room to room, most of the time humming. Scrap ordered him around.

Josha said, "So you're really not crazy about him."

"Scrap?"

"Either."

"I told you."

"Since you don't know his family or anything. Don't know anything about him." He played with her welding torch and gave her a sloppy grin. "I mean, not like how you know me."

She watched the tightropers instead of responding. Josha said "Cricket" quietly to himself a few times. "Cricket must be a genius if he avoids Scrap's stories," he mused.

"A coldhearted genius."

"A genius is a genius. I don't need another heart, anyway. My own is a bitch and a half."

Then the first bombs went off, and they sprang toward each other as if they had previously been stretched apart. Beckan felt some heat on her cheek, like the city was breathing on her, but she couldn't see where the bomb fell, and she couldn't help but think that she expected them to be a little louder. That she had expected to feel a little more.

The day after that first bomb blast (of which there ended up being not so many; it was a quiet war, a starved war), Beckan took her father grocery shopping and found all the stores had been closed down in honor of a bomb that killed no one (no fairies, at least), nor was it meant to. The fairy women and their ancient missing limbs fretted and judged Beckan for her clothes, and Beckan was quickly bored and moved on.

The truth is that fairies are not very attached to the idea of possessions.

In what feels like an unkind bit of irony, given the lack of wings, fairies have a reputation for *flightiness*, for hastiness, for lack of compassion. It's the explanation given for the large number of fairy cities with relatively low populations and no great amount of space in between. Fairies grow old, they grow bored, they leave and settle somewhere new and unnecessary. There is no real reason not to. They have plenty of time.

Ferrum is the oldest and the darkest and it serves as a token, a totem; here is proof that we are not heartless, here is proof that we are not without history, here is our iron city with its cobblestone streets and crackly electricity and a few more crumpled pages of literature than the other cities.

The fairies far away, they likely never think of Ferrum as anything other than a symbol.

They likely never think of it as someone's home.

Before the war, it was the city's secret: that it was loved, that it was beautiful, that it was their entire world and they were never unhappy with that. They liked that they knew who would eat them. They liked that no one outside the city would understand the balance they kept with the gnomes. There was grumbling, there was every once in a while a death of a baby on either side, but most of all there was this odd, buzzing type of harmony that no one who was flighty would ever understand.

It made sense.

Until, well.

A RENAISSANCE PROJECT

Beginning at Amity Park, 10AM Monday

Peace in Ferrum! Let's celebrate!
All help appreciated, all races welcome!
Help usher in a new, free city!

All supplies will be provided.

One flier, representative of many posted throughout
the city starting four days post-cease-fire,
5/10/546 (original)

Beckan goes to help with the renaissance project, of course, and she's been painting for ten minutes when an arm, blue and pink and sparkly and scrawny, appears in her field of vision and dabs a spot of paint onto her nose. She turns around, and Scrap smiles at her.

She can't believe he's here, but more so she can't believe how happy she is to see him. "You came."

"Couldn't miss this!"

"Oh, yeah. Painting. It's really riveting stuff, lemme tell ya."

"We should *actually* rivet something. Would be a lot more interesting." He makes stripes under his eyes and reaches out and drags the back of his hand across the damp surface of the hot-air balloon in the mural she's been working on. Paint gets in his glitter and his glitter gets in the paint.

"That's a fairy balloon," he tells the tightroper women, who are watching in disgust. Even if they came for the fairies, they did not come for the glitter.

They work together for a while, laughing and pouring paint in each other's hair. Beckan considers apologizing for their little fight last night but doesn't, because she doesn't think it will help, and because right now, getting along isn't fake. They aren't ignoring anything. This is just one of their sides. Beckan and Scrap are a lot of things, but they are never not Beckan and Scrap.

Scrap stabilizes himself on the wall with his half arm to reach a spot above his head, but very quickly it starts to shake.

"Does it hurt?" Beckan says. Quietly.

If he were a romantic hero, he would look at her immediately with a dashing smile and say, "No, of course not," in a way that subtly reveals that it does hurt, very much, in fact, but he is strong and brave and rugged.

"Yeah," he says. Straightforward. Calm. He takes the arm off the wall and tugs it back inside his sleeve. "It's ugly, too."

"It's honestly really hideous."

She probably shouldn't have said that. (Did she say that?)

They smile at each other.

Their conversations are all wrong.

What the fuck is going on? The paper's crumpling up and I can keep it straight and more later. Okay. I shouldn't even be out of bed. I need to remember to take this part out. This is ridiculous. Fuck fuck fuck what's wrong with me. I should be doing this in order. This is bad. I think. I think this is bad. Okay, I'm putting this down. More later. (Did that last bit really happen? Did she really smile?) More later.

Sorry about that.

After she saw the bomb site, that second day of the war, she went to Scrap's manhole to meet him. His head slowly came into view as he hauled himself up in the gnomes' elevator. He nodded to the gnome helping him pull (Leak, but she didn't know his name then) and gave his usual tired smile to Beckan before he climbed up into the sunlight. Beckan offered her hand, which he took without pausing.

"No groceries today," she said.

"Lazy?"

"Bomb."

"Oh. Right."

Leak was still there, his orange skin already starting to sweat in the sun. "Good to see you," he said to Beckan. His voice was slimy against the top of his mouth. She didn't know much about gnomes, then, but she knew that they didn't have to talk that way.

She looked at the gnome's teeth, as big and sharp as cleavers, and at Scrap's leg easily within his reach. But she was the one who took a step back.

Scrap chose to go down there, after all. And she didn't ask why. The truth, she realized later, wasn't that she was afraid of what she would find out, but just that she hadn't really cared, and that was a realization that would make it hard for her to sleep sometimes.

They had been friends, once. They played together as children, but never as enthusiastically as she and Josha did a few years later. He went on for more school and she didn't, and neither of them judged the other or thought much of each other or wondered or worried. Scrap kissed a few of the fairy girls with missing feet and Beckan practiced her welding. They had plenty of time.

But now Beckan wanted to read and her neighbor who agreed to help threw up her hands after a few lessons and told her that she should probably ask Scrap, and she remembered the tiny fairy boy in the tiny house all of its hundreds and hundreds of steps away, and she rang his doorbell one day and that was that.

"Ready to go?" she said. She tried not to look at the gnome. The gnome was looking at her.

Scrap rubbed his nose and sneezed at his glitter. Beckan tried not to laugh, but Scrap didn't. His smile was the same as when he was a child. "I'm exhausted," he said. "Clearly."

"Really clearly."

Another smile from him, this one a little sad, and a word, not for the first time, flashed in Beckan's head: disarmed. She once told Josha that when she was around Scrap, she felt disarmed, both in the sense of being overwhelmed and of surrendering shields and weapons.

This, not the bomb site, was where the war first affected Beckan. She was a little fairy who could barely read and the war wormed its way into her words. (This is what history is, Becks.)

"I'll see you tomorrow," Scrap told the gnome.

His grin stretched across his face. "Yeah, have fun off with your chubby little empty."

She stared at him.

"Whoa," Scrap said. "Whoa, hey." He took Beckan's arm and tugged her back. Away. The gnome couldn't grab her and eat her and she couldn't grab him and strangle him.

The first one to ever call Beckan an empty was a fairy boy on the playground by the mall, the one with the two-story slide and the drained swimming pool filled with foam blocks. She didn't know what the word meant, but the tone of his voice made her hit him with her jump rope. Josha finally told her what it meant, after her father refused. He'd learned the slur from his sister, before she left to go live somewhere without gnome girls and traveling girls and lost girls and wandering girls and nymph girls, all of them drifting through the city with their full, kicking bellies.

Beckan wanted to kick the gnome in his horrible teeth.

But she'd been trained out of that harder than she'd been trained to hate the name.

She'd seen this gnome a hundred times. They'd never talked. He'd never called her that.

The war was in their words.

"Get out of here," Scrap said to Leak.

Leak gave him a long look and stepped back into the elevator, and Beckan heard the echoes of his laugh for a long time.

She walked with her arms crossed over her chest. When they got to 7th and Fremont, she crossed the street over the tram tracks and hurried down the sidewalk. A pretty fairy lady she didn't know bumped shoulders with her and didn't pause to apologize.

Beckan breathed out. She dragged her hand over the plate-glass window of a jewelry store she passed and felt a little calmer.

Gradually, she heard Scrap's long strides catch up with her. She knew he would eventually.

"Becks. You okay?"

She shrugged.

"I don't know why you let them bother you."

"Yeah, because the problem is that I'm *letting* them insult me. This is *my* fault. You're so *smart*."

He lowered his voice. "Are you crying?"

"Screw you."

"Beckan."

"No. It's fine." She wiped her cheeks off, hard. "Don't let it bother you or anything."

"I would have beaten him up, but I like my work. And my limbs."

"I don't need you to beat up anyone for me. I can beat up my own assholes."

She felt him smile more than she saw it. "That too," he said.

They crossed the bridge over the bay, trams swerving past them on their tracks, and hiked up the hill until the apartment buildings and the offices faded out and they reached the rim of houses at the top of the hills. The stone walls stretched behind Scrap's house like they were trying to hug the cottages in, make them really a part of the city.

"No tightropes up here yet," Beckan said. She wasn't crying anymore.

"Yeah," Scrap said. "Everyone always forgets we're here."

Beckan eventually pauses in her painting long enough to send Scrap home. She blames it all on the half arm, and that makes him agree, but truly it shakes her seeing him out of the house when he's still weak. Most days he seems, physically, almost like his old self, and she can accept him as a little frailer than he should be when they were only at home, but here, out in the open, whenever he's tired it's so clear that if for whatever reason he needed to fight, he could only make one fist.

She's worried about him. Scrap, with all his darkness and messed-up hair, sometimes calls their little family his pack. Beckan has learned a lot about wolves now from Scrap's books—he loves wolves—and she knows that Scrap is the smallest and the quietest but easily their alpha wolf, with his paws in everything: the dirty dishes in the sink, Josha's hair after a nightmare, the clogged drain in the bathroom, the switchblades, the books. Beckan feels warm and comfortable in her place in the pack, but that doesn't stop her from looking at her wounded alpha and worrying about him now that he's missing a paw.

He's also looking a little sick.

She keeps painting, and the streets flood and fill with more bodies and paintbrushes and voices as tightroper after tightroper drops to the ground. It's still mostly tightroper soldiers in the city with their husbands or wives and small kids. Maybe now their civilians are going to come. She tries to figure out whether or not that would be okay with her and comes up with nothing.

She wonders what it's like up in the tightropes.

She tilts her head back and squints to see the threads more clearly, and at that moment a body drops from a rope and hangs right in front of her, his face suspended inches away. She smells tightroper bread on his breath and cannot look away from his purple, flat, unsparkly eyes.

The tightroper boy smiles like he knows a secret, a nice secret, that she doesn't, and that he might tell her if she smiles back in just the right way, and he says, "Curious?"

Beckan tries a few smiles but doesn't feel like she finds the right one.

"Is it nice?" she says eventually. "Being so high up?"

A rough sketch of the anatomical differences between (a) fairies, (b) gnomes, (c) tightropers, and (d) wolves.

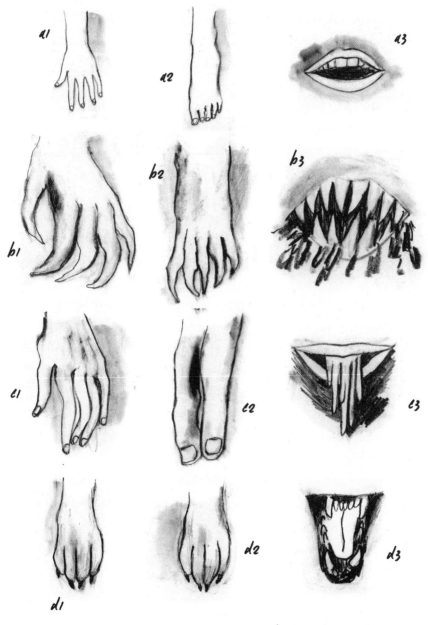

(original, by the author)

"You'd like it," he says, and he zooms back up his rope and into the netting, so fast that he's halfway back to their web before she realizes that that didn't really answer her question.

And that she doesn't really know what just happened.

But her mind clicks, once, and she decides that she's going to find out his name and get him to take her up. Just to *do* something.

It is so, so exhausting, her whole life being the pack.

No wonder Scrap has screwed up so often. (What kind of alpha loses one of his dogs?)

The day after the first bomb, when Scrap still had two arms and Beckan's reading was still mostly sounding-out, he gave her a lesson at his kitchen table. She was learning quite quickly; a few weeks before she'd fluently read her first sentence, one Scrap had once jotted down at the bottom of an old soup recipe: *A long time ago, maybe fairies did have wings.*

Since then she had worked her way through a few of Scrap's stories, but that day after the bomb was the first time she'd read one of Scrap's stories and actually liked it. That had less to do with her taste and more with the fact that most of Scrap's stories were not very good. Dry histories.

"This one is romantic," she'd said, when it was over, and she rested her head on her arm and stretched her fingers out on the kitchen table.

Scrap was lingering by the refrigerator. "That wasn't exactly what I was going for. It's supposed to be . . . realistic." Every few words, he slid his eyes over to the wobbling pile of dishes in the sink.

"I don't like realistic. Just do the dishes if they're bothering you so much."

"It's a waste."

"How?"

"You thought it was romantic?"

"They're in love, aren't they? It's a story and all these terrible things are happening and they're in love the whole time. Why don't you do your dishes?"

"Waste of time."

"They're gross."

"I'll do them later."

Scrap's cousin, rooting through the fridge, said, "He does them in his sleep."

"What?"

Scrap said, "Cricket, bite me a little, why don't you."

Even though Beckan was only a tooth, an eye, and an ear away from living alone, Scrap and Cricket's parentless house felt lawless to her in a way hers never did. Maybe that one eye was enough to make her feel watched—though she had to admit that more and more often, she was leaving her father tucked away in corners or stuffed, as he was now, at the bottom of her tote bag—or maybe it was that her father's apartment could somehow never feel small and bright and reckless in the way of this cottage, where every corner felt filled with something easy and significant, like family.

She could never fill her sink with dishes the way Scrap and Cricket could. There weren't enough dishes in the house. There wasn't enough food in her fridge.

"There's no food at my house," she realized. "I couldn't get groceries."

"Stay here," Cricket said. "I made pasta."

Scrap said, "We cook together. But he does dinner usually. Cricket makes a very good sidekick."

Cricket said, "Too bad you're a shitty superhero. Beckan. Want to be my superhero?"

"I don't know what that is."

Scrap ran his hand over his head. "Like in a book."

"Yes," she said, and she wrote her name and over and over again in the top margin of Scrap's notebook. "Yes."

Scrap took the book away and disappeared to hide it, and Beckan perched on the counter while Cricket warmed up pasta. He sang, to himself, but not as if he cared if she heard. His voice was deep and thick.

"A gnome called me an empty today," she said. She didn't know why.

Cricket set the bowl down.

He said, "How do you feel?"

She watched her feet where they swung back and forth and scraped an itchy bit of glitter off her thigh. "I feel like I shouldn't give a shit."

"I can't have a baby either, you know?" Cricket said, with a smile that Beckan appreciated but didn't quite respect. At least Cricket could give someone else a baby. At least Cricket could make pasta. And sing. All she could do was melt things and dream about flying.

She knew that having a baby was no way to measure success. She knew that it wouldn't make her a more fulfilled person and that lying awake wanting one makes her a useless, stupid cliché.

She also knew that she just wanted a fucking baby, okay?

She lived with that.

She said, "I feel like I don't know what a good goal is. What I should be doing with my life."

"Write a book like Scrap."

"I don't even know what a real book is like."

He grinned. "Then write something stupid and romantic like he does."

"Screw you!" Scrap called from the living room, and Cricket laughed and laughed.

"He's trying to write a serious book," Cricket said. "But he keeps writing love stories. Bad ones. I won't read them. I don't even think he'd let me. He writes them creepily in secret. But they're bad. I can just tell."

"Bad?"

"Substanceless."

"He's never been in love," she guessed.

"Probably not. Have you?"

She nodded. She still was, because Josha was her world then.

"Scrap thinks it must be horrible," he said. "You can tell from the stories."

"It is."

"I think it sounds nice."

"No." A thought edged its way out of her mouth. "You're substanceless, a little, I think."

And he was, but he smiled, and she decided she forgave him. That afternoon, the three of them ate pasta and the gnomes officially declared war.

And now Beckan has fixed the city enough for one day, she still smells like paint, her thoughts are still on the tightroper boy, but she's riding the mines down to work and she remembers that day and that story and that sink full of dishes and that Scrap with his arms and that *story*.

That fucking day after the bomb, it was a love story.

And now he's back to writing lists of dates. When before all of this, before he'd ever felt anything in his whole little life, he'd once written a love story.

She would grab Scrap and shake him, if touching in the elevator weren't silently but very strictly forbidden nowadays. (More on that later.)

It was a love story.

Just a little one.

5

"JUST . . . HERE." Beckan picks up Tier's hands and holds them on the sides of her neck. "Like you're so happy you could just choke me. Like you can't even help it. Except don't actually choke me, come on." She adjusts his fingers. "Here, one thumb up on my chin, casually, like my face is so pretty you want to touch it but you're afraid to. Don't laugh." He doesn't, but there isn't anything complimentary about his seriousness; his heart just isn't in it.

She says, "Now you say, *I can't believe it's you.*"

"That doesn't make sense."

"You're so surprised to see her that you say things that don't make sense."

"We're planning it out in advance, Beckan. We have time to figure out something that makes sense."

"*I've dreamed about this every night.*"

"All right, something that isn't horrible."

She sits on the bed. "I'm thinking."

They are quiet for a long time. Beckan hears something dripping. It sounds deep and distant.

"Maybe I should just say her name," Tier says, after a while.

"Rig?"

"Not like that. Soft. Full of meaning and nuance and . . . all of that. *Rig.*"

"*Rig.*"

"*Rig.*"

"*Riiiiig.*"

Tier nods. "Yes."

"No, that's horrible."

"It's impossible. This. This is impossible."

"You'll see her and it'll all come back. You'll know exactly what to say as soon as she walks through the door. Any minute now."

"I will?"

"It'll be just like in the book."

"Which one?"

"With the girl who couldn't speak while he was gone. Thought she would die with no voice. And then he came back."

"Don't fall for that, Beckan, okay? You cannot just use the things those books tell you. Don't ever stop talking because of a boy. A boy who makes you talk less is not the kind of boy you want anything to do with."

"Lectures from a boy with a prostitute."

"Yeah."

"You learned that from a book too, didn't you?"

"I live in a hole. Where else do I learn anything."

"The girl in the book, she didn't do it on purpose."

"That is my point exactly. That is my point times a hundred."

"You should say something about her boobs."

He ignores her, which she recognizes as probably his best option. "She grew up down the hall. My father betrothed us when we were groundgrubbers. Children," he clarifies.

"I figured that out from context." Scrap taught her that. Context.

"We read the same books and played the same games, Rig and I. We were the same creature. And now . . ." He sighs. "The problem is, the only honest thing I could say to her is, 'Hi, how was your war?' "

"Yeah, don't say that."

"There you have the problem."

"It's just one thing. This war is the only thing you haven't had in common. One thing."

"I don't know how to get past this."

"Because you've never had to get past anything before. You'll deal. She was up there, you were down here, bit by bit you'll tell your stories to each other and you'll forget the rest."

"I don't know what it was like up there." He sits next to her. "What she knew about the war. If she could hear anything. Or see us. If they hurt her."

"You'll know soon."

"She won't understand," he says, softly. "What it was like to be on the ground for this."

You were underground, she doesn't say. You barely ever come up. You felt the explosions and you lived with the cave-ins and maybe you were hungry, but you never had to see anything.

You didn't see carnage and rotting organs.

You just waited for someone to feed them to you.

He says, "The problem is, with regards to the war, I understand you and you understand me, and everything else in the world points toward Rig."

"I don't want you," she says. Her voice doesn't sound like hers. "I point toward Rig, too."

"Except—"

"We had different wars too," she says. Hard. "No one did it like me and Scrap and Josha and Cricket."

Tier studies himself in the mirror, then frowns, pulls his sleeve over his hand, and scrubs at the glass. "When your fairies come back, the war will be common fairy experience. Scrap can let them read that war he wrote, and then the elders will take the stories and insert their own little anecdotes. Lie about it so it seems real. Run away and find new fairy cities and tell them their valiant war stories."

"Don't."

"Don't what?"

"Act like all fairies run away, like it's some given. Because I'm pretty sure there's a fairy girl sitting on your bed right now."

"Yeah."

"Why do you always bring him up?" she says.

"Who?"

"Scrap."

Tier doesn't say anything.

"The jealous thing?" she says. "Do you pay extra for that, or what?"

"Noted." He bites off the word.

And she looks down. "Rig will be here any minute." She stands up. "Grab my face again and then I'll go."

He grabs her face again, and they keep working until the gnomes announce the women coming back, and then she slips out, arms around herself, and does not look for the one face she would recognize. She reminds herself, over and over again, that Rig will not recognize her, but she can't quite believe it.

Josha's favorite memory isn't very old at all. Four months ago, in the dead of winter, bombs rolling in the mines like thunder, they sat in the kitchen with flashlights and cups of hot water and laughed themselves through card games. Cricket found a bit of bug-infested flour under the sink, and they drowned the bugs and filled napkins with wet flour and threw them at each other. They made Beckan

An important thing to consider when crafting a work of fiction is the question of point of view! Who is telling your story? From whose eyes is the reader expected to experience the novel's events? The point of view will not only determine what information the reader is privy to (the point of view character cannot, of course, consciously relay anything to the reader that he himself does not know) but will also affect the way the reader experiences all of the characters in the story! A character might be quite sympathetic from one point of view while not so much from another! By far the most important thing to keep in mind is consistency—be sure to avoid "head-hopping," where the narration suddenly jumps from one point of view to another! You should select the point of view that makes the most sense for the story. For beginners, we recommend using the point of view of your most sympathetic character—likely your protagonist.

Anish Lyza Kornblass, *Fiction Writing for Beginners!* (538 A.F.), p. 8 (author's note: why is this book in my library/why does she use so many exclamation points!!!!)

scream with half-dead bugs in her face, and Josha picked up Scrap and threw him in the bathtub with a bucketful of white, pasty water. They all ended up coated and disgusting with sore stomachs from laughing, and they stood on chairs in the kitchen and pounced to squish the bugs flat. Then Cricket stopped them all and crawled across the floor with a cup and a jack of spades, and he gathered up all the live bugs and put them in a jar by the window. They lit up. They were fireflies.

"Beckan."

It's the tightroper boy. He hangs upside down from an ankle, his head only inches above hers.

"Why are you walking alone this late?" he says.

She shakes her head.

He says, "Shit, you're brave. Do you know that?"

She hadn't stopped shaking her head, but she does, now, very slowly.

He gives his ankle a few tugs and clatters to the ground with a noise like a xylophone. When he straightens up, he is half as wide as Beckan but several inches taller, and she can't stop looking at his hair, black and thin and free, like something spilled on him.

"Hi, Beckan. I'm Piccolo."

"How do you know my name?" she says, which is stupid, because there are three fairies and they are celebrities. He doesn't answer, which she takes as a compliment.

She tilts her head up and tries to find where he was hanging, but she's so quickly disoriented by the hundreds of threads, all nearly translucent and thinner than her fingers.

Piccolo looks up with her.

"You've never been up there?" he says.

"I don't know how. How do you balance?"

He picks a foot up and shows it to her. Where she has five toes, he has two, dividing his foot in half with a narrow slit. "We slide," he says.

"But me."

"You hold on. And you can slide, with practice."

She takes a step back. "Thank you. I'm all right." She does not want to hold on to anyone.

"I'm not going to hurt you."

"Yes. I know, maybe you won't." She shakes her head. "But my friends are waiting for me."

"Scrap's still underground."

"Oh."

"You really want to walk home alone?"

"Is that an offer?"

He shakes his head. "I can't. I can't wander off, I'm ridiculously controlled, it's this whole thing." He chews on the inside of his cheek. "It's bullshit. Anyway. But I'll wait here with you if you want."

And all of a sudden, she trusts him. There's something about a boy who isn't allowed to wander off. There's something about a boy in a sky who has limits.

"You can wait with me," she says.

He nods. She shifts so she is next to him, and they stand together in the darkness. His way of breathing is louder than hers. She can't believe how tall he is.

"You know," she says, and he jumps. "You know," she says again, "We could see better from up there, maybe?"

"We could."

"So." It's Josha's speech pattern, the unaccompanied *so,* but it seems in place here. She feels like Josha would be better at this than she is. It's hard to be herself around new creatures. She always forgets how she is.

His face breaks into a smile, and then hers, and she looks up at the stars and at Piccolo spitting a new thread into his hand, and something inside her pounds like a drum.

He yanks a length of thread out of his throat, bites it off, and whips one end up to the sky. It sticks.

He offers his hand. She takes it so quickly that it isn't until her fingers are in his that she realizes she cannot remember the last time she did anything with this little thought.

She thinks about Tier, probably holding hands with Rig. The different secret handshakes Cricket had with Scrap and Josha. About how Scrap will sometimes grab her knuckles when they're walking home at night and something moves and they are afraid.

"Just hold on to me," Piccolo says. He moves Beckan's hands to his shoulders, slips the thread between his fingers, and zips up the line with Beckan on his back. The thread glides through his hands. Air whistles down Beckan's throat—this is so fast. Has she ever gone this fast?

She watches the building beside her, the ruined mess of a skyscraper, as row after row of windows pass and disappear beneath them. It is so much higher than when she used to go up to the roof of her apartment building, before everything, to get a good view of the sunset while she melted scrap metal into sculptures. She'd dance around while her metal cooled and feel free, as if that was something otherwise hard to feel.

"It's so blue up here," she says.

"Hmm?"

"I thought it would be black."

"Nah," he says. "Not this time of night."

"Nah?"

He laughs. "Yeah. Nah. Like no."

"I've never heard that before."

"You guys all talk really pretty."

"Thank you."

Piccolo says, "Hold on here," and they surface through a hole in the massive net. The threads feel like water on Beckan's skin, and they only cling for a fraction of a second before they let go.

"Is my glitter going to get all over. . . ?"

"You're fine. I don't mind. You're safe now. Here, sit."

She blinks the last threads out of her eyes. Around them, the net spins into a floor, with edges that curl up like the edges of a bowl. Everything under her gives and bounces and scares her. The air feels thicker here, and she smells smoke.

"Where is everyone?" she says.

"By the fire. See?"

She follows his finger across the sky, buildings and buildings away, where a low-slung hammock hosts the fire she could barely see from the ground. She can see a few tightropers laughing, but she can't hear it.

"There really aren't many of us here, you know?" he says. "Just army. And we lost a lot of guys."

"You're in the army?"

"No, my dad's a general. I'm a messboy."

"What's a messboy?"

"I clean up after them and stuff. Spills and things, after meals, latrine."

"That sounds . . ."

"Oh, it's shit. My dad volunteered me." He flashes her a smile and flops down on the web. "We don't get along. You can walk here. It's packed together. Thick."

She takes a few careful steps. Her feet feel so wide.

"Here." He stands up and ties a thread around her wrist. "Lifeline. It won't snap if you fall. You'll hang."

"Like you were."

"Mmmhmm."

His fingers are cool on her wrist. Her glitter gets all over his skin, but he doesn't brush it off.

He doesn't seem to mind.

He's good at messes, though.

"My dad's here," she says, to share something with him. She roots around her bag but doesn't find the jar. "Oh. I left him at home."

"Your dad . . . is really small?"

"He's in a jar. There's not a lot of him."

"Oh. I'm sorry."

She shakes her head. "He's alive."

"Aren't you guys always alive?"

"He communicates. Blinks. That's how we know."

"So if he couldn't blink at you, then he'd be dead?"

She doesn't like this conversation, but she knows he can't tell. "If I couldn't talk to him, he'd be dead."

"That sounds arbitrary."

"We're an arbitrary species." She knows how to be glib about this the same way she knows to ignore the feeling of her glitter falling to the ground.

"Do you like it up here?"

"I can't see anything."

He points toward the edge of the web. "Lead the way."

She does, on her hands and knees to feel a bit more secure. She sits at the edge of the web and holds a thread slung above her head for support. She checks the line tied to her wrist again and again.

"Stop worrying," she whispers. He looks up. She says, "Tell me to stop worrying."

He laughs. "No way."

And she looks up and down and out at the world.

Nothing is gray from here. The city sparkles with blues, and she sees pockets of light from streetlamps and a few buildings still lit throughout the city.

"Are all of those your shops?" she says.

"And headquarters and stuff. There's an office just for planning rebuilding. Selling paintbrushes and stuff."

She finds the light of their cabin. "That's us. I live nearly outside the city now. But I grew up right in the middle." She tries to point, but doesn't know where to start. There's a yellow glow rising up, as if something underground is breathing out gas. "What is that?"

"Something the gnomes do," he says. "No idea what. Every few days it pops up. Glittery smoke, look at it."

"You can't see it from down there. . . ."

"Hmm. Dunno."

She shakes her head a little.

"You've never seen them do anything weird?" he says.

"I . . . go to one room down there. I don't wander. I don't even know what's on the other floors. Scrap does."

"I guess he would have mentioned if it were important."

She nods, though she isn't sure.

"Because, I mean, he clearly told you exactly what it's like up here."

She realizes he's being sarcastic.

"He's my friend," she says.

"Oh, yeah, he seems like a good guy, I wouldn't worry about it."

Now she can't tell if he means it. There's something about his voice that catches her in a place that isn't prepared to be touched. He talks too quickly or too steadily. He doesn't trip over his words. He possibly doesn't think enough.

The last one she knew who didn't think enough . . . well, it didn't work out well for him.

As if reading her mind, Piccolo says, "I saw him, Scrap. And you. The day the gnome king died. And that other one, Cricket?"

"Yes."

"I just . . . I've been interested in you guys since then. I don't know. In you."

And she doesn't wonder *why her*, and she doesn't wonder what his watching means, and she doesn't spiral into flashbacks about that day (she doesn't she doesn't) she just thinks, *What kind of interested?*

"Anyway, I just wondered what you were like. And there's the tall one. Josha? Same color as you. Is it okay to say this stuff? The color thing? I'm not trying to be controversial."

"No, it's fine. That's Josha."

"He's the one who applied for our army."

"He wanted to be helpful. He doesn't trick like us."

But it wasn't just that. Josha was desperate and detached and alone and all he wanted was a gun on his shoulder and someone to stand beside him and squeeze his arm and tell him he was doing a good job.

Instead he was alone every day in that cabin.

"They didn't give him a fucking chance," Piccolo says. "Laughed him away. Just 'cause he's not a tightroper. Fucking moronic, all this racial stuff, the prejudices . . ." He shakes his head. "I look exactly like all the other tightropers, and I don't think anyone's ever felt less like . . . anyway. Less like anything but a messboy. Anyway. Do you like it?" He gestures out toward the view.

"Yes. Absolutely, yes." She shakes her head a little. "*Yes* isn't the right word."

"Try *yeah*."

She laughs. "We say *yeah*. Just . . . not when we're talking to strangers."

"Oh yeah?"

She bites her lip and looks at him.

"Yeah," she says.

Something stirring underneath them breaks the moment, and she sees Scrap walking toward home, alone. He looks small but not scared. He's limping a little.

"I have to go," she says.

"No problem." He doesn't try to help her stand. She doesn't need it.

"I'll . . . see you again?"

"I'll be here. You ever want to come back up . . . you know? You should come back up. Just—"

Scrap is walking faster. "I have to go," Beckan says.

"Just that it's your city. So you more than anyone deserve to be up here to see it."

"You sound like a fairy."

"I wish." He laughs. "Get outta here, kid."

He leads her to a hole in the net and talks her through lowering herself down on the threads. She shakes the whole time, and twenty feet from the ground she looks down and sees Scrap underneath her, watching, his arms crossed. Ten feet later, the rope around her wrist won't stretch anymore. She loosens it and lands on top of Scrap. She feels as useless as a pillow. Somehow he catches her with one arm.

She's on her feet as if he had never held her. She dusts herself off.

"What the fuck?" Scrap says. Gentle. Curious. Suspicious. A lot of things.

"What do the gnomes do underground?"

"Sleep, eat, us—"

"The yellow smoke."

They stand there and stare at each other. It's so much darker than it was half an hour ago.

"We should go home," Scrap says.

"Yeah. Let's go home."

Back to the cottage. Away from her city.

Her city.

When they get home, Josha is putting together an old puzzle at the kitchen table. Scrap, who Beckan had thought would hole up in his room all night with a cigarette (he gets them from the gnomes) and a bad mood, sits right down next to him and starts to help.

"I'm bad at this," Josha says, after a minute.

"Beckan's amazing. Beckan, c'mere, fix it?" Scrap takes his hand off the table and pulls at the bandage on the rest of his other arm. It's been so slow to heal.

She sits and tugs apart the pieces they forced and clicks the real ones in place. Josha and Scrap watch her, fascinated like little boys. She blows glitter off a piece. Josha laughs at Scrap sneezing, and Scrap shoves his head to the side when he stands up.

"Are you hungry?" he says.

Josha and Beckan nod, together, their heads bent over the puzzle still.

Scrap digs through the cupboards and announces, "I'm making bread!"

Their heads snap up like they're on strings. "Noooo you're not," Beckan says. "No no no, you're not." They've been living on stale, molded pieces, a new loaf once a month, *maybe,* through the war, but the loaf they have now is only three-quarters done and almost still soft enough to chew. Making new bread now sounds decadent, incredible, reckless, *peaceful.*

He smiles big, and soon the whole kitchen smells hot and deep. Josha shows them pictures that he drew today, and they aren't nearly as good as the ones he used to do (and he's never been as good as Tier) but it is so good to see him drawing again. They knock their heads together and Josha makes them laugh with stories about Cricket that they pretend they don't already know, and Scrap sends Beckan secret smiles across the table and lets himself trace shapes and write letters on her arm, lets himself daydream, and maybe this is how things get better, Beckan thinks, maybe one loaf of bread, maybe one piece of the puzzle at a time.

Scrap's hand on her feels warm, burning.

"Aren't you eating?" Josha says to Scrap, when both he and Beckan are full.

Scrap rests his head on the table. "I'm not feeling very good."

Beckan stops eating. "You can't get sick."

"I know."

Last time Scrap was sick, it was from a bad reaction to a drug one of the gnomes had slipped under his tongue. He threw up for hours while Cricket held him and made jokes and told Beckan and Josha not to worry, he knew his cousin, he got sick quickly and dramatically and it would be okay. But now Cricket isn't here.

"You can't get sick," Beckan said. "We don't know what to do."

That night, Beckan finds Scrap in the basement with the blue notebook and a fever, writing so fast his hand is shaking.

"Hey," she says, gently. "Come on. Up."

She takes the book and puts it away. "No," he says. "No, I need it." She caves and gives it back. He clutches it to his chest like a baby.

She pulls him up and to the kitchen and pours him glass after glass of water. His teeth chatter.

"You're an idiot," she says. "How high is your fever?" She puts her hand on his forehead. He is immediately icy with sweat and then quickly burning, scalding hot.

He doesn't say anything, and her mind and her eyes travel to his stump of an arm. He pulls away as if she'd touched it.

She sighs. "Is it infected?"

"I don't know."

"Scrap."

"I mean it, I honestly don't know. I need to write."

"Yeah, what's with that 'how to write fiction' book anyway?" she says, mostly just to distract him as she keeps edging him along, but he doesn't answer.

She takes him to the bathroom and sits him on the floor. She's used his first-aid kit a hundred times, but only for little things—a broken finger that time Cricket was shoved, a burn on Josha's face from a bomb too close the day before he decided to apply for the army, various whoring injuries of Scrap's. She hasn't touched his arm since it was bitten off. It's been his own project.

She unwraps it. A sliver of skin falls to the ground and keeps shivering. She pets it gently and Scrap calms a little.

He can still feel that arm.

"I think they're planning something," he mumbles.

"What?"

He's breathing so hard. "That they want something from me. They won't say . . ."

"Okay, you have a fever. Calm down." She leaves her hand on his back.

His arm has healed more than she thought, but the jagged cuts of the teeth are red and swollen. She sees thin skin that sparkles. "The glitter's in it," she says. "It got in the cuts."

She wets a towel with peroxide and dabs his arm. He doesn't cry out, just grits his teeth to make them stop rattling and pushes his forehead into the wall.

"If you weren't sick, you'd be doing this," she says. Because she knows it will comfort him.

"I know."

"You don't need me. You could do it all on your own."

Then he starts to cry.

"No, no, stop." Her lips shake. "No, stop. You don't cry."

He wipes his face, hard.

"No, I cry when you cry. Don't cry. Please stop."

He does.

"I'm done now," she says. "It's clean, all done. Tomorrow I'll go underground and get medicine and you'll be okay."

Then he leans over the toilet and throws up.

"Don't cry." Her voice breaks. "Don't cry. I'll fix it."

Josha stands outside the bathroom and listens. He wants to be close, but the bathroom is small and so is his throat, trying to breathe, trying to swallow, reminding himself over and over that Crate is dead and nobody knows where Scrap's arm is (or if maybe there are bits of Cricket, bloodboneglitter*anything* clinging to it) and that there is nothing he can do. But if Crate weren't already dead. Shit, if Crate weren't already dead, the things Josha would do to that fucking gnome king. The things he would do.

But there is nothing left for him to do.

He hasn't done a single fucking thing for his pack.

The problem is that he alternates between wanting to hug Scrap and wanting to hit him, and hearing Scrap weak and desperate pushes him firmly and horribly into the latter category. Because there it is, the reason for all of his anger, the reason everything is fucked up: Scrap was weak. Scrap turned Cricket into a prostitute. Scrap got his Cricket killed.

Scrap wanted someone to go down into the dark with him and he took the only two things Josha ever loved and one never came back.

"It's going to be okay, buddy," he calls through the door, and Beckan says, "Hear that? Josha is always looking out for us."

What is there to be scared of, anyway, from a sick fairy? They do not die. (That is not how they die.)

I can't remember much more of this part, anyway.

6

AFTER THAT FIRST BOMB, Beckan spent a week and
a half wondering where the war was, because she heard just faint
gunfire far away and saw no carnage.

"Then there'll probably be a big meeting with all the fairies," Josha
said. "And they'll tell us what's going on." Fairies love big meetings.

"I guess we have to go."

"You don't sound like you're dying to know what's going on."

She pushed a handful of her hair back and put her welding
goggles back on. "Doesn't feel real."

But it was only a few days after that when the fairies gathered
for a meeting in the school building on the south end. The flier
plastered to the front door of Beckan's apartment assured them that
there would be protection at the event, and sure enough, when she
approached the auditorium with Josha, two fairies stayed by the
double doors, longer shotguns than Beckan had ever seen slung
over their shoulders.

She'd fired a gun, once, the day a set of gnome teeth snapped a
few inches from her arm on her way home from Josha's house. She
was nine. Her father, still intact, took her on the tram to the edge of
the city, and they proceeded on foot to the outskirts of the farmland,

where sheep grazed on dandelions. He held her arms in place and pushed her finger down on the trigger. "Next time you do this alone," he mumbled in her ear. "I'm not your safety net." He kissed her cheek as the recoil launched them back.

He helped her carry the sheep back to the city. They handed it to the gnome clearing trash by the hospital. He took it and promised to remember her face, and they didn't eat Beckan that day.

"Nice guns," she told the fairies by the door, with a coy little smile, even though they were much too old for her. Josha smacked her. He'd learned to shoot when he was barely out of diapers. Guns were a lot of things for Josha, he told her a few days later. Sexy was not one of them.

Inside, three hundred fairies milled around with juice and bread, mumbling to each other, comparing old battle scars, telling stories of the dozens and hundreds of wars they'd all lived through (most of them lying). Beckan knew many of their ages by heart, as a matter of principle. She knew that the youngest was three, the oldest was four hundred forty-seven and a half (kept in an envelope) and that there were only four who were intact.

Beckan, Scrap, Cricket, Josha. All of them sitting together, somewhat coincidentally, waiting for the meeting to start. All of them without a scratch.

Four. And none of them over twenty, because how long could any fairy truly escape being torn up?

Not very long. Not even in Ferrum, and if you couldn't do it in Ferrum you couldn't do it anywhere.

The thing is that Ferrum was the only place that had never been abandoned.

The thing is that those four thought that that really meant something.

Jenamah, the oldest fairy in Ferrum who could still speak, stood on a chair and called the meeting to order. Scrap recorded this and the time in his notebook, and Beckan rolled her eyes at him and pretended to fall asleep on Josha's shoulder. Scrap shoved her and stuck his tongue in his cheek as he smiled.

One by one, the eldest fairies stood up and gave great speeches that meandered and fought to their deaths against making a real point. Beckan slid down in her chair and traced the edges of the tiles with her heels.

It was one of the younger ones, a fairy man who couldn't have been older than one hundred, who finally said, "Ferrum is a lost cause."

While the four of them looked up, everyone else nodded.

"It's undersized and out of date, and its history isn't worth dealing with these escalating threats."

"History," Scrap scoffed. "Fucking mythical history, maybe if there were more than ten fairies who could fucking spell *history.*"

Cricket said, "Shut *uuuup.*"

"We've held on to Ferrum for as long as we could," the man continued. "I know we all feel an affection for the place, but we can't stay here just to prove a point."

"Prove what point?" Beckan said.

Josha played with his cuticle. He was not interested. "That fairies don't always leave."

The thing is that fairies always leave.

"It's time we evacuate the city and settle somewhere stronger," the man said.

"This is why books are written about us and not by us," Scrap mumbled.

"No one cares about books," Beckan said to him.

Cricket leaned over to whisper, "I have to listen to this shit all the time," in Beckan's ear.

Another woman stood up and started talking. "We've already talked to some of the major nearby cities. Kelleran and Rankel have both agreed to absorb parts of our population. Kelleran offered wagons to help with the journeys. We would be around thousands of other fairies. We're not demanding a permanent relocation. And of course nothing is mandatory. You could take your family and move to a hill town, if you can arrange for deliveries from one of the other cities, since we will be shutting down production here next week."

Beckan narrowed her eyes.

"Where will we get food if we stay here?" Scrap said.

The man exhaled. "Have you been listening, boy? We're not staying here."

"I was listening. Well enough to hear that this isn't compulsory. Which is a better word than mandatory. In this context."

Beckan wasn't so rattled that she couldn't hear in her head a small bit of bitchy victory music for her small, bitchy friend.

Scrap said, "But shutting down production makes it compulsory. It makes the city unlivable."

"We can't order fairies to stay in an unsafe city to serve the stragglers who choose to stay behind," the man said. "Anyone who wants to come back after the war can come back. But we expect many of you will find your new situations far more comfortable."

Cricket sat up straighter. "You can't leave the city for the war and expect to come back and pick up where we left off."

The man sighed. "I don't think anyone's suggesting that."

"They're very young," Jenemah said, in a voice she probably thought was gracious.

Josha said, "This war is for us. Did you see the fliers? The tight-ropers came for us."

Cricket grabbed his hand and squeezed it. It was so small that Beckan almost didn't see, but she could never have missed the look on Josha's face, the world disappearing for him as he looked from his hand to Cricket's hand to Cricket's eyes.

"We've spoken with the tightropers and expressed our desire for peace, and both parties have determined that the best way to ensure fairy safety is for us to vacate Ferrum."

"This is our city," Beckan said.

Jenemah shook her head. "No city is worth losing limbs." She crossed one ankle over where her other would have been. "Just because you four are whole, you think you're invincible. You stay here? You won't be whole for long."

"We are invincible," Scrap whispered. "We all are. That's what being a fairy means."

Scrap didn't know shit.

The meeting progressed. The elders kept saying the same things. Josha and Cricket continued to fall in love in the middle of the auditorium.

Scrap is still so sick and the three of them spend the night in Josha's bed. Josha sleeps between them, clinging. Scrap stays awake, sweating and mumbling and picking at his bandage. Beckan thought she would be too worried, but she sleeps like the dead until morning.

She carefully sits up, holding Josha close so she doesn't startle him, and looks at Scrap. He's watching her, whispering a little to himself, breathing like he's been running.

"Hey, kiddo."

He pushes his face into the mattress and huffs out a breath that sounds like a sob.

"Okay. Hey. Okay." She shakes Josha gently and says, "Josha. Help me with breakfast."

He wakes up and shakes his head and looks down at his feet in their socks and shakes his head again.

"Scrap needs us. Family first."

"Family first," Josha repeats, rolling the words around in his mouth, and he gets up, slowly, like everything hurts. Like he's the one who's sick. "I'll make coffee."

Beckan sits next to Scrap and puts a warm hand on his chest. She leaves it there and lies down next to him. They hold eye contact for a long time. He is tired and the way he looks at her, his eyes big and unblinking with fever, makes her feel like she is the only thing in the whole world.

"It's okay," she whispers.

He nods.

"You got Josha out of bed," she says. "You're a hero."

He shakes his head.

"Yeah, though," she says.

"I want to fix Josha. Help?"

"I'm doing all I can."

"Okay." He sounds so unsure.

"I'm going down to get medicine."

"No! Don't go underground alone."

"I'll be fine."

"No . . ." He sneezes.

"Scrap."

"Not alone." He's big again, big in that small, terrifying way he always has been, voice deep and teeth clenched and . . . well. Like he could do anything. Fever or not.

"Just stay in bed. Josha will bring you breakfast. You can whine at him if you want."

"Why are you mad at me?"

She rolls her eyes but stops when her hand meets his forehead. "Your fever's really high." She hurries into her shoes. "I'm going. Drink water."

"I led you in," he mumbles. "Underground. It was me."

She stops. "Don't."

"I'm so sorry. Never should have taught you. That day I did the walk . . ."

"Stop."

"Sexed you up in the elevator—"

"*Stop*," she says. "You did what you had to do. Nothing more. You needed a third one to go down there and I did a fucking good job and it was nothing more than exactly what we had to do, and why are you worrying about this now?"

"Gave Cricket nightmares. I'm sorry." He shivers into his pillow. "I'm sorry, Becks."

"You kept us from starving, asshole."

"I killed him."

Suddenly the room is cold, and Josha's quilt is ugly, and nothing in the whole world has ever smelled as fiercely like Cricket.

"I'm not doing this today," she says. "I'm not having this conversation with you. I can't."

"*I killed him!*" Scrap sits up. "I killed him and I'm trying to be good now and it still won't go away."

And Beckan realizes that he isn't talking about Cricket. That he isn't thinking about Cricket. That for who knows how long, Scrap has not been thinking about Cricket.

"Nobody cares that Crate's dead, Scrap, we just care about how killing him fucked you up!"

Scrap wheezes for a while and doesn't say anything.

"You *are* fucked up," she says. "And you shouldn't be, because you didn't do anything you didn't have to do."

"I don't know if that makes it okay." He puts his chin on his knees and looks very young for a minute. He's not big. He couldn't do anything. He's a kid who could never kill anyone.

A kid who would be way too messed up to function if he ever had to. Not like someone who could get up and clean the bathroom and make dinner and keep on living like he was normal, like there wasn't a line separating him from anyone else, a line that has nothing to do with a dead cousin. Nothing to do with the missing arm and everything to do with what he was doing when he lost it.

"Could you ever kill someone?" he says.

"I can't do this," she says. "Not when you're sick. You don't really want to talk about this, and I'm not going to do this to you."

"I don't." And then he's shaking hard. "I don't want to talk about this. I don't. I don't."

She stands there for a minute, watching him. She doesn't know in which direction to move.

Then she clears her throat. "You'll feel so much better with some medicine in you. I'll be back soon."

"Yeah."

She walks past Josha, who's frozen halfway through coffee-making. She stops at the front door and looks at him.

"Give him a book if he won't calm down. One of the big old ones. It's just the fever. He's fine. He's not saying anything we didn't know."

He doesn't answer.

"You can do it. You can make breakfast. I know you can."

She's controlling them, telling them that they're capable. She knows that. But there's nothing else she knows how to say.

And anyway, men have been doing that to her since she was a girl in a field with a gun.

She doesn't have time for this. She leaves. She has work to do, medicine to find, things that she can fix.

She hasn't changed.

She was shocked by how quickly the streets cleared after the fairies left. How efficiently the stores closed, how old the newspapers and store displays seemed.

And she was shocked by how quiet, how simply occupied, the city was for a long time.

She didn't grocery shop anymore. She brought her tote bag and her father across town—she walked, such a long walk—over to the farm and took whatever she wanted from the dying stalks. She missed chocolate and jam and cheese, things she had no idea how to make for herself.

The explosions hit the city walls from above—all the better to cave in the gnome tunnels—and were few and far between and so her city was not decimated; it was just ignored. It was a gray and empty space in between the buzzing above and below her. She hurried down the dusty sidewalks and felt drilling beneath her feet. She felt fleeting shade as tightropers above her zipped between her and the sun.

She thought maybe the fairies had been stupid, that this war wasn't really going to happen. Just an isolated incident. Just a typical fairy flee.

Girls with infinite time don't typically factor in planning stages.

She still hadn't seen a tightroper up close. She was never much of an artist, but she tried to draw one, one night, from her imagination. It was a colder night than they'd had since early spring, and she was alone. She curled up with an extra blanket over her feet and drew while her father slept in the corner.

She got a mouth and a rope before she gave up.

The war was quiet then. Her city was occupied, so Beckan tried to be too. She melted metal and made things she couldn't sell.

Josha stands at the door and Scrap buries his red-hot head between the pillows.

"What is this?" Josha says, holding up Scrap's only fairy history book.

The pages are cut out.

"What the fuck have you been doing?"

"Don't tell Beckan," Scrap says, without moving.

"He's running a fever?" Tier calls over his shoulder. He's digging through the gnomes' enormous medicine chest down the hallway from his room. When he was a child, Tier had a cough that lasted years and a constant ear infection on his left side. He says that's why he was forced into this hall, so close to the ground. The son of the king should be much farther down. But Crate never cared much for propriety when his youngest, useless son was concerned.

"Yes," Beckan says. "High. He's delirious. It's his arm." The medicine chest smells like dust and old wood. Home to Beckan used to be glass and high chrome, but since she's moved to the cabin, this smell, like something organic, something that lives and dies, makes her want to curl up in the bottom of the cabinet and go to sleep.

"Is it infected?"

"The glitter's getting in it."

"It gets everywhere, I swear."

She crosses her arms once, then the other way. "Scrap's drives him crazy," she says. "Gets in his eyes, makes him sneeze. He's bad at fairies."

He says, "Shouldn't you guys have figured out how to get rid of it?"

"We have creams."

"You know those don't work. The glitter just causes us all a lot of trouble, you know?"

"It's a defense mechanism," she says. "Biological. Probably."

"It gets in your cuts and makes you sick."

"It makes you less likely to eat us."

He doesn't say anything.

"Glitter doesn't taste good," she says. "You told me."

"Yeah, but not tasting good will only get you so far when underneath the glitter you're . . . you know. Nutritious." Beckan knows this already, that a tiny bit of a fairy will satisfy a gnome faster than ten tightroper bodies, or ten backpacker bodies, or the bits of animals the fairies used to throw down when they had any to spare and were feeling generous, or protective of their appendages.

He digs something out of the closet. "Let's bring him this. And these. These will fight the infection, the gel will help with the pain."

"Oh. I . . . you don't have to come."

Tier closes the doors, and immediately it's just the dust and granite of the tunnels and it doesn't smell like home, not at all.

"I haven't seen Scrap in a long time."

She nods a little, still swallowing, still confused.

Tier gives her eye contact and a small sigh. "It'll be good to see him," he says.

"Let me carry the medicine?"

"No . . . no. You should just stay a little behind me." He leads her around, his hand on her head, like she is a toy he has borrowed and doesn't want to break.

She wants to tell him she's been up in the sky, so high that you can't see the holes to enter this dirty waste of a palace.

She stays behind him and avoids eye contact with every gnome that passes them on their way to the elevator. One man stops Tier with a hand on his chest. "You sick?" he says.

Tier says, "It's for Scrap."

The gnome is quiet for a minute, then says, "Well."

Tier says, "So we'll be going now." The gnome lets them by.

The elevator growls as the gnome at the top pulls them up. "Thank you," Beckan says to Tier.

"Hmm?"

"I was scared."

"Lan isn't the friendliest, no."

"He knows Scrap?"

"He's one of Scrap's clients. Who isn't?"

She should have guessed that.

"But he sounded afraid of him."

Tier gives her a look.

She clears her throat. "Right." Why wouldn't a gnome be afraid of Scrap? He killed the fucking king. It's a wonder he's still allowed down.

Tier says, "Lan shouldn't have hassled you. He . . . was looking out for me, really. Ever since my father died, it's everyone's job to babysit me."

"Oh."

"It's just . . . we're not meant to be without a king. We're antsy and upset. We can't get anything done. We're meant to be led."

"Like how we're meant to run away?"

"Exactly. It's how we are."

"Oh," she says, again. Because what else is there to say? *I'm sorry my best friend killed your dad and ruined your species?*

"It isn't so bad. If we had a new king, I probably wouldn't be able to skip out on my girlfriend to go aboveground with a fairy girl, would I?" He steps out into the open air, nods at Leak by his post. "Remind me which way to your house?" he says.

She'd forgotten all about Rig.

Tier hadn't mentioned her.

Josha says, "I wish I'd killed Crate. I wish it had been me."

"Noooo." Scrap's voice is muffled in his pillow.

"It would have been perfect if it were me. It would have been *right*. And I wouldn't be making myself sick over it." He watches Scrap. "I would have eaten him alive."

"Shouldn't have happened," Scrap says. "None of it. I shouldn't've let it happen."

"Yeah. That's the other reason I should have been the one to kill him. If you hadn't had that minute of playing hero, everyone would have figured out by now that you are not a good guy."

Scrap makes a noise like he's been hit, and Josha runs his hand over his face and says. "Shit."

And then, two months after the fairies left, it happened.

The bomb that morning was the sound of a shovel hitting snow, scratchy and long and low. Beckan had covered her ears without thinking. She and Josha stood absolutely still in his apartment, staring at each other. Didn't yell.

They ran through the empty city, but they knew already it was Beckan's block. Her apartment building was all over the street. Thousands of pounds of brick and steel and furniture that was not hers. Occasional bits of something she recognized. A bit of carpet was the color of the one in her room. A leg of a chair that might have once been her father's. Even though she knew he was with her, she reached into her tote bag and felt around until she grasped her father's jar. Just to be sure.

What if she hadn't brought him that day?

Next to her, Josha was cursing so constantly it sounded like a chant.

A piece of metal shifted on the ground, and Beckan jumped backward. It slid to reveal a pit in the ground, and four gnome heads stuck out and lifted four roughly constructed guns. They ignored Josha and Beckan. They aimed at the sky and waited.

Far above their heads, it sounded like someone was laughing.

"Move," a gnome growled at her.

She did, faster than she'd ever done anything.

"Come live with us," Scrap said, so gentle, when she showed up, shaking, for her reading lesson, because she didn't know what else to do. "Are you kidding? Come in right now. Come live with us."

Tier is quiet, so after a few blocks, Beckan says, "Well . . . ?"

He's distracted, peering around all the streets, shielding himself from the sun. A tightroper at a shop stand yells something at them and Tier hisses, but Beckan gives them each a gentle smile.

"Well?" she says again.

"Hmm?"

"Rig. What about Rig?"

"Must we?"

"Yes. We must."

He groans and rolls his head back. "I don't know. I don't know what to do. We have nothing to talk about. She's scared and she's been through so much and she just needs me to be there for her. That's all she needs. We were in love."

"Were?"

"And literally all she needs is for me to sit next to her and hold her hand and tell her I know, and I understand, and I . . . can't do it."

"Just do it."

"I *can't*. I know exactly how I sound. I do." He runs his hand over his head and looks through a broken window to an old shop. "And I don't know why I can't do it. She starts talking, and she'll say something, and it's like I'm not even there. Like I'm back underneath 8th Street loading my gun or buried in the east wing under that pile of rubble or tearing apart some dead tightroper or looking and looking and looking for bits of Cricket and I just . . . I need what she went through to mesh with what I went through, and it doesn't."

"You haven't even tried. Maybe it does."

"You said it yourself. No one experienced this the same way."

"So talk about something else."

"There's nothing else to talk about. Everything is different now. I can't connect."

"You can, though. You're just talking in all these abstractions and making it sound impossible."

"Abstractions. I taught you that word."

"Scrap did. When really it's just a matter of actually making yourself do it. Just start somewhere. Just hold her hand."

He breathes out.

"Stop running off with fairy girls or something, I don't know."

"I'm here to fix Scrap."

"Uh-huh."

He looks at her hard. "I'm not in love with you, Beckan."

She shrinks inside of herself. "I know that."

And it isn't that she's in love with him, or even that she wanted him to be in love with her. But believing that he might be has been like a hand reaching out to her, ready to catch her in case she fell.

A lifeline.

"I know that," she says.

"Okay. I'm sorry. That was uncalled for."

"Welcome to our relationship. It's fine."

They hike up the hill to the cottage, and maybe it's just having Tier with her, but for the first time in months she really feels herself taking these steps up and *from* the city proper and into the outskirts. The center city has a smell, now, from the produce the tightropers ship in, and there's the buzz of music from up on their ropes and the consistent drone of chain saws and nail guns repairing their buildings. "For you," a tightroper said to Beckan yesterday, with a smile. "All for you, Miss Fairy." She can't hear any of that out here.

She figures she's past the point of believing their bullshit. She will die in that cottage and that's all right.

Josha, back in the kitchen, looks up when the front door opens. He snarls at Tier and stomps over to the refrigerator.

"Josha," Beckan says. "Come on."

He sucks some glitter off the back of his hand and spits it toward them.

"Charming," Beckan says.

"What the fuck is he doing here?"

"I'm just here for Scrap," Tier says. "I'm not trying to do anything."

"Scrap doesn't want to see you."

Beckan says, "Oh, he told you that?"

"He doesn't want to see any of you." Josha gestures at Tier. "He's miserable going down there, and the last thing he needs is one of you lurking around here when he's sick. Becks, you should go see him, he's shaking. I'm out of things to say to him. I don't know."

Beckan doesn't push. Josha and Scrap have always had the most strained relationship in their pack, but they are largely all right and that isn't something she wants to compromise. Scrap is going to be okay, but this illness is messing with their precarious semblance of calm.

"Okay," Beckan says. "That's fine. But Tier brought medicine and he wants to check Scrap to make sure we have everything he needs."

Tier says, "If he doesn't want to see me, I'll leave. Quietly. Okay?"

"Doesn't the smell of blood get you all riled up?"

Beckan says, "Shut *up*, Josha."

"They eat fairies."

"I'm not hungry," Tier says. "Okay?"

Josha slams the door to the refrigerator and storms out to the living room.

"Don't worry about him," Beckan says, but Tier has already disappeared down the other hall. He knocks on each door until he hears the sleepy voice telling him to come in. Beckan trails behind. She isn't nervous. Of course she isn't.

Tier would never eat Scrap.

Even though Scrap killed his father.

Nothing to worry about.

Except the feeling in her stomach isn't nervousness as much as it is anticipation, as if something inside her is cranking to slip something else into place. The horrible thought she can't shake is that, if Tier were to eat Scrap, there would be something correct about it, something final, something meaningful.

It would go nicely in a book.

On the other hand, Scrap is her best friend.

"Come in," Scrap says again.

Tier opens the door and says, "Hello."

Scrap sits up, his face pink, his eyes shiny and wild like a small animal's. "Hi." He scoots over on the bed, makes room. "Tier, hi."

"Hi. Heard you're not feeling well."

Scrap looks up. "Hey, Beckan."

She cocks her head toward Tier. "Pay attention to him."

Scrap watches Tier unwind the bandage on his arm. "It hurts," he says, softly. "I'm not being brave."

"Sure you are."

"No."

"This is going to be okay," Tier says. He examines the wound and spreads lotion on his fingers and dabs Scrap's arm. Scrap doesn't wince. "You should be resting more."

"I can't. I have to keep going down there."

"I'll tell them you're sick."

"No!" Scrap's head snaps up. "No, no, don't. Please don't."

"Okay, hey. Hey. Calm down."

Beckan sits on Scrap's other side and puts her hand on his forehead. He doesn't feel so hot anymore.

"Don't," Scrap says. "Please."

Tier says, "Okay. I won't. It's all right."

Scrap takes a long time to calm down. It isn't until Tier is done rebandaging his arm that Scrap slumps into his shoulder, shaking, and puts his arm around him.

"Oh." Tier hugs him, slowly. "Oh."

"I'm sorry," Scrap says.

"Oh."

"I'm so sorry. I don't know what to do with these things I've done."

I don't know if I can write any more today.

I'm so tired, Beckan.

Beckan moved in, and it wasn't long before Josha, who was spending all his time with them anyway, did as well. His father had already abandoned the city (he thought Josha was behind him and for whatever reason it appeared he'd never turned around to check) and they were already a pack.

Cricket and Scrap left sometimes and came back with money—Scrap always with more—and she never thought much about it. She had no idea that soon she'd be going too, and she had no idea what it would do to her and what it would come to. She didn't know she should start hating Scrap with every bit of her, that she couldn't have started hating him fast enough, she really couldn't.

Scrap sleeps, but Tier shows no signs of leaving, no matter how long Beckan lets the silences sit or how many times she drifts toward the front door. Something about the cottage, or possibly about Josha still sulking in the next room, adds a level of discomfort to their relationship that she's never felt down in the mines. Tier seems completely oblivious.

"Can I see the library?" he says brightly, drinking juice Scrap squeezed from tightroper limes.

"Oh, of course. Of course."

She leads him down to the damp basement, and she sees tension she hadn't seen in him unfurl and settle down. He smiles. "It's dark," he says.

"You're weird, you know?"

"Yeah." He runs his fingers over the spines and nods at the ones he recognizes. "It's funny seeing my books here with Scrap's. Does he read them ever?"

"When he thinks we're not looking. I think he secretly loves them."

Tier laughs a little. "Noooo. They're fiction."

"Maybe that's what he likes."

He shakes his head. "That's not Scrap."

"Like you know him so well," she says, and she can see that hurts him, but really, most of his experiences with Scrap have been filtered through Beckan. She hands books from one to the other. She tells them stories that will make them trust each other and trust her when she's with them.

"What is that?" Tier says, pointing to the corner.

"My welding bench. Cricket set it up for me. A long time ago. So much better than my old apartment. I did it at the dining room table."

He drifts over. "What are you working on?"

"An arm for Scrap. Made out of old pots and pans. He asked for a hook, but . . . I want him to be able to move the fingers. Well, not move. Pose. With his other hand."

Tier goes back to the bookshelf, where he is more comfortable, she assumes, and she stays over and looks at the arm. It isn't much yet.

Tier pauses on one book—*Ferrum: A Brief History.* "Could I borrow this one?"

He flips through the book and says, without looking at her, "There are pages missing from this. Torn out."

"Oh. I don't know."

"My father has some gnome history book I've never read. Scrap might like it. I'll bring it."

Josha's voice startles them. "Why are you trying to make nice with Scrap?"

Tier looks up. "I'm not—"

"Why don't you hate him?"

Tier breathes out. "Because what's the point? What good would it do?"

"He killed your dad. You can't be rational."

Beckan says, "Josha, stop."

Tier says, "It was war."

"Can we keep using that excuse forever? It was war? How long do we say that? Is that going in the history books, Beckan?"

"Stop."

"A thousand years from now, we'll be chewed up gnome food, and someone will open up a book, what, Scrap's book? And they'll say, it's okay, it's just a war. It's just history. Crate and Scrap's arm and Cricket and everybody."

Beckan doesn't mention that there is no way any of them but Crate will make history books.

Does that mean Crate wins?

Who would have to write that book, anyway? (Please no, please no, please.)

Tier says. "I get that you're restless."

Beckan puts her hand on Josha's arm, because she senses he's about to explode, but he doesn't. She watches him exhale something, and he says, "I am. I'm restless." He shakes his head a little. "And I'm mad at Scrap."

"Me too," Beckan says quietly, because the truth is that Scrap killed someone, and the fact that who he killed was horrible doesn't change that. And it doesn't make him sexy and dangerous, it makes him scary, and she wants to hold him and get rid of the fever and she wants to hit him and she wants to run away.

Tier says, "Guys, give him a break. He's suffering for it."

"Suffering doesn't do shit," Josha said, and really, he would know.

Tier looks at Beckan hard and says, "He takes care of you. You tell me that all the time. He makes you food and cleans the house and worries about you. Do you know how rare that is? Do you know how few of us are left who are at all capable of taking care of anyone?"

It was amazing how quickly things became normal. Beckan and Josha shared a room, officially, and they tended house while Cricket and Scrap went out and came home with enough food to get them through the day, or fabric for a new shirt for Beckan, or pills for Josha's cold. They got used to chasing the mice around, staying up late singing folk songs their fathers had taught them, comparing imperceptible battle scars and finding the bits of them that looked like the other species they all were.

They were just so close and all so crazy about each other, so quickly. Beckan had a space on Cricket's shoulder that she told Josha was only for her, and she would rest her head there when she was tired and kiss it over and over when she wasn't. She had a favorite place on the floor to stretch out with Josha and take a nap. And Scrap. Scrap was giggles through the walls, secret smiles, notes passed back and forth, but they were slow, they were childish about it, they never stepped over any kind of line. For some reason, it felt important to them both that they be careful. Because they would look at Cricket and Josha and see how crazy they were for each other and wake up gasping hard in bed, freezing cold, thinking about how dangerous it was to love someone that much during a war.

Anyway. They had plenty of time.

The guns got louder and louder and closer and there was more blood and gradually, around the time Josha started spending more nights in Cricket's room than Beckan's, they began to live their lives in new pairs. Josha and Beckan were still, in their way, ridiculously in love, but they spent less and less time together as Cricket and Josha threw themselves into shared sweatshirts and last-bite-of-ice-cream kisses, and Beckan and Scrap lived like (mythical) parents, teasing each other for sleepwalking and flat gnome noses, curling up together with a book after the kids were in bed.

It wasn't long before Beckan found out about tricking; Cricket had told Josha within days—the kind of indiscretion Cricket lived and died with—and Scrap never made much of an effort to hide it, coming home with half his glitter rubbed off, sometimes drugged and giggly, always in the mood for a kiss on the cheek and a bit of babying before he was sent off to bed. They never talked about it. Beckan washed bloodstains out of his underwear and rubbed his shoulders when he looked tense and comforted him after nightmares and Josha worried the three days a week Cricket accompanied each-night-every-night Scrap. "I don't make as much as Scrap does," Cricket said once to Beckan, explaining his part-time work. "He's the best little whore in Ferrum."

A few weeks into the war, the tightropers invaded the mines and took the women captive, and business boomed for Cricket and Scrap. The gnome men had been wanting before, surrounded by women who instead of getting into bed with them waited around and dreamed about fairy boys and fairy babies—a piece of immortality—instead of another generation in the mines, but now with the women gone entirely they needed Cricket and Scrap more than ever, and the boys were happy to oblige. During that initial surge, when sex was valuable and food wasn't, quite, they ate and drank and fucked like kings.

And somehow, in the war, Scrap came alive. While Josha and Cricket nervously discussed weapons and production, Scrap tried three-ingredient recipes with whatever three ingredients they had left and made Beckan guess what he was trying to make. He invented card games called Treewoman and Cabaret and lied when he said he would let Beckan win. He once lay half naked on the kitchen floor and laughed hysterically while the other three rubbed him as hard as they could to get glitter off him, and he kicked and screamed and tackled them back on the floor.

And one night he and Cricket came home too late and nearly empty-handed for the fourth night in a row and sat in the kitchen in silence, their fingers laced together and Josha and Beckan sat with them and eventually there was no way to avoid the fact that two prostitutes was no longer enough, in a time when the gnomes were clinging to each bit of meat like it was made of gold and licking their teeth and smacking their lips whenever Cricket and Scrap came down, to secure food for four mouths.

"Teach me," Beckan said, and most of her was excited, most of her had been waiting, most of her wanted to feel everything that Scrap had ever felt, because that was where she was then. "I'll go."

7

BECKAN BROWSES the tightroper shops and is wandering around, looking up at the sky, when a hand pushes down hard on her shoulder and a little blue and pink fairy catapults over her shoulders and onto the ground.

She hauls him off the ground. "Someone's feeling better."

"Much." Scrap bends over and pants. The brass locket she made jingles around his neck. "Had to run ages to catch up to you. What are you doing out? Are you working today?"

"No." Now that the girls are back, Beckan goes down much less frequently, despite the silence still between Tier and Rig. "What, are you?"

"Yeah."

"You're still sick."

"No."

"Their girls are back. Why do they still need you?"

"They love me. I went down back when the girls were still here, remember?"

"Well . . . I guess we need the money."

"Yeah. Hey." He grabs her, suddenly, and hugs her. "Thank you for taking care of me. You're amazing. I owe you. Really big."

"Shh, no. You sure you're better? You're still all pant-y."

"Yeah, I'm going to hit Tier up for another one of those pills when I'm down there. But I'm much better."

"You look good."

He smiles at her. "Hey," he says. "I found some old board game in the basement. Want to play tonight? I think we can get Josha to. He's having one of his better days."

"Absolutely."

"I'll invite Tier if you want," he says.

"No, no, he needs to stay down there. Girlfriend and all."

"You got it." He stands up, finally done panting, and smacks a kiss on her cheek. "See you. Thank you, Beckan. You help with all of it."

She touches her cheek for a while before she starts scanning the sky again. It isn't long before she finds him, that smiling figure in the sky, leaning against the rope. Patient, hopeful, incredibly young.

What bothers her, she realizes, is that's the most happy Scrap's been since the war ended, and it is a far cry from tickling him on the floor.

But there's a boy in the sky smiling at her.

Scrap brings Tier's history book home and sits down and tears through it, and Josha takes the opportunity to steal Scrap's notebook. Not the one he kept during the war, not the boring three-line descriptions of each day, but the blue one he keeps hidden under his pillow, the one with loose pages and glued-in ripped-out paragraphs and spaces for illustrations and horrible, fevered handwriting.

Josha reads it and now he knows everything.

Scrap sees him and his mouth opens, and he is very quiet for a minute.

"I didn't know it was this bad," Josha says. "I thought you were just . . ."

"Don't tell Beckan," Scrap says, eventually. "For the love of . . . please don't tell Beckan."

"Shouldn't you tell her?"

"I do," Scrap says. "Every day."

"You're a coward."

"This is . . . this is all we can handle right now." He looks down. "I'm getting there. I'm working on it."

YOU ARE LIKE TWENTY THOUSAND STARS ALL IN ONE GIRL.

A note, slipped under Beckan's door, three months into the war. Handwriting reproduced exactly (which was not difficult, for the obvious reason. I'm a fucking idiot).

"That's abuse," Piccolo says. "Pushing you into prostitution like that. You know that, right? You could pretty much arrest him or have him killed or whatever for being a sexual predator."

"He's younger than me."

"Oh. Well then you have no case, sorry."

Beckan rolls her eyes and cranes her neck further over the rope under her chin. In the afternoon sun, the city looks so much different from the last time she was up here, when everything twinkled with an imaginary magic. Now, everything is sharp, real, and almost comical in its smallness. It must be so easy to come into a city, to invade, to kill, when you see how small everything can really be.

He says, "There's something inside you, Beckan. I can see it. You have something. A spark."

"It's called glitter."

He laughs. "All of you have that. This is just you."

"I'm the only girl. I know how these things work. It makes me look more special. Process of elimination. You know Scrap used to think he was interested in me? And I used to think I was interested in him? Just because we were the only ones not paired off."

Piccolo says, "There are a lot of soldier's daughters and a lot of cute nurses up here and I'm talking to you. What does that say?"

She looks away and rolls her eyes and feels so much different from when Scrap kissed her cheek. "That you have a thing for fairies."

He laughs. "That's not what makes you interesting. The fairy thing or the girl thing. They listen to you. And that's really interesting."

"Who?"

"The other ones. Scrap especially."

"You *are* a bad spy."

"Nah."

"Scrap's our leader, no question."

"That's not how it looks from up here."

"You're reaaally far away, Piccolo."

"They listen to you. They're careful with you."

"I'm crazy. They think I'll explode. Too much spark."

"Scrap wouldn't have gone down to the mines just now if you'd told him not to. Or he would have given up on that board game. Or believed you if you said Josha wasn't having a good day."

"You saw that?"

"I was hanging right there," he says. "*You're* a bad spy."

She flops back and laughs. Her legs slip down a little, her feet dangling in the air, and she feels dangerous and amazing.

"Is Josha okay?" Piccolo says, softly.

"No."

Piccolo is quiet for a minute, then he says, "Anyway, the little one. He was waiting for you to ask why he had to go ho around in the middle of the day, or to tell him where you were going, but you didn't and he wasn't about to push you. He tried to cheer you up a little and then he left you alone. You're in charge."

"Maybe."

"And Josha doesn't even come out without you."

"He's not okay."

"The loud one. Cricket? He liked you, too," he says. "The one who used to come up here."

"The dead one."

"So he counts as dead."

"It's just . . . the easiest way to call it what it is." And it's so much easier than saying, *Yes, there have to be parts of Cricket somewhere but we can't find them.* So much easier than thinking about bones and fingernails calcified in a dead man's stomach, the digested bits rotting in the stale air of the mines, the thousands and thousands of specks of glitter buried and blown who knows where, but not to Josha, not to any of them.

(Let's just call it dead, okay?)

Piccolo squeezes her hand.

"We don't even look for him anymore," she says.

"Why not?"

"Because . . . it's a whole city that's getting more and more cleaned up every day and he's tiny bits of one fairy. It's impossible. And because . . ."

"Because now's not the time you want to risk poking around making the gnomes mad."

"Yes." She feels horrible. "And it wasn't working anyway."

"It's horrible," he says, quietly. "This war. It was horrible for all of us."

"I know." And she does. She saw dead tightropers in the streets, heard Leak mumbling about the gnomes killed in a mine explosion. She knows that losing one fairy, even if that fairy was a quarter of their tiny population, does not make them the race with the most lost. "But it's over now," she says.

Piccolo very obviously does not say anything and does not look away.

Something sinks its way to the bottom of Beckan's stomach.

"Isn't it?" she says, softly.

"Is this your first war, Beckan?" he says.

"Yes."

"It's mine, too. So I want it to end. Not to peter out. Not for us to still be plotting up here and them to still be plotting down there. Finished. Done. No more occupation. No more."

"What does ending the occupation even mean? You just go away?"

"Yep."

"But . . ." *But you're my friend.* She feels young and stupid and fluttery. "But why can't we just share it? You stay, the fairies come back, and . . ."

He's looking at her, waiting for her to figure it out. Patient.

"You guys aren't going to let the fairies come back," she says.

"No."

"I knew that liberation stuff was . . ."

"Yeah. Tightropers are conquerers, not liberators. No one expected any fairies to stick around, and we thought the gnomes would be easy to take out."

"So why are you different?"

"I asked my father that once, and he told me my lack of ability to correctly size up an enemy is why I'll always be a messboy."

"There go your dreams of being a warlord."

"Right?"

"How do I know . . ."

"How do you know if you can trust me," he fills in.

"Yes."

He's quiet for a minute, stretching his arms over his head. Then he says, "Why didn't you run away with the rest of them?"

"Mmm. Fair enough."

"We're big ol' blood traitors, you and me."

She nods.

He says, "And the thing is nothing's ever going to change if we keep clinging to the ideas of these stupid races. Because you guys are what, half fairy? A quarter now? A sixty-fourth? You get all diluted . . ."

"It doesn't work that way."

"Bullshit."

"There aren't that many generations of us. We live forever."

"What's your other half?"

She doesn't say anything.

"Well, what was your father's?" he says.

"I don't know. It isn't something we talk about."

"But he wasn't full fairy. He couldn't be. No one is."

"It doesn't work like that."

"So you have to be less than half. And unless he's the, what, proto-fairy, he would have to be too."

"It doesn't *work* like that. It's different for us. It's any amount of fairy blood."

"No, Beckan." He's gentle. "That's not different. That's just racism."

"I'll live forever and you won't," she says. "That's not me being an asshole. That's genetics."

"Genetics is an asshole."

"Fair enough."

"So you don't know anyone's other half?"

"Well, I know *theirs*. My pack. We don't have secrets," she says. (Yeah, sure.) She's known Josha's for a long time, because it is something they eagerly talked about as children before they learned that it is improper. Beckan found out she was half gnome from the things they would yell at her when she walked by the mines with her father. When she was very small, she thought they were being friendly, calling her *sister*.

"I knew him," Piccolo says abruptly. "Cricket. I don't think we were what he expected. Cricket came thinking we'd whore him out like the gnomes do, but . . . I guess there aren't as many of us, and we're soldiers. We're used to nice long dry spells."

"But you're not a soldier."

"No, I'm too young to be a soldier, and I would never be anyway. But it's the same deal with messboys. We're also not, you know, monsters. We weren't going to take advantage of some kid."

"Cricket was older than you, I think."

"Barely. Really he just wanted to make sure we wouldn't let Josha into the army. And of course we wouldn't. He's a kid too. But in exchange for promising him that, he told the guys—my dad, his friends—that they could sleep with him for free. And they laughed at him. So I think that surprised Cricket at first, but then he . . . he kept coming up, which at first was really confusing." He laughs. "But we like fairies. You know that, right? We like you guys."

"You don't know us," she says, to do anything but think about Cricket coming up here and how stupid he was and how brave he was and how much she wishes she'd asked him to stop.

"Cricket came up a lot. The officers . . . I don't know. There was something about him they liked. He got around really easily up here and they admired that, they'd give him cigars and things. He made money selling rings and stuff."

"Oh. I made those."

"And Scrap goes to our shops, like you." He clears his throat. Scrap's name, like every time he's said it, sounds funny, and he must notice, because he says, "I don't feel like I can use their names, because . . . you don't think that I know you."

She looks at him.

He has a sad little smile. "Cricket talked about you."

"We were fine." She kicks her feet and watches specks of glitter float down to the ground. "I didn't know him like the others," she says. "I mean, I knew him really well. I just . . . Scrap was like his brother. They grew up together. And he and Josha were in love like nobody I've ever seen."

"What about Scrap and Josha?"

"They fought over Cricket like it was a game and now Cricket's dead and they have nothing to fight about and no more games."

"Sucks."

"Scrap killed the guy who killed Cricket, and we all want that to be some positive heroic thing, except now we're living with a killer and Scrap has to keep this with him, and Josha's half in love with Scrap for killing Crate and half furious at him for having Cricket in the mines with him in the first place. Josha and Scrap had to have a relationship because the rest of us all did, so they made that as easy a relationship as they could just to be a convenience to everyone, and now the reason they had to have a relationship is gone and they're still living six feet away from each other and they still care about each other and that's no longer convenient, because Josha would rather hate him and Scrap would rather disappear."

"And you're still there. And they both love you."

She flops down on her back, and Piccolo grabs her before she slips. She says, "Why is that always how it works? Cricket dying. The ones who are in love the most die, the ones who are going through the motions live forever and never really care about it."

"Like fairies."

"We care."

Piccolo says, "I think that's only in stories. I don't think those who die are any better than those who stay alive. They just look better. They can't mess anything up anymore."

"I only know stories."

He laughs. "I need to teach you how to live."

It's a stupid line, but she looks at him and she believes it. The only other lessons she's had, after all, have been from a man in a jar, a boy who lives underground, and a boy who can live forever.

Never a girl.

Every once in a while, a book.

Cricket got Beckan ready on her first night of tricking. While Scrap and Josha argued in the kitchen, he put her hair up and set to work scrubbing the glitter off her neck. "They hate it," he said. "You want as little as possible."

"I thought glitter keeps them from eating us."

"They won't eat you. You're too expensive." He took glitter from her chin and pressed it onto her eyelids instead.

"What are they fighting about?" Beckan said.

Cricket rolled his eyes. "You know them. Josha's being bitchy. He's just worried about you," Cricket said. "And me. But now that it's both of us . . . really, now that it's all of us, I guess. You know how he feels about tricking. Like we have much of a choice."

But Cricket didn't hate it.

Cricket took stupid risks and liked to feel important.

Cricket was alive.

"He does care about Scrap," Beckan said.

Cricket shrugged and said, "I guess," because whether or not Josha cared about Scrap was the subject of the majority of Cricket and Josha's arguments. While the other two trusted Scrap as their leader, even if Josha's acceptance was typically begrudging, Cricket still thought of Scrap as his little brother. Withdrawing that protective arm from around Scrap's shoulders was one of the few things that Cricket would not do for Josha.

"He does," Beckan said. "He loves him."

Because how else was there to describe how they were than to say they loved each other? Even on Josha and Scrap's worst days, one would have run into a burning building for the other. Beckan had long thought of family as a concept so simple she could keep it in a jar in the bottom of her tote bag. She hadn't known much at all about love and now she was in love with the concept of it, in love with hugging her boys and watching them hug each other, and she didn't want to believe that it could really be so much more complicated than that.

Cricket said, "They don't know what to do with each other. Scrap's willing to compromise a lot to keep us alive. Josha isn't."

"I'm with Scrap on this."

"Josha thinks there are more important things than staying alive."

"Like what?"

Cricket laughed. "Fuck if I know. I hope the gnomes drug me tonight. Makes it easier. I'm so tired."

When they left, Cricket said, "We'll be fine," softly in Josha's ear, and somehow tonight that was enough for Josha to lower his shoulders, to nod a little, to breathe.

"Don't be delicious," he yelled to Cricket, as always, as he left.

"Only thing I know how to be!" Cricket called back. As always. Every night, now.

"Listen," Piccolo says. "Can I ask you something?"

"Mmmhmm."

"That gnome I saw you with yesterday. Are you . . . friends?"

"Good friends, yeah."

"That's amazing. Beckan, that's amazing." He smiles. "This is perfect."

"What?"

"I probably sound crazy. I sound crazy. I just . . . I would really love to get a group of us together, and it will work so much better if we have a gnome too. Me, you guys, a gnome."

"Like a study group?"

He laughs. "You're thinking book club, I'm guessing."

"Shut up."

He keeps laughing lightly and gives his head a shake. "An antiwar group."

"The war is over. Shit. Shit." She looks through the ropes. "That's Josha down there. He sees us. I should go."

Piccolo glances down, but then looks immediately back to her. "Beckan, listen. This isn't peace. The gnomes are still scared to go aboveground, the tightropers are opening up shops like this isn't your city anymore, you're afraid to be seen with me. There can't be real peace during an occupation. We need to integrate, all of us. That's why we need a group. Being peaceful on your own, being quietly antiwar, it doesn't work." He ties another rope to her wrist to help her down. "Just think it over? I'm really not asking anything. Just to get to sit down with all of you together, meet your gnome friend, maybe? See if we can get a few gnomes together who want peace?"

"Maybe," she says, but she doesn't see any reason why not.

"Us young ones . . . we're the ones who can change things. We're not jaded and horrible and willing to accept that this will keep going and going. We feel things."

Yes.

Yes, Beckan feels things.

And right now she feels that Piccolo is a little beautiful.

He rips something off his jacket and hands it to her. "Here. It's our flag. Get a gnome flag too. And a fairy flag."

"There is no fairy flag."

"We'll make one! Perfect. Now our group has a mission." He smiles. "And then we'll make a joined flag. Combining features from all of them, stuff like that. It'll be a great way to bring us together at the beginning. Plus crafts are fun. Plus," he says, again, more quietly. "I wouldn't hate spending more time with you."

She says, "That's not the only mission I want to do."

"Yeah?"

She clings to the rope with both hands and says, "I want to find Cricket."

"Then we will."

Josha is still standing there when they drop down from the ropes, arms crossed. But he doesn't seem angry. He seems playful.

"So who's this?" he says.

"Piccolo." He offers his hand, and they shake. Josha is trying to be polite, but Beckan can see him sneaking glances at Piccolo. The last time he saw a tightroper was probably when they were laughing at him when he tried to join their army.

"What are you doing out?" she says.

"Scrap wanted me to come find you. He has a headache and he's all freaking out, worried because you said you'd be home."

"Oh. Shit."

He looks surprised. He expects her to be more formal in front of strangers. And now he's realizing that she knows Piccolo fairly well if she's cursing in front of him.

"So you made a friend, I see," he says.

"He knew Cricket."

"We're going to find him," Piccolo says. "We'll get something organized. Search parties. I'm going to work on it."

"Wow," Josha says, quietly.

"He was lovely," Piccolo says. "He had vision."

Josha breathes out. "He totally had vision."

She mills around while the two of them exchange small talk. They work in some more compliments of Cricket and some gentle ribs at Beckan's gnome-nose or lack of climbing skills.

"Do you want to come by to the cottage?" Beckan says. "Grab a drink or something? Better than talking on the streets."

Josha hesitates, and Beckan is confused; she thought they were getting along wonderfully, but he says, "It's just Scrap. I think he . . . will want to talk to us alone about this. It's not about you, it's just, you know. Business."

Piccolo nods.

Josha says, "Hanging out with tightropers . . . you know, it . . . didn't do Cricket any favors."

Piccolo looks down and swallows and says, "I'm so sorry."

Josha is quiet for a long time, and Beckan waits, wringing her hands, knowing that the next thing Josha says will be very important.

"I believe you," Josha says, softly, like he's a little surprised.

No one had ever been louder than Josha. And then she met Cricket.

They used the word *loud*, but it wasn't volume that came from Cricket, it was magnitude. Words fell out of his mouth like it hurt to keep them contained, and he constantly laughed and touched and

Cricket

stole your clothes and tried them on in front of you and determined they looked much better on him than on you. He would tell anybody everything.

Stupid boy.

It was a fucking *war*.

Josha is very quiet on the walk back to the cottage.

"Sorry if I scared you," Beckan says.

Josha startles and looks up. "What?"

She gives up. He isn't with her. He hasn't been in so long.

Scrap is in the kitchen, throwing dirty plates into the sink and scrubbing them with his whole arm. Nobody used to do dishes, since they all knew they were the first thing he headed for when he sleepwalked. They'd wake up to a spotless kitchen.

But he hasn't sleepwalked in weeks, and the dishes are piling up, and nobody knows what to say about it.

"How's your head?" Josha says.

"It's fine," Scrap snaps, shoving the dishrag back and forth across the counter. "I don't have a headache." The little wince he gives when he turns to look at Beckan isn't very convincing. "Where were you?"

"Whoa."

"You've been gone *all* day. Tier hadn't seen you, Josha hadn't, who the fuck else was I supposed to ask, your father? *Where were you?*"

"Maybe I'll tell you if you calm down." She takes the towel from him and shoves him toward a chair. "Will you sit down? You're still all hot."

He balls his hand into a fist and pushes it into his forehead.

This morning, everything was fine. They were fine.

This is why it's easier not to give a shit. To just be high above it all.

"Did something happen today?" she says.

"What?"

"In the mines? You were all calm earlier—"

"Where were you?"

She says, "Scrap, come on. I was up on the ropes. I made friends with a tightroper boy. That one you caught a glimpse of last time. He knows you. You've met him."

"Which one?"

"Piccolo."

"Piccolo?" He sits up straight and stares at her. "You go make a new friend, and you choose the son of the major general?"

"No," Beckan says. "No, he's not like that. He hates war. He hates the tightropers, for fuck's sake. He's their messboy."

Josha says, "Listen to her, Scrap."

"No. This is bullshit. Go hang out with Tier."

"Are you kidding me?" She stares at him. "Don't get me wrong here, okay? I love Tier. But he's a gnome. You'd rather I be friends with a fairy-eating gnome—"

"Don't say that about Tier," Scrap says, and she feels bad, she does, but Josha is over Scrap's shoulder, nodding, egging her on.

"—than a tightroper when they've never done shit to us . . . he bought my ring from Cricket, did you know that? He bought my ring. He's trying to start a peace movement. He wants to talk to you. To get to know you for real. To help us find Cricket. He's, I mean, he's a messboy, right? He has a broom. He can sweep the streets and everything, maybe find a little bit of Cricket." She's fishing, obviously, and she knows it—they don't need a tightroper to show them how to push a broom—but Beckan knows the cards to play to shut Scrap up and plays them well.

Because he does still think about Cricket. He thinks about too much. He gets headaches.

And right now he doesn't say anything. Because Beckan knew Cricket and she knows how to use him. And she hates herself a little for it.

Beckan says, "Piccolo said he's met you. What did you think of him?"

He breathes out, long and slow.

"I thought he seemed nice," he says, quietly. He adds, "But I've talked to him all of twice. I don't know the guy."

"But he wants to know you. So maybe you could give him a chance before you freak completely out? I think you might actually like him if you took a second to stretch outside these weird prejudices you seem to have developed all of a sudden."

Scrap looks like he's about to say something, but instead he deflates. "Yeah," he says. "You're right." He chews his cheek for a minute and says, "Sorry for yelling."

"Did you have a bad day or something?"

He laughs, once. "Yeah. Yeah, you could say that."

"Shit, honey. Did they hurt you?"

He shakes his head. "No. Everything's fine. Nothing you need to worry about."

"Please?"

He shakes his head again.

She gives up. She's done enough today. She goes to her room and takes her father out of her nightstand, where she's had him locked for so long it makes guilt pool in her stomach. She holds the jar and feels like a girl in a book, and for once that doesn't make her happy. She's not a hero anymore. She's just helpless and written.

8

SCRAP COMES UP from the mines the next day with the news that Tier is looking for Beckan, so she resists the instinct to make herself pretty and goes down in her sweatshirt and sneakers, even though it's too hot to be that covered up. The point is that they're not whoring clothes.

"You have to stop hiring me," she says, stripping off the sweatshirt as she enters his cave. But he isn't alone. There is Rig, beside him, one ankle crossed over the other.

She is big and brown, like she was carved right out of rock.

Beckan stuffs her sweatshirt in her tote bag. She is nervous in a way she hasn't been with Tier in a very long time.

"I'm sorry," she says, to Rig. "If I'd known you were here, I wouldn't have come."

"Beckan," Tier says.

"No, come on, she doesn't want to see me."

"I asked him to get you," Rig says.

Beckan stops.

Rig says, "I wanted to talk to you."

Tier leans over and gives Rig a miniscule kiss on the cheek before he scoots off the bed and out of his room. He doesn't touch Beckan.

Rig doesn't indicate if Beckan should sit next to her, so she doesn't. Rig stays still, and Beckan wanders the room like it's new to her, touching books on the shelves that she's read and ones that she's never noticed before, a picture Tier drew of his father, the picture of Rig.

"Beckan?" Rig says.

She snaps her head up.

"Are you afraid of me?"

She tries to find the words.

Rig says, "Please don't be."

"What do you have to eat?"

"You're hungry?"

Beckan shakes her head, and Rig seems to understand.

She says, "There's . . . carnage from the war, still. Tightropers. Some of our own. It's better than what we got while we were . . . The tightropers, they don't eat meat. They don't have the stomachs for it."

"And there aren't any fairies."

"No. You'd know if we had one. You could tell from up above. The glitter cooks off and . . . it makes that yellow smoke."

Her breath catches.

They do have a fairy.

They had one a few days ago.

She saw the smoke.

Rig is lying.

Beckan takes a step back.

Bad bad this is bad. Bad.

Where did they get a fairy?

They haven't found the smallest crumb of Cricket.

Beckan forces herself to calm down. Tier wouldn't hurt her, she thinks. Tier wouldn't even hurt Scrap. He would never leave her somewhere unsafe. He loves her.

And maybe Rig knows that.

"You're scared of me," Rig says. "I knew it. You're scared of me?"

Beckan nods before she can stop herself.

"No, Beckan, don't be. I just . . . I wanted to talk to someone. About Tier, and . . . well. You know him. And there just aren't many girls around. There were nurses up there who spit at us and there were the gnome girls stolen with me, but we were locked separately, we never . . . I need to talk to a girl."

"I know," Beckan says. Because she does too. Every day she feels words inside her that she wants to tell a girl, that she wants to giggle to her old neighbor or the women at the grocery store. She wants someone she can say the word *empty* to without getting rolled eyes or blank stares or a Cricket-style speech about how she shouldn't let the demands of society and masculine influence trick her into thinking that she wants a baby. She wants someone she can just tell that she wants a fucking baby.

If she does. Sometimes she does. She should be allowed to want one.

Except standing here, fearing for every bit of her, she would never wish being a fairy on anyone.

But then Rig says, "I always thought fairies were so beautiful. You're beautiful, Beckan." She smiles through tears and says, "I see why he loves you."

"He doesn't."

"Teach me how to love him again?"

"But I don't love him," Beckan says.

It's important to remember that when Beckan went down to the mines the first time, things were not very bleak yet. She was not even hungry, not really.

Riding down on that elevator for the first time, she still felt safe because she was with Cricket and Scrap. Even the floors passing by, layer after layer of dirt and steel, didn't scare her, because she hadn't seen any gnomes yet.

But she still couldn't help asking, "How do you know they won't eat you?"

"They need us," Cricket said, immediately. "Without us they're aaaaaall aloooone. And the glitter, they don't like that. And they can still get meat from a few animals they have out in the farms, and they'd have to eat all of us at the same time or else waste all of us because it's not like we'd come back," and Cricket kept talking to himself, quietly, while he bounced on his toes and watched the darkness grow through the elevator's bars, because that was what Cricket did. He talked.

So Beckan looked at Scrap, who said, with a small shrug, "We don't know. That's part of it."

Beckan thought that he meant "part of the risk," or "part of the job." It wasn't until later that she realized he meant part of the thrill, for a gnome and a fairy alike.

That it was just one second, just one pound of pressure difference between kissing and devouring that made the fairies worth every bit of the food they took. It was the reason that the fairies went home feeling disgusted and sick and sore but also alive, fucking brimming with it. It was the reason that, when Scrap and Cricket got drunk and told whoring stories, only half the time was it full of dizzy, drowned self-loathing. Sometimes they really were laughing because they were happy. Sometimes they didn't hate it.

Things weren't bleak yet.

"Okay," Scrap said as the elevator stopped. "They have some system among themselves to determine who gets each of us. It changes. We don't ask questions. I told them last time that you're coming, so they're probably going to be . . . excited."

She chewed on the inside of her cheek.

Scrap said, "So all you have to do is stand there, keep your mouth shut, and try to look charming. Tell him what you want up front—we need bread, Beckan. Get bread. If he thinks you're asking too much, he'll tell you. They've never done that to us, though. You should be fine." He nods. "You'll be fine."

The elevator finally groaned to a stop at the lowest floor. She wanted to trail behind the boys, but Cricket gestured for her to get off first, so she did, slowly.

And there they were, in front of her, as if they'd come from nowhere. Thirty gnome men, each twice her size, gnashing their teeth and pulling their hair back in their hands and rubbing their arms. She stood very still as Scrap and Cricket took their spots on either side again.

And then she saw him.

Crate.

He wore a gold crown and a necklace of heavy, uncarved diamonds. His teeth seemed longer and brighter than those of the others, his eyes redder, his thick legs so much thicker. He was something out of a storybook.

He nodded at Scrap, who nodded back.

"The new one?" Crate asked the crowd. "Who wants her?"

Beckan wrapped her arms around herself. Scrap immediately tugged them loose, but it didn't seem to help. Not a single gnome volunteered, or seemed to be considering her, or even looked up.

Beckan's heart hurt.

"For Cricket?"

Cricket, beside her, giggled and waved a little, and three gnomes—two halfheartedly, one eagerly—requested him, and Crate gave Cricket to the third, who clamped a heavy hand on Cricket's shoulder as he led him away.

Then Crate smiled, slowly, with all his teeth.

"And for Scrap?"

And everyone started cheering, howling, begging, licking their lips and reaching grimy hands out to Scrap, and Beckan looked at Scrap to see what had changed, where her tiny, pink friend had gone, but he was still there. He had a looseness to his hips and shoulders that wasn't natural, and his smile wasn't one she'd ever seen on him, but he was still Scrap. He was still mangy. He still was not beautiful.

But he would make them feel beautiful, and that was why they wanted him.

Crate laughed a little and shook his head. "No," he said. "No, today he's mine."

Scrap smiled at him.

Crate reached an arm over Scrap's shoulder like a proud parent and called, "You can go, fairy girl," over his shoulder. "There's no need for you tonight."

And she was left alone with the gnome men, who rolled their eyes and let her be, and she was not afraid.

She was embarrassed.

She was jealous.

She was so stupid. Beckan.

Rig drives her toe into the ground. "I listened to them rape the other girls. The smaller ones. They didn't want me."

"That's good," Beckan says. "You know that's good, right?"

"I know it. I don't feel it."

"Why would you want horrible tightroper military bastards to want you?"

"To . . . feel something at the same time as someone." She swallows. "You'd see the girls crying and comforting each other, and they'd stare at me like they'd never seen me. We grew up together. And now all of a sudden I was the outsider. Like I wasn't suffering.

Like I hadn't been kidnapped." She shakes her head. "I'm horrible. They went through something horrible. I know that. I don't want that."

But Rig *does* want that, and Beckan hates her a little. It's the same hate that made her scream at Josha the time he told her that she loved being a prostitute. It is guilty and self-aware. Of course Rig wanted to be hurt in a way she could qualify. Of course Beckan wanted to feel useful. There were so many truths, and those two were not acceptable.

(And then you are shoved back against the wall and pinned to rock and a dirty mouth finds yours and you are broken and used and adored and you crawl home and are cleaned up and loved beyond all reason and you scream from nightmares, how is anything supposed to be simple nowadays?)

"You have Tier. Tier loves you," Beckan says. "Look." She holds out the drawing.

"I don't feel it," Rig says. She takes the picture between her fingers, like it's fragile. "I feel them," she said. "I feel their hands on me, and they didn't even touch me. No one has touched me in so long."

"Teach me!" Beckan begged Scrap, the next day, while he was frying the two handfuls of meat Crate could spare in a skillet on the stove. "Teach me how to do it."

"The sex part is easy," Cricket said. "They have nothing to compare it to, you know?" He was on his stomach on the floor, reading through Scrap's red notebook, the war journal. "Gnome girls are teases. Scrap."

"Whaaaaat?"

"I'm bored. I am so bored." He held up the book. "This is so boring. Where's the sex?"

Josha came in from the hallway and lay on top of Cricket, curving himself to fit Cricket's body, his belly in the small of Cricket's back. "Sex?"

Cricket hit him with the notebook.

"That's not the part I'm worried about," Beckan said, though of course she was. How could she not be? She'd never seen anyone naked besides a glimpse of her fairy boys here and there, and those contexts were always too safe to feel sexual. She always thought sex would be something incredibly different, and she always thought her first time, her best time, would be with a devastatingly handsome wandering stranger who held her tightly and went weak when she kissed him.

Beckan could have written lovely sex scenes into Scrap's notebooks, they just would have had nothing to do with sex.

"Don't listen to him," Scrap said. He turned around, arms crossed. "Look. The sex part is important. And it's going to be terrifying at first. And it's going to hurt. Your clothes will feel heavy afterward, and you'll walk differently, and you'll wake up the next morning with marks and places that are sore and you can't remember why. You will feel like you missed something. You'll feel like you slept through some of it."

"But first they have to want me," she said.

"That's just semantics," Scrap said. "How you stand. How you walk."

"Teach me."

He shook his head.

"Please," she said, quietly.

Scrap took a few practice steps, crossing each foot in front of the other. The meat hissed on the stove.

Beckan got up and tried to copy him. "Like this?"

"No . . ." Scrap tried again, his brow furrowed. "Like this, more."

"I'm doing what you're doing."

Josha was watching Scrap's ass. "You're definitely not doing what he's doing."

Cricket hit him. "Give it up, Becks," he says. "It's not something he can teach. It's something about him. Gnomes think he's hot, I don't know."

Josha stood up and palmed the top of Scrap's head.

"Well," Scrap said. "I guess it's nice that someone does."

"Scrap fairy," Cricket said, affectionately.

"Yeah," Scrap said. "Scrap fairy." He was so short, but so was Beckan. He was messy hair and pink glitter. He still had both his arms then, but they were pale and not as muscular as Cricket's, and his eyes were too big and too dark. . . .

But there was something about him.

(Please, please, let there be something about him.)

Beckan scribbles down an address. She uses the back of Tier's drawing of Rig. "Come here tomorrow night," she says.

Rig looks at it. "Where is this? I don't know your addresses."

"Right. It's on the hills, at the edge, nearly out of the city." She sketches a map in the floor. The dirt gives easily under her fingernail, surprising her.

Rig's face says *There's an out of the city?*

"Tier knows the way. Bring him." She pauses. "Did you meet a boy named Piccolo when you were up there?"

She shakes her head.

"None of the girls mentioned him?"

"No. We weren't with any boys. We were with the men."

"He picks up trash."

Her face changes. "Oh. Oh, him." She nods. "I remember him."

"In a good way?"

Rig chokes out a laugh. "I don't think I know any good ways anymore."

"In a not-bad way."

"Yes. Not bad."

"I don't think Piccolo would ever hurt anyone," Beckan says. She hands Rig the piece of paper. "Piccolo likes art. We'll have tea and then . . . there's stuff to do. Anyway. You should come. With Tier. Tomorrow night. Around six?"

Beckan never got the walk exactly right. But the second time she went down to the mines, she brushed out her hair and put on sluttier clothes and she went on a night Cricket was off. Scrap kept studying her in the elevator, and it took her a minute to realize that what was confusing him was the two-and-a-half extra inches she got from her shoes.

"I like you short," he mumbled, which was stupid, because even barefoot she was a hair taller.

"I look like I know what I'm doing."

"You don't know shit," he said.

"I know how to stand and that it's going to hurt. What else is there?"

And then he grabbed her by her wrists and pinned her against the wall. He gripped the chest of her T-shirt, yanked her down to his level, and stopped. His hands were caught in her perfect hair and she was struggling out of her shoes and they were forehead-to-forehead, nose-to-nose, gasping into each other's mouths.

Beckan had kissed two boys before this: Josha, once, drunk, two years ago, and Scrap himself, small, snotty, spitty, when they were six years old, crashed in beds next to each other at the clinic, everything muffled by coughs and high fevers. She was so aware now of every bit of Scrap, from his dark dark hair to the chapped spot on his lip that he could never stop aggravating. Every part of him that was no longer a sweet, sick little boy. She ran her tongue over the chip in her front tooth, and then they were imperfect mouth against imperfect mouth, as hard and as deep as they possibly could.

He was cold, cold like water, and he made her so thirsty and she wanted to drink all of him, pull him into her mouth, suck him dry and carry all of his weight. Sounds vibrated out of her throat and into Scrap's lips and glitter scraped off his cheek and onto hers. She hit her ear against the wall and grabbed his ear so he could feel it too, so they would feel absolutely everything in this moment at exactly the same time. Their bodies were all elbows and sweat but this kiss was perfect. She was in love with this kiss in a way she had never been in love with anyone or anything; her whole life had come to this kiss, not the boy but the kiss, face-burning, clothes-ripping, heart-vibrating in love. And she bit Scrap's lip and he bit back and pinned her against the bars with his knee. And she had always thought it would be safe, would be horribly boring, would be an impossible, hideous life sentence to be in love with a fairy, to never die, to never hurt, and right now his nails dug her skin and his hipbones collided with hers and how did she ever think he was too short or too cold or too buttoned—*undo the fucking buttons*—or too near? For this second, he was perfect because he was half of this kiss, and this kiss was something rare and special. And his hands, his hands were everywhere, his hands were holding her and grabbing her and begging her closer and closer to him and longer and harder. His arms were around her neck with his hands on either side of her head, squeezing every bit of her out that he could get, begging every bit of her into his mouth, then grabbing her shoulder blades and squeezing her chest to his so hard they couldn't breathe and the elevator jerked to a stop at their floor.

They flew away from each other. Scrap wiped her lipstick off his mouth.

He said, "Now you know what you're doing."

And maybe it was the messed-up hair and smeared lipstick and the high heels she shoved back on as the elevator stopped, maybe it was her face, still a little dazed, or maybe it was just that Cricket wasn't there that day or that Tier had said something that either greatly pleased or gravely disappointed his father, but today Crate passed Scrap off to an attendant and gave Beckan a shrug. "Tier can have you," he said.

The crowd parted and on the floor sat a boy, chubby and small, a heavy book in his lap, a smudge of dust down his nose. He looked up and said, "Me?" and he looked at Beckan, and he was young and so much more terrified than she was.

And maybe she fell just a little in love.

It's so hard to picture now.

There is nothing in the history books about love.

Except Beckan would say that there's all that is.

Sometimes I think that Beckan is full of shit. Are you reading this, Beckan? Sometimes I think you're full of shit, and sometimes I can't believe how shortsighted you are, and sometimes I want to take you and pin you up against that wall again but I can't because Cricket's dead and the world is for shit and this was never about me. This will never, ever be about me.

And now I have so much else to worry about. I don't think you could ever know what I would give to have you be my biggest problem, Becks.

Fuck, I can't believe Josha was right, I can't believe this is a story about you.

9

AN HOUR BEFORE EVERYONE is scheduled to arrive, Beckan is a mess. She pushes the chairs in at the kitchen table, pulls them out to readjust the cushions, trips over Josha's shoe on the way to make the beds. "Do the fucking dishes!" she yells at Scrap, who is sitting uselessly at the kitchen table during all of this, head in his hands, reading Tier's history book.

"Shouldn't you be writing or something?" she says.

He looks up. "What?"

"All you've been doing lately is writing."

"I'm not writing anything," he says, absently, vaguely, turns a page.

"You're cutting and pasting. Making a scrapbook, Scrap? Should I take pictures? Come on. Do the dishes."

"I'll do them later."

"You don't even sleepwalk anymore."

The first problem is Josha. Beckan has been preparing him for hours, but as soon as Tier and Rig walk in, he is snarling his way to a corner of the kitchen. Rig flinches and watches him.

"He's fine," Beckan says. "Don't worry about him."

Tier says something in Rig's ear. Beckan listens for Cricket's name, but instead hears her own. Rig loosens and nods, and on the way to the table, she grabs Beckan's hand for a second and squeezes, and Beckan is confused that this makes her feel comfortable and big.

The second problem is Piccolo, who arrives late, but he shows up before anyone gets too suspicious. "Sorry, I got so lost," he says, with a smile like Beckan hasn't seen, on anyone, in months. He comes up behind her and gives her a hug that lifts her a few inches off the ground.

The third problem is Scrap, who watches this hug with one eyebrow arched, his arm wrapped around himself while he leans against the refrigerator.

"It's good to see you, Scrap," Piccolo says. He offers his hand—his left, to match Scrap's—and Beckan is nervous for a split of a second that Scrap won't take it. But he does, immediately.

Tier and Scrap make eye contact across the room.

Maybe she notices, maybe she doesn't.

"How are you?" Tier says, very softly.

Scrap nods a little.

"He's doing great," Beckan says, brightly, squirming out of Piccolo's arms. "He healed right up. Fever's gone and everything! He never gets sick. It was a fluke, yeah, Scrap?"

"Yeah."

Yeah, Piccolo mouths to her. She bites her lip.

"I like your house," Rig says, and Beckan scurries off to give her a tour while Piccolo greets Josha like an old friend.

They all sit around the table, Beckan between Rig and Piccolo, Josha on Piccolo's right, where he can best fawn over the big silver buttons on his military coat. "A hand-me-down of my dad's," Piccolo says. "Pretty much the only good thing he's given me."

"Mine left me some buckle-shaped scars on my back and a dry sense of humor," Josha says.

"Mine left most of that kid," Tier says, pointing at Scrap, who rolls his eyes and sticks his tongue in his cheek and finally sits down, next to Tier.

Beckan runs off to get her father.

When she gets back, everyone is focused on Scrap's arm, or where his arm would be. Rig touches a space a few inches under his ripped shoulder, like she thinks the arm might be invisible. Scrap gives her a small smile.

"Can I see it?" Piccolo says, and Scrap offers the stump of his arm as best he can, and Piccolo gives it a quick look before he shakes his head. "Disgusting," he says. "It's fucking sick."

"Oh," Rig says when he curses, not like she disapproves, not even like she's surprised, but like it is dawning on her that *this is what this is. This is how we are going to talk about this.*

Scrap pulls back.

Beckan isn't sure she's ever, ever seen him embarrassed before.

"No," Piccolo says. "No, I didn't mean you. I'm sorry. I mean . . . what happened to you. This is the kind of shit that war does," Piccolo says.

"Exactly," Josha says. "Exactly."

Scrap says, "Gnomes always ate fairies. The war didn't cause that."

"The war was the reason Cricket was anywhere near Crate," Piccolo says, as if Scrap needs this explained and he is the one to do it. No one mentions that Scrap and Cricket tricked for a year before the war started. That all it took was one dirty comment spat at Cricket while he was grocery shopping to make them realize it would be a pretty easy way to afford to eat like kings and sleep in late, which were the kinds of job perks they liked at that point.

"I really admire that you can be calm about it," Piccolo says to Scrap. "It's really incredible. I don't know how I could move on if something like that happened to me."

"We're fairies. We're used to having pieces missing."

Piccolo says, "It must be such a hard thing, this immortality of yours. Especially now, seeing that it . . . that's not a guarantee that you're going to live forever. It just means you won't die from natural causes."

"We always knew that," Scrap says.

"We won't die at all," Beckan says. "Just be lost." She peeks at her father and wonders about the rest of him, stuck in a dead gnome's stomach.

"You know a lot about fairies," Scrap says.

Piccolo is still smiling. "My mom used to tell me stories about a few fairies she met one time. I always thought you guys sounded amazing."

"Josha likes you guys, too!" Beckan says. "That's why he wanted to be in your army."

"What's the state of the gnome army, anyway?" Piccolo says, his tone changed, no longer light.

"Gnomes need leaders," Rig says quietly. "It's just . . . how we are. We like to be led."

"So now that the king's dead, they're not gonna be trying anything again?"

"I can't imagine so, no."

Tier and Scrap are looking at each other again, like they know something the others don't, and Beckan does not like this.

What kind of secret could the two possibly share? (Fuck, Beckan, I'm so sorry.)

"But truly," Piccolo says to Scrap. "That you're able to deal with losing that arm. It's incredible."

"It's killing him," Josha says. "He's just trying not to hurt Tier's feelings."

Scrap says, "Josha, would you shut up?"

"Bite me."

Tier looks up.

Josha growls.

"Tea," Beckan says, jumping up. "I'm making tea. Do you guys like tea?"

Tier says, "Yeah, we do."

"Piccolo?"

"I don't know what it is."

"It's good. You'll love it."

Beckan gets up to put the kettle on, and they're quiet for a minute at the table. Tier plays with Rig's fingers, and Josha keeps admiring Piccolo's jacket. Scrap sits perfectly still and somehow seems a hundred times calmer than the rest, and Beckan looks at him and thinks maybe it's because he just does not care.

You're always cold.

"It was my dad," Tier says, eventually. "Who ripped off Scrap's arm."

Piccolo nods, slowly.

"Tier's a good guy," Scrap says.

Beckan says, "He is," and Josha gives the smallest grunt of agreement, and Tier smiles at Josha with everything in him.

"Oh, God, of course," Piccolo says. The others look at each other in confusion, but Piccolo just scoots his chair farther into the table, leans more toward Tier. "Of course. Trust me, if I took after my father, I'd be ripping arms out too."

Tier watches him. He isn't smiling anymore, but his eyes still are.

"It really can skip a generation," Piccolo says. "Hopefully more."

"What can skip?" Rig says.

"War," he says. "Someone just has to make it happen."

They all are quiet. They look at each other.

And together, they start making a flag.

"The gnomes think the tightropers are planning something," Tier says, marker in one hand, teacup in the other.

"Tier," Scrap says. He looks up from Tier's history book, which he's been devouring instead of drawing. "Don't."

Tier takes a deep breath. "They don't know anything, really. But there's talking . . . there's always talking. Everyone's suspicious, no one's happy."

Piccolo nods. "I figured. I have no way of knowing what the tightropers are up to. They hide everything when I'm anywhere close."

"Why?" Rig says.

Scrap says quietly, to Tier, underneath everything, "We should talk later."

"Okay," Tier says. No one else notices.

Piccolo says to Rig, "Because . . . back at our last city, I had a . . . a someone. In my life. Who wasn't a tightroper."

"A fairy?" Beckan says.

"No, I've never been to a fairy city before. A fire-breather. We're nomads, y'know, we travel around, dropping in over other cities. We're so charming." He ruffles the hair on the back of his head. "Anyway, they broke us up, but . . . they weren't happy about that. Called me a blood traitor. These fucking bloodlines. That's how all of this crap gets started."

Tier says, "But some of it's good. Racial strengths—we have the teeth and talons, the fairies live forever, that stuff isn't worthless."

"It's not at all worthless. That's the problem. It's powerful. It's hideous scary shitty powerful. What's really important right now is that we're a united front. The group of us."

"A pack," Scrap says, softly.

Beckan lights up.

"Yeah," Piccolo says. "Yeah, totally like that."

"The thing is that I tend to screw up packs," Scrap says.

They talk and draw late into the night, Scrap fraying at the edges. He starts out calmly distant from the crafts and plans, but after a few hours he is restless, even twitchy, jumping up every few minutes to check that the stove is off or that the window in his bedroom wasn't left open. "Scrap," Beckan says. "Calm down?"

Eventually he opens up Tier's book and puts it on the table.

"Look at this," he says. His voice is scratchy. "Someone else please look at this. It's killing me."

"You were here first," Scrap says. "We pushed *you* underground. *We're* ruling *you*."

Beckan says, "No. No. They *eat* us. I'm sorry, Tier, but you eat us."

"I know." Tier puts his hand on Scrap's. "Hey. It's just one book. It's one truth. It's ancient history, anyway."

"But *I don't know which one is right.* How the fuck am I supposed to write a book if I don't know what the real truth is?" He's even quieter now. "How am I supposed to . . . make any decisions? It's not even a matter of choosing what side to be on, it's . . . how do you even keep track of what the sides are when you can't even get the whole story?"

Scrap starts falling asleep at the table—maybe still worn out from being sick, Beckan thinks, because she can't figure out any other reason for him to be so out of sorts—and they send him off to bed, but the rest of them stay up, drinking cups of tea. They make maps for where they will look for Cricket. Beckan assumes they'll be sneaking around, like she and Scrap used to (why did they stop? Why did

Ferrum was once the largest gnome city in the world, but a fairy invasion in 1390 forced them underground and into a lower-class position. Gnomes in Ferrum are subjected to terrible conditions underground and are at the mercy of a tyrannical fairy rule. Half starved, they have no choice but to fall to predatory instincts, and many remain oblivious to the superior conditions of gnomes outside of Ferrum. What was once a great city for gnomes is now merely one more fairy city. There is nothing remarkable about Ferrum besides the longevity of its injustices.

Bol Trav, *The Rise and Fall of Gnome Culture,* 1936, p. 183.

(I have no idea what 1936 means. I have no idea when they started counting their years. I have no idea what is important to them. I had no idea they were around that long. I'm so sorry, Tier.)

the end of the war make them stop?), but Piccolo says no, that being visible is part of the plan. Being visible lets them know that every member of a resistance is important and together.

Piccolo says, "We need to stay safe, but we also need to send the message that we're going to be doing that *together*. That we're not going to let any kind of threat turn us into fairy versus gnome versus tightroper. Do you mind if I do those dishes? They're driving me crazy."

Beckan and Josha look sadly at the sink. They nod a little.

It was a running joke, the sink full of dishes, because it was one of the most blatant examples of the bizarre routines that made everything bearable. Whether they wolfed down sudden feasts of food or licked yesterday's remnants off tea saucers, they always knew that they could throw their plates in the sink and let them pile high and disgusting, and when they woke up, they would be clean and put away. Because they had a sleepwalker, and their sleepwalker was as predictable by night as he was by day.

He was so harmless. He'd get up from bed, do the dishes, and go back to sleep. Sometimes he would dance a little around the kitchen, humming. Beckan liked to catch him at that and lead him back to bed. She wouldn't wake him up. She kept that a secret for a long time.

Three hours later, they have given up on all things serious and are rolling around on the floor, playing cards, when Scrap comes in from the bedroom. He looks exhausted and nervous and confused.

"Is he okay?" Tier says.

"He's sleepwalking," Josha says. "He's all right. He never leaves the house."

Rig watches him. "Does he do this a lot?"

"No." Beckan is watching him too. "No, not anymore." She smiles. "It's good. It's . . . Scrap. He's being like Scrap."

Scrap wanders over to the sink. They giggle and pretend they're going to trip him. "What's he going to do?" Josha says. "There are no dishes!"

"Poor thing's going to be confused," Rig says.

Scrap turns on the tap and reaches his hand out for the first dish. He grasps around in the dead space, opening and closing his fingers again and again.

They keep laughing.

And Scrap, fast asleep, leans over the empty sink and starts to cry.

There is a rush to get to him, but Josha gets there first, and he puts a cautious hand on each of Scrap's shoulders.

"Okay, Scrap. Shh shh shh. You're okay, buddy."

Tier holds Beckan back and whispers, "Let them."

For the first few weeks, Beckan and Tier did not talk.

It was a business relationship. Beckan knew that going in, but she had still expected to get a certain thrill out of prostitution, and all she felt was sore and lonely. Scrap and Cricket lived dangerously, bouncing from gnome to gnome, not knowing who they would have and who would be cruel, but Beckan, stuck night after night with only Tier, had nothing to fear from the nervous, cautious boy who made sure she always had a pillow under her head, who sometimes sobbed another girl's name at the end.

Eventually they shared a few words, the occasional smile, maybe a kiss now and then, and with the promise of food at the end of the night the sex became fine, nothing special, but nothing that would keep her awake shaking and sweating and whimpering in pain and fear like it sometimes would the boys. She enjoyed it as much as she could and found other things to focus on. Usually, those things were the drawing of Rig and Tier's massive bookshelf.

"Do you read?" was the first real thing Tier ever said to her.

She was pulling her pants back on. She looked up.

And he looked down. "I'm sorry," he said. "You always drift over to them. I only wondered."

She bit down on her lip. Tier already probably thought she was stupid since she never talked. What would he think of her when he learned she couldn't really read?

"Fairies can read," she said.

"Some of my books are by fairies."

"Really?"

"Mmmhmm. Look at the names."

She found the names of the authors and sounded them out to herself as quietly as she could. Most of the names did sound like fairies, but it wasn't always easy to tell. Beckan always worried, irrationally, that the hard sounds in her name betrayed that she was half gnome, that it took Cricket's litheness for a fairy to carry a name that sounded so fierce. Beckan was short, soft, solid. Names could be unfairly transparent, after all. She knew for sure that Scrap's name betrayed he was just a bit of something.

Tier went to the bed and shook glitter off the sheets. He spat a bit out of his mouth. "Do you know how much our women love . . . loved fairies?"

Beckan touched her hair.

"They'd do anything to have a fairy baby. They toss it aboveground and no one will ever care that the child is half gnome. They will call it a fairy and the thing will grow up to hate gnomes and live forever. Like you, correct?"

"What?"

"You. You're half gnome."

"You judge your women for wanting to have fairy babies—maybe you should stop eating their kids."

"Do you know your mother's name? Did your father ever tell you? He was a diplomat, yes?"

She liked the way he ended sentences. She liked that he sounded uncomfortable. It made her feel powerful.

"My dad is a diplomat," she said. "He's in a jar."

"What was your mother's name?"

"I only know her first name. She's dead now. That's all my dad told me."

Tier was quiet for a minute. "You're the last one," he said. "The last half-gnome."

"I know. There will be more."

"There haven't been. Not for sixteen years. You're the last link between gnomes and fairies." He laughed, once, to himself. Then he stopped. "What did you say her name was?"

"Spark. Dad said Spark. She's dead, right?"

He closed his eyes and said, "Yes. I . . . yes. "

He hurried to the bookshelf and started to read the spines, then he shook his head and said, "Take one. Take any of them."

"What?"

"The books. Take whatever you want." He forced a stack into her hands. "Take them. Take anything."

Beckan shakes free and is the one to lead Scrap back to bed. She knows not to wake him up, but her hand brushes his half arm accidentally and it jerks him awake.

"Sorry," she says. "Sorry."

". . . Beckan?"

"You were sleepwalking. Just bringing you back to bed. Don't worry."

"Am I crying?"

"There weren't any dirty dishes. It scared you. Josha hugged you. Let's get you in bed, okay?"

She eases him between the covers, but he stiffens a little and says, "Oh, Becks, I'm fine I'm fine I'm fine," and gets under himself.

He brings his knees up and tucks his chin on top. "I'm sorry," he says. "Really embarrassing. I cry all the time lately."

"Not really. Not as much as me."

"No way."

"I cried this morning because I couldn't find my hairbrush."

Scrap laughs a little. "It's hard at night," he says. "Everything's harder at night. Your friends seem nice. But angry."

"You mean Piccolo."

"Yeah."

"Josha's angry too," Beckan says. "It will be nice for him to have someone to be angry with. I don't even know how to be angry for more than a minute anymore. It's there and then it's gone."

"I'm not even angry, just sad all the time."

"Me too. It's harder at night."

"It's so much harder at night."

Beckan squeezes his hand. "I have something for you. I think now might be the time."

Scrap looks up. "Yeah?"

"Yeah. Hold on." She runs down to the basement and grabs it from her welding bench. It's not perfect, but neither is Scrap.

She brings it to him. "See, see," she says. "It's an arm. I made it for you. It has straps to go to your shoulder."

Scrap stares at it, his eyes enormous. "Oh . . . Beckan . . ." he says, and she is concerned, and he says, "No, no, it's a good *oh*. Fuck, Becks, I can't believe you did this. I wondered how a hook was taking you this long."

She laughs and helps him attach it to his shoulder. "The fingers don't move, of course. I'm not a genius. But you can move them with the other hand. If you wear a sleeve, it will just look like you have a metal hand, like the rest of your arm is still there, and that's pretty cool, isn't it? And if you wore a glove . . ."

He plays with the fingers. "I can't believe this."

"You like it?"

And he grabs her, two arms, one enormous hug.

"Love you," he says. "You're incredible."

"You're gonna get glitter all over it," she says. "It'll look just like your real arm. Wherever that is."

Scrap is suspiciously quiet.

A throat-clearing from the doorway. They turn around, startled, like they were doing something wrong, but it's only Josha.

"Everyone left," he said. "Help me clean up?"

Josha having the energy and motivation to clean is not something Beckan wants to scare away. She looks at Scrap.

"Go ahead. I'm fine. I promise."

Maybe she doesn't believe him. But she says, "Don't let them get you."

(They used to say that, bloody and ground down at the end of a long night, when there was nothing else they could take from them and no other ways they could be broken, they said *Don't let them get you,* like that would make them have something left.)

"I won't." He looks at her. "I promise that I won't."

"Sleep."

"I will."

"Nice arm, kid," Josha says.

Scrap shoots him a hesitant smile, not sure if he's joking, and they close the door on him cradling his arm to his chest like it is precious, like it is perfect.

The next morning, when Beckan is out at the tightroper shops and Scrap is about to, like every morning, like every afternoon, go down to the mines, Josha goes to the closet in the basement where they've stuffed Cricket's things and starts rooting through. He startles when Scrap walks by.

"I thought you were gone," Josha says.

"Just about. What are you doing?"

"Just looking through his papers and things. Does it matter?"

"That's my stuff," Scrap says. "I keep it in here. That's mine."

Josha drops the pages, quickly. "Oh," he says. "Sorry."

Scrap says, "I thought you were going to give me a break about this. I'll let you read it when it's done."

"Like I want to read that."

"Why else would you be going through my shit?"

"I thought it was Cricket's. I'm sorry." He stands up. "You're going to the mines?"

"Yeah. Josha?"

"Hmm?"

"If you and Beckan were to want to get out of the city for a while . . . just, do you know how you might do that?"

"What?"

"I'm just asking. If you have any idea what direction would be the way to go."

"The city's blocked off. Gnomes are lining the place, posts set up in front of all the gates, tracing the walls. You didn't know?"

Scrap freezes. "What?"

Scrap had not known that.

That had not been in Scrap's book.

"They went out there a few days ago. You need to get out from underground more. Hey, get cash from them and get more stuff at the shops, okay? I forgot to tell Beckan I really want taffy. You like taffy, right?"

"Yeah. I'll . . . see what I can do."

"How come you don't bring anything up anymore?"

"Shut up, Josha."

A few weeks before he died, Cricket started coming home with twice, three times as much food as usual.

"Don't you wonder how he's getting that?" Beckan asked Scrap.

"Yeah," Scrap said. "But it's probably some risky shit. Two at once, taking some of the syrups instead of the pills." All the stuff that Scrap had told Beckan, before she had even gotten dressed that first day, that she was not allowed to do.

"He goes up to the ropes all the time."

"Yeah. Hmm. Maybe he's tricking for them too."

"Don't you want to know?" Beckan said.

"No. I don't."

"I'm going to talk to him," Beckan said, and maybe she did, but Scrap didn't and he never checked up, because no one has ever been as horrible at leading a pack as Scrap was.

(Remember to take that out in the final draft, that's stupid, I've got to stop making things that aren't about Cricket about Cricket. That's not even where that scene should go. It has nothing to do with anything. Remember to cross that out. Cricket, I miss you. I miss you so much, you stupid bastard.)

10

SHE CAME HOME rather early that evening after Tier first handed her the stacks of books, tottering under the pile. Scrap had told her earlier not to wait up; Cricket was taking the night off, and he was pulling double duty to compensate. It had taken her hours earlier that day of wondering why Scrap wasn't angry at Cricket before she realized that the night off was not Cricket's doing.

She wasn't afraid of walking home alone, though a part of her did wish that Josha cared enough to keep her home, too. She could hear the quick snicks above her of tightropes being stretched and cut and new ones strung at twice the speed.

She heard giggling as soon as she opened the front door. "You're not alone anymore!" she yelled. She dropped the books on the floor, all except one that was bright yellow and looked the most loved that she'd already decided was her favorite, and she ran into Cricket and Josha's room.

They were both under the comforter, Josha drowsy with his head on Cricket's chest, his eyes closed, his mouth in a smile, and Cricket whispering in his ear while he played with his hair. They had a candle lit on the nightstand and Beckan thought they were so pathetic and so lovely.

She pounced on the bed beside them, and they groaned and laughed.

"Miss me?" she said.

"Desperately," Cricket said. "Right, kid?"

"Desperately," Josha said.

She gave them her biggest smile. "Tier gave me a book."

"Tier?" Cricket said. He never paid attention.

"Her gnome." Josha wasn't smiling anymore.

Cricket said, "Ew, Beckan, go take a shower."

"He's nice. He gave me tons of books, actually. I'm going to make Scrap read them all with me all the time and then he won't have any time to make me read his horrible stories. Everyone wins."

"But Scrap," Cricket pointed out.

"Hmm. Yes. Poor Scrap. But he never wins anyway. Not even in his stupid stories."

"He's in the stories?" Josha said.

"No, no. Of course not really. But you can always tell which one is supposed to be him," Cricket said.

"He doesn't even write stories anymore," Beckan said. "He's a big historian now. You piss him off when you keep mentioning them."

"That's why I do it! My little Scrap used to make things up and he's so *embarrassed* about it. Where is he?" Cricket said. He climbed out of bed—Beckan was surprised to see that he was dressed, since they weren't very careful at this point, now that they'd seen each other kissed and touched and stripped down— and pulled on another sweatshirt. They had a wood-burning stove, but it did little to keep the house warm in the middle of winter. And the later in the year it became, the darker and longer the nights and the weaker their candles seemed.

Were they starting to lose hope already? I can't remember.

"He's probably still down in the mines," Beckan said.

"I hope he brings soup," Cricket said. "Or something we can make soup out of. Or a recipe for how to make soup out of the bread and old cheese we didn't eat last night."

Josha pressed his lips to the top of Cricket's head. "In the mood for soup, are we?"

"Yeah."

And then the world exploded.

The house shook, the vase fell off Josha's dresser, and Beckan's father, in her room, rolled around in his jar. Half a mile away, something cracked and fell, and half a mile beneath that, mines collapsed.

Gnomes suffocated.

"Scrap," they said. "Scrap."

I don't want to write about back then anymore.

I don't want to write this fucking book anymore.

He didn't come back for a day and a half.

They thought that if the tightropers bombing the mines hadn't killed him, the gnomes surely would have eaten him by then. It was a long time before she learned why they hadn't.

He had been trapped alone.

After Cricket stood on the streets and screamed at the sky that a fairy was trapped underground, the tightropers took to the ground with jackhammers and shovels and dynamite. They blew holes in the ground and sent down gun-laden search parties and Cricket screamed at them *what is wrong with you what is taking so long I hear your guys up there still drinking and laughing why aren't you saving him why aren't you liberating us* and finally the soldiers emerged in the middle of the night with a half-starved, shaking little fairy.

They were awake when Scrap came through the door. They'd been awake for thirty-four hours.

They tried to touch him, but he shook them off. He went to the sink and washed his face over the dirty dishes, again and again and again.

"We're so glad you're okay," they said, and they didn't know what else to do when the only thing they wanted in the whole world was to touch him and he wouldn't let them.

That night, Beckan stood at his doorway and looked in on him. He was curled around the pillow, lying on his side, his eyes squeezed shut. He was so very not asleep.

"Scrap," she said.

He startled.

"Can we read together?"

He sat up and nodded. She climbed up on the bed next to him, and while she sounded out the words, he lay his head on her chest and took deep breaths she could feel in her own body.

"I missed you," she said. "Don't ever disappear like that again."

He was breathing so carefully.

"Is Tier okay?" she whispered, as he was falling asleep.

He cleared his throat. "His side didn't collapse," he said. His first words since he came home, and Beckan wished they'd been something more significant. Something about her. Something about him.

"I love you," she said.

He looked up at her. "I love you, too."

The next day he locked himself in his room and wouldn't come out. It was too much. It was all just too much.

Tier gave Beckan a book to bring to him.

I don't want to write about back then anymore.

I don't want to write any of this anymore.

Josha is lingering by a bombed-out building with Tier, Rig, and Piccolo, waiting for Beckan to show up. He should have waited for her.

He looks up toward the cottage, that tiny blur in the distance. She'll be okay walking down alone. There isn't anything to worry about anymore.

Piccolo says, "So . . . Beckan welds."

"She made an arm for Scrap. It's amazing. I've never seen anything like it."

"You sound happy," Piccolo says, and Josha blushes.

Piccolo is very pretty, is the thing.

He says, "Do you think she could . . . I'm talking hypothetically. But if we needed her to. Do you think she could make us armor of some kind?"

Josha says, "Shields, helmets? Yeah."

"Good. That's good." He pauses. "Do you think she could make weapons?"

Piccolo divides their map of the city in sections for the Cricket search. He tells Tier and Rig and Josha to take the inner circle and the mines while he and Beckan scan the perimeter.

"Look under *everything*," he tells them. "Try calling him. It can't hurt. This is so, so important, guys."

Josha gives him a small smile.

"I want to stay with you two," he says to Piccolo, and Rig and Tier are planning a strategy.

Piccolo puts a hand on Josha's shoulder. "I need you to look out for them," he says. "Look, they seem like good kids, but this is all really new to them. I want to make sure they're invested."

"This is really new to all of us," Beckan says, not quite sure what this is.

"I know I can trust you two." Piccolo smiles at Josha. "I know I can trust you, kid."

Josha grins and runs off, and Beckan says, "No one's trusted him for a long time."

Piccolo plays with her fingers. "I figured. We've got to get up on the ropes real quick, ready?"

"Oh . . ."

"I just need to see if the tightropers know anything. Play lookout."

"About Cricket?"

"About anything."

"Stop looking at me!" Piccolo says, laughing.

"I'm not looking!"

"You're supposed to be looking *out*. Out *there*."

But she is just loving this, loving watching him root through the stacks, mumbling to himself, singing bars of songs she doesn't know. He's alive, quick-fingered, enjoying himself.

And there's no one around. They are in their own world.

He emerges triumphant with a stack of papers and they run, and she is so good at the tightropes now, and he picks her up and twirls her like she is a little thing.

"You're amazing," he says. "God, look at you."

She doesn't know that word. *God.* She doesn't care. "You are so much better than them," Beckan says, talking about the tightropers, the gnomes, everyone they have stolen from, everything. "You give a shit. I like that you give a shit."

"I like that you smile," Piccolo says, and right now she is lit up like twenty thousand stars. And then they are kissing, then they are on top of each other, sinking into the net of the ropes, then they are touching and holding and clawing at each other and Beckan starts laughing, she is so happy, she hasn't been this happy in so long, nobody else makes her this happy and nobody else ever has. Nobody. She needs happy right now. It is what she should handle and all she should have to.

And then they hit the streets. They're not subtle and they're not quiet and they scream Cricket's name and they hear Josha and Rig and Tier doing the same. They don't find Cricket, but Beckan finds strength and excitement and power that she didn't know she had.

Josha and the gnomes come back with paperwork about possible new tunnels the gnomes are building, possible access routes to open areas, possible formulas for explosives, and they crowd in an empty lot that once was not an empty lot and tear through what they've found and Piccolo tells them how proud he is.

She and Josha get home very late. Scrap is already asleep, on top of his covers, all of his clothes still on, even his shoes. "We should feed and water him," Josha grumbles. "Like a plant."

"Like your bean sprouts."

"They died."

Beckan wakes Scrap up and hands him a glass of water. He sips. He is so tired.

"You didn't come home for ages," he says.

"We were out," Josha says. "Having fun. You should try it."

Scrap rubs his eyes. He looks confused. "What did you guys do? I saw you"—he points to Josha—"and Rig and Tier in the mines."

"We were looking for Cricket," Josha says. "You were in the mines? Why are you down there all the time?"

"We've gotta eat," he says weakly.

"Then where's the money?"

"Josha . . ."

"We did missions!" Beckan says. "Josha and Rig and Tier in the mines, me and Piccolo up on the ropes, and then all of us on the ground."

"What kind of missions?"

Josha says, "Looking for Cricket, I fucking told you."

Beckan says, "We did some reconnaissance stuff too, gathered information."

"Stealing?"

"Well . . ."

Scrap rubs his forehead. "You guys stole from the gnomes? Do you know what a horrible idea that is? And the tightropers?"

Beckan and Josha look at each other quickly.

Like they know something Scrap doesn't.

(Scrap doesn't pay any fucking attention because Scrap is an idiot.)

Josha says, "We didn't steal anything important. Just paperwork. It's not a big deal. Scrap, seriously, what is this? I sure as fuck don't need another dad, and—"

"Neither do I!" Beckan says brightly. "Mine's getting sun on the windowsill."

"What'd you find?" Scrap says. "Are they planning an attack? Are the tightropers . . . are they doing something against the gnomes?"

Josha clucks his tongue. "Awfully protective of gnomes lately, aren't we?"

Scrap stares him down.

Josha sighs. "The gnomes haven't given up. They're waiting for the right time or something, but they're making plans. We went over it all with Piccolo. It's just what Tier was hearing whispers of. They're trying to organize . . . get some kind of new king. And after that they want to do a huge press aboveground. But they're not going to do it until they feel like the tightropers are weak and until they have their new king. They're pretty much impotent without this king."

Beckan says, "Piccolo says as long as we figure out what we're doing before they have the new king, we have an advantage. Then it just comes down to making the tightropers think it's time for them to clear out, maybe alter their paperwork, make them think there's some more lucrative city out there. And if their ropes are torn down, that'll help with that because starting over in a new city would be practically as easy as staying."

"Did it say who?" Scrap says.

Josha says, "What?"

"The king. Who they want for the king."

Josha looks at him funny. "No. There was nothing in the papers we found. You think they have someone in particular in mind?"

Beckan says, "They want Tier, don't they." She looks at Scrap. "Scrap, we can't let them have Tier. They'll break him."

Scrap says, "I'll try to make sure they don't bring his name up. I haven't heard anything about him."

"One of his brothers would be more likely. . . ," Beckan says to herself.

Josha's still watching Scrap. "You'll make sure they don't bring his name up? You have a lot of pull down there or something?"

Scrap groans. "Josha, I'm just down there a lot."

"Yeah, and *why*? You didn't used to go down nearly this much—"

"There's only two of us tricking now!"

"Wow, *really*? You think I didn't know that?"

Beckan looks at Scrap and shakes her head. "Not cool."

"I wasn't trying . . . to be cool."

Beckan gets up and hugs Josha.

Scrap says, "Look. What happened to Cricket is all the more reason for us to be really careful. To not be running around stealing things."

Again, another moment where Beckan and Josha look at each other.

'Foreshadowing' is an important narrative trick that plays with the power the writer has over his characters! A plot point that foreshadows something still to come may at the time seem small and insignificant, and the reader—similarly to the characters themselves—may have no idea that this point will have any significance! Skilled authors use foreshadowing to emphasize a theme or to make future plot events integrate themselves more naturally into the existing plot; one of the benefits of fiction is that any good author has already planned how each event will predict those in the future! Imagine a book where the author didn't know what would come next! How would he know what to emphasize!

Anish Lyza Kornblass, Fiction Writing for Beginners! (538 A.F.), p. 71

(author's note: fuck. everything.)

"You're overreacting," Beckan says. "The war's over. We're just try-ing to keep it that way."

"I hope I'm overreacting. I seriously hope so. Are you sure no one saw you go down?"

Josha says, "Stop hovering."

"There are ways to have fun, okay? There are ways to have fun—"

"We're *looking for Cricket,* you asshole," Josha says.

"So the paperwork is what, then? What does that have to do with Cricket?"

"You've been trying to get me out of the house for weeks, you think you'd be okay with me freaking multitasking. And you want to talk about intentions?"

Scrap says "What're you talking about" like it's a statement, not a question. Like he already knows exactly what Josha's talking about and doesn't have the words to stop him.

And sure enough, Josha takes the blue notebook off Scrap's nightstand and throws it at the bed before he walks out. The pages flutter open, and clippings from newspapers and older books come loose and fall onto the comforter.

"*Shit.*" Scrap starts stuffing everything back in. He is very adept now with his fake arm. He balances the notebook on it, uses the wrist to tuck pages back into the pockets, scoops up pages between the fingers.

But Beckan stops him. "What is this?" she says.

"It's nothing. Just something I've been working on. A journal."

"I saw my name."

"It's nothing," he says, but he doesn't fight when she takes it out of his hands.

She opens it near the beginning and reads a little.

"Even though Beckan was only a tooth, an eye, and an ear away from living alone, Scrap and Cricket's parentless house felt lawless to

her in a way hers never did. Maybe that one eye was enough to make her feel watched—though she had to admit that, more and more often, she was leaving her father tucked away in corners or stuffed, as he was now, at the bottom of her tote bag—or maybe it was that her father's apartment could somehow never feel small and bright and reckless in the way of this cottage, where every corner felt filled with something easy and significant, like family."

"You're writing about me?" she says.

"No, it isn't about you. It's about the war. I'm using us, but just as a device."

"What? I'm not a device!"

"No, that's not what I—"

"No, but you're pretending to be in my head," she says. "You're writing as me."

"And Josha! Josha, too. And sometimes Cricket, even. Not just you. It's just . . . easier than being in my own head. I don't know." He runs his hand through his hair. "I can't write from me right now."

She flips through the pages. "Some of this is familiar."

"Yeah, from the old notebook, parts of it, some of the descriptions from back then, a few pages from Tier's books, and the conversations we've had, the scenes I'm in, those should look familiar, I have a good memory, the dialogue's off some of the time I'm sure, but it's close—"

"This must have taken you ages."

He keeps talking like he didn't hear her. "The stuff from during the war is in past tense, the stuff happening now is in present tense, but that's just to make it clearer. I'm a few days behind, always, I'm always a few days behind, and I don't know if that's good because then maybe I can have some perspective, but on the other hand it would be nice to be at the same time as something and I'm writing about you meeting Rig, now, the parts when I was sick were tricky and the parts I wrote when I was sick are these crazy ramblings, but I think I figured it out from how we talked later—"

"Writing about me meeting . . ." She tries to find the passage in question, but he finally comes to his senses and takes the book away. "You write about things you're not there for?" she says. "Things that I do? Are you spying on me?"

His eyes get huge. "No, no! It's made up. Here." He opens the notebook. "Here, here. Here's you talking to Rig."

She reads for a minute, mouthing the words to herself. Then she shakes her head. "No. I didn't say this. We never said this."

"I know. I'm not trying to . . ." He breathes out. "I'm just trying to write what makes sense." He shakes his head. "I'm just trying to get it out of my mind."

She touches the notebook and hands it back.

He says, "I'm trying to put it together in a way that makes sense."

"But you're not in my head really. So you're going to miss stuff. This isn't really me."

"I know. . . ."

"Stuff is going to happen that you weren't expecting and it's not gonna work with what you've already written and then what? Books are supposed to make *sense*. Stuff is going to come out of *nowhere*."

He's breathing fast. "I don't know. Shit, I don't know. It's just to keep my mind clear. It isn't important."

She shakes her head for a minute, slow.

"You can keep doing it," she says. "If it helps. Just don't forget you're getting everything wrong."

Get out of my head get out of my head get out of my head get out of my head

11

AFTER SCRAP WAS TRAPPED, the war changed.

It was no longer a harmless little thing, an inconvenience keeping them inside, like a thunderstorm or a case of the flu. It was a gray monster hanging over the city, with growls like bomb blasts and claws as sharp as gnome teeth. They had never felt more disconnected from the city, up in their little cottage, and Josha and Beckan responded by locking themselves inside, and Cricket and Scrap stopped coming home every night and started sleeping in shattered doorways and the remains of blasted sidewalk benches.

"We're the ones who grew up in the city," Josha said. "What the fuck are they trying to prove?"

They couldn't explain it, and neither could Beckan, but somehow it seemed to keep both Scrap and Cricket's nightmares at bay when they crashed in the city, together but not together, each on the opposite side of a destroyed grocery store, empty tin cans and cardboard displays upturned around them like covers, feet stretched out toward each other like they were trying to reach across the rows of black-and-once-white tiles. They found bits of food the armies had left behind. They brought most of it back up to the house. They ate some of it crouched in corners, devouring old coffee grounds and stale jelly beans. They made pinky promises, like they did when they were six and seven, that they would not tell Beckan and Josha. "I love you most," Scrap told him. "Don't ever forget."

"I don't," Cricket said, but he did sometimes. The city smelled like smoke and something rotten, something sick, something growing in the sores on their skin.

"You look like shit," Beckan said on one of those days.

Scrap was drinking coffee beans mixed with rain water, swirled in an empty can of split pea soup, wrapped in one of the tightroper army's homemade newspapers.

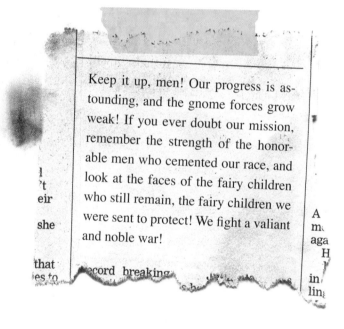

Keep it up, men! Our progress is astounding, and the gnome forces grow weak! If you ever doubt our mission, remember the strength of the honorable men who cemented our race, and look at the faces of the fairy children who still remain, the fairy children we were sent to protect! We fight a valiant and noble war!

An excerpt from the tightroper newspaper, 12/16/345, writer unknown (couldn't be Piccolo)

"I'm just tired," he said.

"And cold. And skinny as fuck."

"We're all skinny. There's no fucking food." He pulled a mouthful from the cup, swished it around his mouth, and spit it out.

"Charming," she said.

He coughed a little.

"We're all freaked out from you being trapped, okay?" she says. "You don't have to do this wounded mysterious act. We know what's going on. Come home."

But they were headed to work.

He said, "I'm not pulling any act. I'm not trying to make any sort of point. I'm just . . . doing what makes sense right now."

"Sleeping on the ground in the cold makes sense? When you already have a cough like that?"

"Being here, in the city, where I can see what's going on."

"Where you can die the next time they fling a bomb in the right direction."

He wiped his nose on his hand. "They know we're down here. Cricket talks to them. Haven't been any bombs in forever."

"Yeah, since the one that almost killed you. What about the gnomes?"

"I'm only worth one thing to them now, and it isn't fucking food, I'll tell you that." He pinched his skin. "They couldn't eat me. I'm skinny as fuck."

"Cricket's been bringing home a lot lately," Beckan said. "Did you ever talk to him about how he's getting that much money?"

"No. Did you?"

"Yes."

He looked at her, and he didn't ask.

He said, "I don't want to know. I have this image of Cricket in my head and he's just like a big brother and I don't want that to get ruined, okay?"

"Not fucking okay. What the fuck is wrong with you?"

"I need this. I need this thing to hold on to. He's the one of us who's changed the least and I just want to hold on to that, okay?"

Beckan didn't say anything.

"Just tell me one thing," Scrap said. "Just . . . what he's doing. Is he safe? Is he going to get hurt?"

Beckan was quiet for a minute, then she said, "No. No, I think he'll be fine."

I. Do. Not. Blame. Her.

Just making that clear.

They were rewarded that day with a thigh of something they hoped was a chicken, and they were halfway through promising to bring it, intact, back to the cottage, where Josha had tempted Cricket into an extended visit home with promises of boiled-water baths and bedtime stories, when they both took rabid hungry bites of the meat right there in the mines, holding the carcass between them, chewing with teeth that had forgotten what it was like to do real work.

"Fuck, it's rancid," Beckan said.

"I can't taste anyway."

They heard a small murmur from the floor, and they looked down to see a gnome boy, younger than anyone they'd seen in a very long time, sucking on his dirty fingers and looking up at them. Or at their meat.

He was almost as skinny as Scrap and he looked a little like Beckan.

"We can't," Beckan said. "I'm sorry. Go ask your dad."

"My dad's dead. Just a little?"

Beckan shook her head, her eyes closed, her chin shaking. "No. We can't." She imagined how Scrap would judge her if she gave in. How he would shake his head and tell her she was soft, and stupid, and that she should be sleeping on the streets, that if she were cold and hard like he was, she wouldn't need to hide under her comforter and cry herself to sleep. If she were cold, she wouldn't cry. She would cough dust and dirt and dry air.

The gnome looked at Scrap. "Please?" he said.

Scrap hesitated.

Beckan's eyes snapped open.

"Scrap," she said. "Come on. Let's go."

Scrap said, "I don't know. I don't know I don't know I—"

And then the gnome boy lunged. He wrapped himself around Scrap's leg and stabbed his teeth through his pants.

Scrap yelled and cursed and Beckan shook the gnome boy loose with her foot and flung him across the tunnel, and they heard a guard yelling—at the child, not at them, because they were worth so much more, because there wasn't enough meat on them to bother, they thought, they thought, they thought—all the way to the elevator. Scrap leaned on Beckan for support but they moved quickly.

He left Beckan holding the meat and went to the other side of the elevator and slammed his fist against the bars. "Fuck!" he yelled. "Fuck, this hurts."

She didn't know what to say.

They were perfect. They had nibbles in their shoulders, but none of them had really been touched. But Scrap's pant leg was torn, and what was left was dark and wet with blood. It wasn't an enormous bite, but it was a piece of him that he would not get back. Fairies are good at healing—it would close up and close over—but it would never, ever grow back.

"Fuck, I feel him chewing it." He squeezed his eyes shut and swallowed hard. "I have to harden up," he said. "I have to harden up."

"No," she said. But not because she wanted him to be soft. Because she honestly didn't believe that he could be any harder. His hesitation hadn't been tenderness; it was panic, it was hunger, it was delirium, it was fear, but it was nothing that the war could squeeze out of him, because he didn't have anything left to squeeze. She had never known a sweet Scrap—from diapers he had been pragmatic, fixed, counting out pieces of candy to make sure everyone got the same amount. And she didn't love him, how could she? How could anyone love him?

He came home only to clean his leg with the first-aid kit and finish off his share of the meat.

I don't want to write about back then anymore.

But now I don't know what else to write about.

Cricket, Cricket, Cricket.

A few weeks before he died it was grimy and awful and he was with a skinny gnome he didn't know, and he was surprised when the gnome brought him down to Crate's chambers with Scrap. He'd never been in there before. He'd never imagined the golden walls, the carved marble bed, the smell of earth so much stronger here than anywhere else.

But the strangest part was seeing Scrap. They were used to being separated the second they came down. Of course he knew what Scrap did.

Of course he was curious how Scrap did it so much better than he did.

But he did not want to see this. Scrap making noises in his throat, twisting his hips against the wall, accepting everything, his hands above his head grinding his pelvis into Crate. He was smiling up at him and making his eyes bright and whispering in Crate's ear. He was urging Crate's clothes off, aiming him toward the bed, waiting for the part everyone knew he was best at, when he could moan and move at the right time and think about all the reasons he was doing this: for

Cricket's smile, for food, for notes slipped under her door. He knew why he was here.

And then Cricket was kissed, roughly, and a pill was slipped from the gnome's tongue onto his. He swallowed and turned his head in time to see Scrap accepting an identical pill under his own tongue.

It made Cricket immediately woozy, and Scrap turned and looked at him, his eyes so big.

So Cricket took care of his boy. He put on his big-brother voice and said, "It's okay. We're fine," because Scrap hated being drugged, even after all this time. Scrap had to be present.

Cricket would have rather felt none of it.

Oh yes, write that instead, you fucking genius. Brilliant.

Beckan brings welded trinkets to Piccolo and comes home with a feast for dinner, and she and Josha and Piccolo and Rig and Tier all chatter to each other while they wash stalks of imported corn and the gnomes debate whether they should give in and try a vegetable, if their stomachs could take it, and Piccolo prods the meat that they brought and wisely does not ask what creature it used to be.

Josha is wearing Piccolo's jacket.

"Here, try these," Piccolo says. He grabs a handful of pea pods from a basket and rinses them.

"Raw?" Beckan says.

"Best that way. C'mere, I'll show you." He backs her against the fridge and dangles one over her lips.

She laughs, low, and snaps at it.

Tier and Josha look, together, toward the bedroom where Scrap is reading or writing or something.

Beckan groans. "Oh, guys. Seriously? Give up."

Piccolo says, "What's going on?"

Beckan stands on her toes and kisses him. It isn't comfortable. They haven't been touching nearly long enough for it to be comfortable. It is new and passionate and hot enough that she can imagine steam coming from Piccolo's lips. He is always hot.

"They have a crush on Scrap and me as a couple," Beckan says.

"Oh . . ."

"Which we never were and never will be. Seriously, guys?"

Josha shrugs one shoulder.

Beckan goes back to the sink, munching on the rest of the pea, and rinses potatoes. "There's too much," she says. "Too much stuff. Too much bullshit and . . . history."

"You just described Scrap," Josha says.

She shakes her head. "Me and Scrap." And she goes back to Piccolo and kisses him again, and he puts a hand on her back and a hand in her hair, and he is the perfect height for her, his chin on the top of her head, she fits into him like a glove, and she smiles and is happy.

Josha goes to get Scrap for dinner, and they sit at the table, suddenly quiet with their new addition, exchanging glances as they scrape at their plates. The gnomes try the vegetables and Piccolo tries the meat.

He wipes his mouth on his napkin. "Scrappy," he says.

Scrap is so confused by the nickname that it takes him a minute to look up. Beckan chews on her lip and tries not to laugh.

Piccolo doesn't seem to notice. "Have Josha and Becks filled you in on our plans?"

Beckan says, "Oh, I don't think Scrap's interested—"

Scrap looks at her, steady. "I'm very, very interested," he says.

Piccolo smiles brightly. "Great! We've turned up some great stuff. The gnomes aren't great at security, y'know? They're useless without a king, really."

Tier drops his fork, and Scrap picks it up before Tier can. They exchange a glance and a nervous expression—a chewed cheek, a raised eyebrow—when Scrap hands it back.

Josha and Beckan aren't the only ones who can have secrets.

Piccolo says, "And the tightropers aren't much better, especially with me on the inside."

"Are they planning something?" Scrap says.

"No, they're idiots who think the war is over, but they're also not planning to leave any time soon. That's their weakness; that they're not expecting anything. Between their . . . what's that word you used, Becks?"

"Complacency."

"Yeah! Between their complacency and the gnomes' need to rely on a king they don't have, we have two huge groups that are totally disorganized. Three if we're counting your fairies who aren't here. It makes us six the most cohesive group in the whole city."

"But you're just kids," Scrap says.

Piccolo grins. "That's what makes us so cohesive. We give a shit about each other. That's a kid thing."

"But . . . there aren't very many of us. Of you."

"Not yet, no, but that's always how revolutions start."

Scrap lowers his water glass. "Revolution? I thought the master plan here was finding Cricket."

Piccolo says. "Beckan's been making us some really fantastic armor, and what we're going to do is literally bring the tightropers to the ground."

"Tear the ropes down," Josha says.

Piccolo nods. "As safely as possible, of course, but we need to make sure that we're protected in case *they* start any violence. Plus it sends a good message, you know? They can't just hang out over the city and expect us to be fine with that."

"You're on the ground all the time," Scrap says.

Beckan says, "It's a metaphor."

"Yeah, I'm sure they're gonna be thinking metaphors when they're falling off their ropes," Scrap says. "And what about the gnomes?"

"Without a king, they're immobile."

Scrap says, "But you should have some measure against them, just in case they figure out a way to organize. Or in case they find out the plan somehow. If you guys weren't as careful as you think you were sneaking down—"

Josha says, "I told you, we were really careful."

(They were running around screaming Cricket's name.)

Piccolo says, "Rig and Tier told us that there's no way they can all come together without a leader. I'm not trying to insult anyone, it's just the way their species has been taught to behave. This is the horrible thing about their organization, you know? They're so isolated, they get into this behavior and then they believe that it's something they can't live without. Right, Tier?"

Tier says, very carefully, "No, I don't think there's any way the gnomes could possibly put together any kind of powerful resistance if they didn't have a king."

Scrap tilts his head back and looks at the ceiling.

Piccolo says, "Yeah. So we'll of course keep all of our eyes open for any kind of gnome strike, but it's not our major concern. We need to focus on the tightropers. But you're right, Scrap!" He smiles at him, big. "You're absolutely right that we need to be prepared for everything, which is where Beckan comes in. She's our diplomat. Keeping us all safe, making sure this all stays peaceful. And we'd still love to have you on board."

"What do you need me for?"

Piccolo's smile fades, just a little. "Oh, Scrap, we don't need you *for* anything." He gives a small laugh. "You think I hand-selected these bastards for their special sets of skills or something?" He slings an arm over Josha's shoulders. "We like you. It's nice to have friends, yeah? God knows I've been lonely, up there with the fucking soldiers."

"Not literally fucking," Josha says.

"No, no, that would have been much less boring. Except I would have to clean up after all of it. Fuck, do I hate tightropers."

Scrap says, "I guess I have reading to do. Sorry."

Beckan says, "No, Scrap. Come. We're planning tonight and then we're doing major Cricket searching."

He shakes his head. "I'm sorry. I'm just so tired."

A minute later, they're all set to leave, but Beckan and Josha tell the others to get a head start while they clean the kitchen. As soon as Piccolo and the gnomes are shoved out the door, Scrap says, "Guys, please? Don't do this."

"You should come," Josha says. "I mean it. This is the last fucking helpful thing I'm going to say to you if you keep just giving us that tortured-martyr face."

"Oh, that was helpful?"

"It's been three months, Scrap!" Josha says. "I know you loved him."

Scrap whispers something that sounds suspiciously like *I loved him most.*

"But fucking find something else to think about. That's what we're doing." He throws his dish towel in the sink and heads outside. Beckan fishes it out of the water and makes a face.

"So what about you?" Scrap says.

She doesn't look at him. "There's nothing *about* me."

"Are you doing this for the same reason he is? Looking for a distraction?"

"No. I don't need a distraction. I dealt with Cricket's death when it happened and I was broken down to pieces and I am still sad every day, but I am actually dealing with it, okay? And Josha isn't looking for a distraction, he's looking for something—someone—to put his faith in, because the only two anythings he ever looked up to have fucking bailed on him. That's Cricket and you, if I'm not being clear enough."

"He didn't look up to me."

"Quit being obtuse."

"And I didn't bail on him."

"Bullshit, he was hurting and you couldn't handle it and you hid in the basement and told me to take care of him."

"I made him breakfast," Scrap says. "I went in there some nights without you and held him. You don't know everything I've done. And *what about you*, okay?"

"I didn't bail on him!"

"I know you didn't bail on him. I mean you. And Piccolo. Why are you doing this?"

"I don't know!" She turns to him. "Because it's not a big deal? Because maybe we'll get some of Cricket out of it? Because it's nice to not be so alone? Because I *don't want the tightropers to start another war?*"

"They don't have any plans to! You *just found out* they don't have plans!"

"As soon as the gnomes get a new king, this is all starting over again. You heard them."

"Yes, I heard them," Scrap says. "I fucking heard them. Okay. But this is . . . can you please trust me? *Don't do this.* Someone is going to get hurt. You're going to get hurt. Fuck, everyone is going to get hurt."

"You're being paranoid. Just because Cricket—"

"Don't do this."

"—it doesn't mean Josha and I are suddenly more fragile than we were. Or you. You're not fragile. Stop talking like you think you are."

"Don't do this."

"We're not doing anything!"

"You shouldn't be getting involved."

"Scrap, how the fuck am I not supposed to get involved? It's happening in our city. What the fuck is my other choice, stay here and watch you write and let the only Beckan who's doing anything be the one in your little stories?"

"Shut up," he says. His voice is so quiet.

"Do I even get to do anything? Because pretty-storybook-Beckan probably stays home and never causes any trouble, right?"

"You think that's how I think of you?"

She turns away and rolls her eyes. He's not worth it.

"I love this about you," he says. "That you care."

"No hero of any book ever sits around and doesn't do anything. So pretend I'm doing this for you and your book if that helps. Just leave me alone."

"Are you doing it because of him?" Scrap says.

"What?"

"Piccolo."

"Seriously? Seriously, you want to do this? There's nothing with Piccolo and me."

He crosses his arms.

"*Don't look at me like that!* You know what?" she says. "Fine. Fine. There's *tons* with Piccolo and me. Piccolo and me are having wild passionate sex while you're busy writing your stupid book. We're making out and ripping off each other's clothes and running around like little vagabonds off having the times of our lives and he's showing me all this stuff about being free and being happy that I never would have realized without him, and for once in my whole life I feel happy and wanted and dear, and he's opening my eyes to awesome food and awesome games and awesome sex and nobody invited you because *everybody hates you, poor poor Scrap.*" She shuts the water off and dries her hands on her pants. "There. What you wanted to hear was probably somewhere in there."

"Fuck off."

"You fuck off. And stop acting like my jealous boyfriend." She dumps a whole load of dishes in the sink for him. "Do these yourself. I'm leaving."

"You're going to get hurt."

"I hope I die!"

"I hope we both die!" he yells as the door shuts.

YOU HAVE FIVE DAYS.
DO NOT MAKE THE
WRONG DECISION.

A note in Scrap's pocket, that day.

"It's bullshit," Beckan tells her father on her way down to meet the others. "It's total fucking bullshit, and I'd like to punch him in the face." She shakes him, gently, and peers through the glass at his glitter and his eye. "I wish I knew if you could hear me." It's a windy day, and her hair whips into her eyes as she walks.

The city is transformed more and more every day. The tightroper shops gleam. They're building apartments soon.

They're not going anywhere.

The fairies aren't coming back.

But they probably wouldn't have tried anyway, and Beckan can't regret wanting to hold hands with her gnomes and her tightroper and start something new.

It's a little like when she and her father moved closer to the center of the city (he was never interested in a house on the outskirts. Beckan's father was strong and brave and was crafted like iron in his city) when she was seven. They went back to their old apartment a few days after the move to sign some papers, and gnome construction workers were already rearranging the counters and putting in a nook for the next fairy family who would live there. The furniture was gone, but the burn on the wall—from one of Beckan's earliest welding experiments—was still there. The apartment was still the same shape. It was still the same space. There were still bits of her in it.

But there were only bits, and everything was changing and she had to go to her new home.

"Becks!" Piccolo yells, half a mile above her head, the second she steps into the city. She lifts her head and smiles at everyone and stuffs her father into her bag before she starts the climb. She isn't scared anymore. She isn't scared of anything. She climbs and breathes thinner, cleaner air and forgets about the city and the cottage and the apartments and the bits.

Beckan is invincible.

When she gets to the top, Josha immediately says, "What's wrong?" and hugs her. He's still a bit more shaky on the tightropes than Beckan is, but he's improving. Even the gnomes are beginning to get their sky legs, but for safety they stay sitting, and for other reasons they stay sitting too far apart to touch.

"Nothing," she said. "I'm fine."

"You brought your dad!" Piccolo exclaims, pulling him out of her bag.

"He always liked heights. I used to leave him on our windowsill, back in my apartment."

"Where was your apartment?" Rig says, and Beckan brings her to the edge of the bowl of webbing so she can point out the rubble that was once her building. Up here, she can see the progress the tightropers are making in a way that's so much calmer and more objective.

See, it's pretty. It's all very pretty.

"How are you?" she whispers to Rig.

Rig coughs out a laugh. "Lonely," she says, after a minute.

"Are you two . . ."

She shakes her head. "Not yet."

It's hard for Beckan to understand. The rush of being alive, the passion of fighting for it, makes her want to grab hold of anyone nearby.

She touches Rig's hand, and Rig, after a minute, turns her hand to wrap her fingers around Beckan's.

"I'm afraid of power now," she says.

"What?"

"I'm afraid of sex because I'm afraid of the power. Because I know that either Tier will have power over me or I will have power over him, and I know that should be part of it—I know that is part of it, and I loved it before because everything about sex with him, I loved—but now it's just a part of the war. And I'm scared." She shakes her head. "I can't believe I'm up here after . . ."

"Oh. Shit. Are you—"

"I'm okay."

"You can't be okay. No one can be okay after that."

"I'm breathing in everything and breathing it back out." She points. "That's where they kept us. You can't even see it from here."

"You *are* okay, aren't you?"

She's just so *real*, this girl.

"You sound disappointed," she says.

"I sound amazed, Rig."

Piccolo says, "Hey, lovelies, come here. Something to show you."

They turn around. Piccolo, still with Beckan's dad on his lap, is shooting them a huge grin.

They come and rejoin the circle, and Piccolo reaches deep into the folds of his jacket. "Ta-da," he says, and he pulls out a small silver gun.

It is just so very small.

"Now, don't freak out," he says, though nobody has moved. "It's only for protection. No one's going to get hurt." He passes it to Tier, who rolls it in his hand for a minute before quickly nudging it the rest of its way around the circle. It is heavier than Beckan expected, and she is surprised and confused by her urge to pull the trigger. Just to see what would happen. She doesn't believe it, really.

They had talked about carrying weapons. Cricket wanted to. He said they needed something for protection.

"No," Scrap had said. "No. Carrying a weapon shows you want to fight. We don't want to fight. We do not want to fight."

But Beckan had a knife in her pocket the day Cricket died.

"Where did you get this?" Rig asks.

"Grabbed it from the supply closet when I was putting my mop away. There are dozens and dozens of them. One won't be missed. Neither would five." When the gun gets back to him, Piccolo tucks

Beckan's dad under one arm and stretches his other out over the city. He aims at a crumbling office building, close to Beckan's late apartment, and pulls the trigger.

It's so much louder than any of the fighting Beckan has ever heard. It is right next to her ear. It is right here.

Rig says, "Someone's going to come—"

"Here," Piccolo says. "Give it a try."

"What is it for?" Tier says. "Why do we need guns?"

"We need to be able to hold them like we know what we're doing," he says. "Even if we don't use them, we need to make sure that if there's any trouble, the tightropers and the gnomes think we'll use them. No one takes you seriously without a weapon." He fires the gun again, and this time he lets out a little cheer, like a child's, when it goes off.

And just while Beckan is looking at the others, just when they're all trying to figure out if they are being set up, or they are being sucked in by someone who is beautiful and charismatic but altogether crazy, a voice yells, "Piccolo!" and he shoves the gun back into his coat and runs his hand through his hair. "Shit," he whispers. "Shit."

Beckan says, "What's going on?"

"Shit. My dad. I'm supposed to be working. You guys should leave. Now."

Rig grabs Beckan's hand and Beckan whispers, "It's okay it's okay you're okay."

They scurry toward the ladder they took up, but Josha, the first in line, hasn't made it even a step down before a man, in a jacket identical to Piccolo's but twice as big, with eyes the same color as Piccolo's but twice as mean, barrels toward them and they flinch and huddle together. But he stops at Piccolo and grabs him by both of his shoulders. He shakes his son like Beckan will sometimes shake her father, when she forgets to think of him as still alive.

Beckan's father, who is clutched in Piccolo's hand.

"No," Beckan whispers. "No, stop shaking him."

Piccolo's father begins to scream at him in a language Beckan doesn't know, and even though she's heard the tightroper language before, this is the first time she's really realized that they do not use her language when she's not around, that most foreigners don't, that this is a thing that she takes for granted. Did the gnomes once have their own language, too? (I don't know. I'm working on this one.)

So Beckan does not understand the words. But how his father shoves his mop at him, the way he rips the sleeve of Piccolo's jacket, the slap he plants firmly on Piccolo's cheek . . . those she understands.

And so does Josha. He is pushing through them, separating father and son, jerking Piccolo back into him, and into safety—

—and her father's jar slips from Piccolo's hand and falls through the ropes and crashes to the ground.

She can't breathe. "No. No. No no no no no."

She has to get to him. She has to find every bit of him and sweep him into the jar, she has to make sure not a single speck of his glitter gets lost because it will be alone and it will be frightened, and he trusted her. He thought he would be safe in that jar, she told everyone he would be safe and here he is lying in the dust of the city he knew, blowing around and hitting dirty stone and concrete and unfamiliar shops and whipping back and forth like this city is the world's biggest glass jar. Trapped forever but no lid and no Beckan and she cannot get down there fast enough.

By the time she gets to the ground, there is nothing left. Not a scrap of him. Nothing but slivers of glass. Nothing.

He is somewhere. But he is nowhere.

And she is on the ground, she is bleeding from the glass, she is desperate down in the dust and her nose is running and she is sloughing off her skin clawing the pavement and she is desperate and she is gasping and crying harder than she ever has and scream-ing how sorry she is and how she never meant to and then Tier is beside her, his arms around her, crying like it was his own dad.

"When was the last time you saw Piccolo and everybody?" Scrap says a few days later in a voice that is so genuine and naïve and stupid it could slay her.

"I don't know," she says, and she does nothing but eat and sleep for the rest of the week.

Josha comes home less and less and spends his days with Pic-colo up in the sky. He says the gnomes don't come up anymore. He says one of them couldn't stand it and doesn't say which. Everything broke, so quickly.

Scrap disappears to the mines again and again and he comes up each time looking like someone has sucked out some of his blood. Shaky, pale, somehow smaller. Glitter missing in patches.

Beckan brings herself to care about all of this as much as she can, which is hard when she can barely get herself out of bed.

She gets up at one point to get a glass of milk and Scrap is holding his head at the kitchen table, staring down at an empty mug.

"Becks?" he says, without looking up.

"Yeah?"

"Will you tell me how Cricket made all that money?"

It's his voice. That's the reason she tells him. He sounds like he has given up and what harm will it do now?

"He was a spy," she says.

"Spying on the gnomes?" His voice is resigned, like he'd figured this out.

But: "No," she says. "Spying on the tightropers."

Scrap looks up.

"He took information from the tightropers and brought it down to the gnomes. They paid him for it and he got to stop tricking. The tightropers liked him, never suspected anything. And then that day . . . Cricket was talking to the tightropers and I guess Crate decided he couldn't trust him."

Scrap is frozen, his hands covering his eyes. In this light, his fake one almost looks real.

"You didn't want to know," Beckan says. "So I didn't tell you."

"That's how you guys got your information on the tightropers."

"Cricket's old stuff, and what Piccolo and I stole. None of it turned out to be very useful. If they'd had anything good, Cricket would have found it and the gnomes probably would have won the war while they could."

"While they had a king."

"Right."

Scrap shakes his head for a while, silently.

"That was so stupid," he says. "Why did he do that? If he hated tricking so much . . . he could have stopped, we could have gotten by just the two of us."

"No. We couldn't have."

"We could have made it work. I could have made it better for him. If he'd talked to me, I—I don't know, I could have done something."

Beckan says, "Why did you want to know now?"

"I just thought it might change something. Help somehow. I don't know."

"Well," she says. "Did it help?"

"No. No, it didn't." He clears his throat. "Where's your dad? I haven't seen him lately."

Beckan puts her cup down. She didn't drink any. "You don't know anything."

"What?"

"You're writing a fucking book and you didn't know that Cricket is a spy. How can you write a book that's going to mean anything if you don't know what's going on? If you don't see stuff that's right the fuck in front of you?"

He stares at her.

She says, "What else do you think you're missing?"

He puts his head back in his hands.

"I can't do this," she says. "I'm going back to bed."

"'Night, Beckan."

Shit I'm sorry it's been so long I don't know how the fuck I'm supposed to write now but I'll do my best I don't know how much time I have I wish they were here I wish they were here I would do anything.

12

I'm sorry. I don't have much time.

THE NEXT NIGHT, before she goes to bed, Scrap says, "Wait."

He goes to her and hugs her. He's wearing the locket, and it presses against her chest.

They haven't touched very often lately. They haven't done anything very often but fight.

"I love you," he says.

"What? I love you, too."

"I'm so, so sorry about your dad."

"Josha told you?"

"Finally." He runs his fake arm through his hair. He's getting very good at it. He knows exactly the angle to hold it so the fingers will catch his hair as if they were real.

"I'm sorry about tomorrow," he says.

"What?"

"About what's going to happen."

"Scrap, what?"

"I'm just sorry."

She wakes up to crying, vomiting.

Her first thought is, all that noise could not be coming from only one creature.

Her second is, all that noise is coming from Scrap.

But she falls back asleep, and when she next wakes up, he's gone. The house is empty.

She hauls herself out of bed. Every muscle in her body feels twisted and frozen. It is eighty degrees outside, but she tugs on one of Josha's old sweatshirts. She is so cold.

It's early, much earlier than Scrap usually goes to work, but he isn't here. He's down in the mines every day now, at strange hours, for long stretches. Maybe he has a friend down there.

Maybe he has a girlfriend, boyfriend, something.

Is that so unbelievable?

When was the last time she worked? She runs her finger through days on the calendar. Two weeks ago, back when Piccolo was only a boy on a rope. She misses working, a little, which surprises her. It's not something she would say if she still had to do it, or if prostitution was ever the same for her as it was for Scrap and Cricket. She was never a real whore, not really; she was a girl thrown together with a boy she otherwise would never have loved, but she misses him. Right now she misses Tier so badly, she can taste it.

It tastes like cold mud and bacon grease and skin without glitter.

She needs to get out of this silent house, finally. She puts on a hat and gloves. When she steps outside, she knows she is hot, but for once she doesn't feel it.

And then she hears shouting.

Josha.

She runs toward the noise, because she knows Josha, and it doesn't matter that he is six inches shorter than Piccolo; she doesn't know who else he could be yelling at, who else he cares enough to yell at like that, and no one on the receiving end of Josha's temper stands a chance. And whatever she feels about Piccolo, she does not want him dead. That is one thing she knows, one of the few things: she does not want Piccolo dead.

She runs. Her feet know the places where the cobblestones have been fixed. Her hand knows which lamppost is stable enough to hold her as she vaults herself from 3rd Street to 4th Street from Huntington to Liberty to 5th to Sarosoto and there they are.

But Josha is not yelling at Piccolo.

He is yelling at Scrap.

"Leave me alone!" he screams. *"Go away! Go home!"*

"Not without you!" Scrap yells back. *"Get. The fuck. Home."*

Piccolo puts one hand on Scrap's shoulder and the other on Josha's. "Hey. Guys. Hey."

Scrap hits Piccolo's hand off his shoulder and turns to face him. "No. You. You stop this *now*. You are going to get hurt. You have no idea what you're doing. You are going to *hurt Josha*."

"We're just pulling down some ropes," Piccolo says. "Nobody's going to get hurt."

Scrap says, "If the gnomes see the tightropers are weak—"

Piccolo says, "Scrap, seriously, are we doing this again? *They are useless without a king.*"

"You don't know everything about them!"

"Fucking Scrap, defender of gnomes everywhere," Josha mumbles.

"They don't know we're doing anything." Piccolo says.

"You think you've been *subtle*? You're underground, you're on the ground, you're above the ground, you're everywhere, and they hear you."

"So what if they do?" Piccolo bats him away. "We're just making some noise."

"Before all you were doing was defending yourself, and before that you were looking for my cousin and making a fucking flag!" Scrap pushes him. He is so much more than six inches shorter than Piccolo.

Piccolo says, "Don't push me, kid."

"I'm not a kid!"

Piccolo laughs. It's cold.

"Right," he says. "Right. You're the little den mother. Well, guess what? Josha doesn't need a babysitter, and all Beckan needed was someone to open her eyes—"

"*No!*" she shouts.

They all spin around. Not one of them had noticed her.

"I did not need anyone to open my eyes!" she says. "I am not some sheltered little child, okay? I'm not a little princess just because I'm a girl. I had a knife the day Cricket was killed. *I was there. I could have killed Crate,*" she tells Scrap.

He closes his eyes. "Beckan, go home," he whispers.

"*Screw you.* Both of you! I'm not doing this here. *You* go home," she tells Scrap.

"Make Josha and I will."

"*Make* Josha? Who do you think I am, Cricket?"

"Fuck off," Josha spits at her, but he tells Piccolo, "I'll see you later," and stalks back toward the cottage. Scrap runs after him.

"Aren't you going?" Piccolo says.

She shakes her head. "In a minute. I'm not done with you."

Piccolo crosses his arms and leans against a rope. He's cocky and beautiful and he has that half smile and he is everything she would want if she were different.

She says, "I'm not that girl."

"You're any girl you want to be."

"And I don't want to be that girl."

He watches her and doesn't say anything.

"How do you want me to feel, like I'm cute and young and so glad you're here to show me what's going on, because I'm useless and I can't have kids or wings and . . . that's not me. I'm just more. I have my pack. And I went through all the shit they did. I was there when Cricket died, and I fought Crate off or I would have been killed too. You know that?"

"I saw it," Piccolo says.

"Then give me some fucking credit," she says. This cocky, idiot, beautiful jerk. "Go home, Piccolo."

Maybe she's trying to make him slip, say *I am home*, reveal that this whole time he's been on the tightroper's side, settling in to their city, laughing at the stupid fairies. Maybe she was expecting that.

She wasn't expecting him to say, "Screw you, Beckan," in the most broken voice, spit a rope into his hand, and zip away.

Scrap and Josha stare at each other in the silent kitchen.

"Show her the book," Josha says suddenly.

"She saw it."

"No. *Show* her."

Scrap has his head in his hands. "Shut up."

"Then fucking tell her."

"Give me the locket."

Josha holds it tightly. "No."

I should have told her.

I did it all wrong.

Shit shit shit shit, who writes a fucking book?

Beckan shuts the door quietly behind her. "Okay," she says. "We're going to talk about this. Like adults. Which means you"—she points at Josha—"don't start screaming and leave, and you, you stop acting aloof and bitchy and *superior*. We're in this together, Scrap. This is a family. And you are *not* mother hen. You were our general, and the war's over, so cut it the fuck out."

"I'm trying to be an adult," Scrap says. "I'm *trying* to stop moping around. . . ."

"So tell us what's going on."

"You guys are going to get killed."

Josha snorts. "Scrap, you go down to the mines every day. This has got to be the least dangerous thing we've done this whole war."

"Don't do it."

"I have to do *something*. I'm coming out of my skin."

"You don't understand."

He says, "Then tell me. Fucking tell me."

Scrap pinches the top of his nose, like he does when he has a headache.

Beckan whispers, "What's wrong with you, Scrap?"

He doesn't move.

"Tell her what you're writing," Josha says, and nobody responds, so he says, louder, "Tell her."

"That's not what this—" Scrap starts, and then he shakes his head.

"Just tell her already," Josha says, and then Scrap stands up and throws his blue notebook at the table. Pages scatter across the surface.

"Fine!" he says. *"Fine."*

Beckan says, "I've already seen this."

Scrap looks at Josha. "Can you give us a minute?"

They stare at each other for a moment as though they are about to fight.

Beckan remembers when they loved each other.

"Fine," Josha says. He goes to his room and closes the door.

Scrap says, "I told you it was stories about all of us. I thought that's what it was. But that's not what it is. It's about you." He rakes his hand through his hair. "It's one long story and it's about you."

She can feel her heartbeat. "What?"

"It's Tier's fault . . . those stupid fiction books, I'm trying to write something real, trying to write about this war, and I can't get this love story out of my mind."

Her voice breaks. "A love story? You're writing . . . about Josha and Cricket?"

He sinks to the table and puts his head back in his hands, and she gets it.

"This is creepy," she says. "You're creepy."

"I know."

"You're in love with me?"

"I don't know."

"You don't *know*? You're writing a love story about me!"

And he looks up. "I want you out of my head!" He throws the book open and flips through the pages. He cuts his finger. "I have written so many pages, look at this, just trying to get you out of me. I thought I could write this stupid little thing and get it out of my system and then start writing my real book, if I could just figure out a happy ending, some way this could work, but I can't. I keep just writing all the bullshit that is really happening and anything I can plug in that makes it make sense, but I'm always behind, I'm always missing things, and here you are, you're everywhere and I *cannot stop writing this.*"

"Because you put me there!" She pulls back. "*This* is why you didn't want me to hang out with Piccolo! I *told* you, there's nothing—"

He says, "No. This has nothing to do with that."

"What, you expect me to believe you were just looking out for the gnomes? You want to know why I can't be in love with you?"

He doesn't move.

"Not because I'm in love with Piccolo, not because I'm scared of getting hurt the way Josha was if *somethinghappenedtoyou*, because I am in love with one fucking thing, and that thing is *not being at war*, and I can't forget that, I can't let myself forget about that for one second."

"You don't understand."

"This isn't supposed to be a love story! History isn't a love story. Do you know who taught me that?"

"I don't want to write this." He presses his palms into his eyes. "I don't want to write this."

"This is a shitty way to tell me you're in love with me," she says.

"I didn't know how else to do it."

She walks to the sink because she doesn't know what else to do.

"You could have just told me," she says after a minute. "You could have just said something outright. But you've never been that guy. You don't know how to be that guy. What the fuck kind of romantic hero . . ."

"I've told you I love you, don't give me that."

"Yeah, the way we tell Josha and we used to tell Cricket! You could have just *told me*. Just stopped thinking and stopped writing for a minute and just *told me something!*"

And he says, as fast and as loud as he's ever said anything, "I have to tell the gnomes today that I'll be their king or they're going to eat me."

She hears all these things that she'd never noticed before.

The click of the clock above the stove.

The dripping sink.

Scrap's heartbeat.

And Josha heard it, Josha is out of the room, Josha is yelling at him like this is all Scrap's fault and he has doomed them and like he has already decided what the fuck he's going to do.

"It's protocol," Scrap says. His voice is so hoarse. "Protocol . . . I killed the last king, I have to succeed—"

"It was self-defense!" Beckan cries. "You weren't trying to—"

"It doesn't matter." Scrap sits down, hard. "They don't have organization, and they think they need this huge push through the ground to get any sort of headway, and they've let me in on all this stuff. And they know about you guys. They know you guys are planning."

Josha says, "You told them."

Beckan stares at Scrap.

Scrap says, "What?" like he's so exhausted.

"You told them about me and Piccolo and Beckan. You tipped them off that the tightropers are going to be weak."

"No," Scrap says. "Leak did."

"Leak?"

"He runs the elevator. He saw you going down to the mines, he knows you're involved with Piccolo, they heard you and Rig and Tier talking. You guys were not careful." He breathes out. "The gnomes are just waiting for you to weaken the tightropers, and then they're going to take over. All of the tightropers are going to get hurt, and you could be too, now that they realize you give a shit."

"You're *betraying us!*" Josha yells. "You're going to be their king and make this a gnome city."

"That's the idea," Scrap says. Quietly.

Beckan makes her eyes as narrow as they will go. "You're bringing the war back. They're starting the war up again. You're going to lead them in it."

He nods heavily. "But—"

"You asshole!" Josha knocks a chair to the floor. "You had us tell you all our plans so you could use them against us."

"So I could *figure out how to keep you alive.*"

"Who knows that they're making you be king?" Beckan says.

He rubs his forehead. "All the gnomes. Most of them haven't known for as long as I have."

"Tier?"

"Only recently. They . . . don't tell him much. They were afraid he'd want the job."

"They're going to eat you?" she says.

"Only if I don't take it."

Scrap stays still for a minute, then he shakes off his boot and then his sock and holds out what remains of his foot. Three of the toes and half the side are missing.

He was what was cooking. He was the yellow smoke.

Beckan sinks to the floor.

"They already destroyed most of the arm," Scrap says.

"What happens if they eat you?" Josha says. "Who's king then?"

"One of Tier's brothers. No better for the city."

Josha says, "This is fucked up."

And then something inside of Scrap breaks.

"You think I don't know?" he says. "Why are you standing here telling me it's my fault? Why are you fucking lecturing me like you disapprove? *I didn't ask for this.* There *isn't* a good outcome here— do you think I can't see that? There is no getting out of this."

"Get out of the fucking city!" Josha yells.

"And leave you here to get yourselves killed with Crate's sons in charge?"

"At least that would buy us some time, wouldn't it?" Beckan says. "While they figure out how to organize around one of Tier's brothers . . . we need time." She sits down at the table. "I need to think."

Josha says, "We could plan a strike against them while they try to organize."

"They'd eat you. They know they're about to be back on top. They wouldn't hesitate."

"Maybe we should all leave?" Beckan says, quietly.

Josha says, "We're not leaving this city to be destroyed."

Scrap shakes his head, breathing hard. "We can't get out. You know they have guards around the entire edge of the city. They're adding more every day. Th-the only solution I can see right now is to try to get the fairies back, and I've been making this gnome kid who owes me a favor go out every day looking for them, feeding this fucking kid all I have and he's traveling farther and farther every day but he hasn't found them." He shakes his head quickly, then says, "Maybe if I did it . . . took the job. Maybe I could protect us. Protect you guys. They would never touch you."

"We'd be two fairies in a gnome-dominated city. You couldn't babysit us every second," Josha says.

Scrap says, "Becks is half gnome."

And for a second, they are quiet.

"That might help you," Scrap says.

"Shut up," she says.

"Did you ever think that this type of racial pride is what got us into this war in the first place?"

"Don't talk to me about what started this war when you're about to profit from it."

"Being half gnome is going to save you," he says. "The same way being half fairy saved all of us."

"We're not half. . . . ," she says, because fairy is fairy, this is what she has been taught, this is what is real, this is the one thing she has never really thought to question and she will leave forever so shutup-shutupshutup.

"What about me?" Josha says. He sounds like a kid for a moment, sounds like when he would chase after Beckan when her father came to pick her up from play group: *what about me?*

Scrap starts, again, "But I'm—"

Beckan feels the sudden overwhelming urge to go to sleep, to curl up on the floor while they yell and have to do nothing but close her eyes.

Scrap is very quiet now. "I didn't know how to tell you guys," he says. "You seemed happy lately."

And Beckan's about to laugh before she realizes that, yes, she has been happy lately.

I don't hate gnomes, she thinks to herself. *Not anymore.*

"I have to find Piccolo," Josha says, and he's out the door.

Beckan breathes into her hands.

"What should I do?" He looks up at her. "What do I do now?"

"You take the job," she says. "Because you're not an idiot."

He shakes his head a bit.

She says, "And then I hate you a little for the rest of my life."

Beckan.

"You should have told us," she says. "You shouldn't keep secrets from us. How'd that work out for Cricket? Why didn't you tell us, baby?"

He looks at his book.

"I thought I had time," he says.

She runs after Josha.

Beckan.

Becks.

Beckan.

She is on the street now, charging toward Josha down this street, left on this one, right on this one, right on this one, and there he is, talking to the boy dangling from the ropes.

"Josha," she says. "We have to go."

He doesn't look at her. "No."

Piccolo says, "Beckan, get out of here."

"No. We have to go."

"I'm not going home."

"I'm not talking about home! We need to get out of the city. We need to find the other fairies and we need to bring them back."

"No one knows where they are," Josha says.

"They said they were going—"

"And *nobody's* heard from them. They sent no word that they reached their destination. They've made no contact. They could all be fucking dead. We don't know."

Beckan watches Piccolo. "He knows."

Piccolo makes eye contact.

"I swear to you," he says. "I swear to you that I don't. I've been through all the papers. No one's heard from them. I'm guessing they got absorbed right into the big cities. Your fairies don't want to be found, Becks."

"No . . ." That can't be true. It just cannot be.

Piccolo takes the gun out of the pocket of his jacket. She notices, for the first time, that Josha is wearing one just like it. How long has he had it?

Why hasn't she been watching him?

Piccolo loads the gun. "You need to go, Beckan."

"What are you doing?"

Josha says, "What do you think we're doing? We're saving Scrap."

Beckan looks at Josha and sees something in him that she hasn't in a long time.

"He's going to be okay," she says.

"Look." Josha points.

There is Scrap, aboveground, at the end of the block. He is arguing with a gnome they don't recognize. He is being pushed and pulled around. The gnome is laughing at him.

Piccolo says, "Go home, Beckan. Somewhere safe."

"Home isn't safe."

And then she hears Scrap's voice, louder than anything she's ever heard—*"NO!"*

And the last she sees before the ground explodes, before there are gunshots, crying, screaming, is Scrap's face, at the end of the block, as he is finally, finally overwhelmed.

So much happens at once.

There's yelling, there's growling as the gnomes drill up through the ground, there's Josha and Piccolo's absolute panic. There's tightropers coming down from the skies with rifles and orders belted in that language Beckan doesn't speak, and there's dust, so much dust in her throat, and she coughs, it's in her eyes, and she can't see anything.

Josha's voice, somehow far away: "What do we do?" and she doesn't know, she doesn't know, because she has no idea what's happening.

She hears ropes break, and feels nets coming down on top of her, and it sounds almost like wings—

And she's thrown to the ground. She sees orange bodies coming up, climbing with pickaxes and bare hands and horrible smiles. She feels the ground crumble underneath her and she falls, hard, into what was once the top level of the gnome tunnels.

She sees Leak.

And he says, "Are you all right?" and he looks like he might really care (so many days in the elevator and he never drops her), but she can barely hear him.

The gnomes have broken through. She is lying in what was once a tunnel but is now open to the sky and only a ditch in the ground. The gnome beds, their clothes, their books, are scattered to the streets, are blowing everywhere.

The gnomes are snatching up tightroper soldiers and bringing them to their mouths—

"*Josha!*" she hears, but she doesn't know if it's her voice or Scrap's or Piccolo's or a hungry gnome's—

"*Beckan!*"

"*Scrap!*"

It's chaos, it's dust, it's three races in the same space at the same time. This is what Piccolo wanted and he thought it would be so different. This is what Beckan was afraid of and she hoped that she was wrong. This is what Josha needed to finally be a part of.

And she sees glitter.

More glitter than she has seen in so long, and a young voice she doesn't know yelling, *Scrap, I did it! I found them! King Scrap!* and what is *happening*—

Then there's a hand on her arm, it's a body, it's someone, and she falls into it and she clings and she does not care who it is, but then she feels the roughness of the clothes and the height of the shoulders and the curls in her hair and it is Rig, it is Rig, it is Rig.

And then there is another set of hands on her, this one so familiar, this one bringing her back to familiar and dirty places, to nights in his room, to the way it hurt the first time and the boys never asked her if it had, the way she cried and they teased her because she was so lucky, because he looked gentle, and now his hand is on her shoulder, not gentle, but not scary, necessary, near, the only possible option—

And they run, through a hole that was once a tunnel, through the smallest passageways Beckan has seen. They gasp behind boulders, they run themselves ragged and out of the city.

fuck fuck what was that noise I'm sorry I'm sorry this is it the end

the end

13

Sorry about that.

Here's what happened.

BEFORE LONG, the tunnels close off again, where the city has not been exploded, where they are maybe not still in the city, and Beckan and Rig and Tier can slow to a walk because there is no one else. They inch along in the total dark, Beckan between the gnomes, all of them clasping hands. Beckan doesn't know where she is, only that this is a part of the tunnels she's never been to before. Maybe there are rooms back here. Maybe gnomes live here that she's never met, and never thought about.

But there's no one here now. The silence is so heavy, Beckan feels it on her skin. There's no noise from the city. There is no city.

They do not talk because there isn't anything much to say.

Eventually, they all say, at once, "I'm so thirsty," only Rig says *very*.

They stop walking then and pant, holding on to each other.

"We've got to go up," Tier says.

"What?"

"Up. Aboveground. The air."

Beckan tilts her head back. She can't see the sides or the ceiling of the tunnel. She has no idea how tall it is. It's hard to imagine that there is an above the ground, anymore. She stretches her arms out, still holding their hands, and does not hit the sides of the tunnel.

"Up," she says.

"Yes."

"How?"

She can feel them look at each other, then hear them start to laugh.

"We dig," Rig says.

"With what?"

They laugh again, and she is momentarily terrified, and then they lift themselves up, they climb the walls, and they begin to dig with their mouths and their nails. They are faster than the tightropers' jackhammers. How did she think they made all their tunnels?

She'd never considered that gnomes might have natural talents, that there are ways that they do not need to teach themselves— that they do not need fairies to teach them—to be good. Her stomach hurts.

"I'm sorry," she says, and they don't ask why.

They emerge, coughing. Beckan chokes on dry glitter.

Around them is something Beckan hasn't seen, in anywhere near this abundance, since long before the war, when she used to take the trolley out of the city, when she would bring her father and eat a peach and think of nothing.

Grass.

She'd forgotten the smell, how it tickles the inside of her nose, and the feel of it around her ankles, how sleepy it makes her. She'd forgotten bugs and earthworms.

These are the things that they lose. They're so aware of the big things, and they miss them constantly and loudly and mumble about them in their sleep—the fresh food, the heat, the family. They miss them so sorely that in a way they're not gone. When you miss something as much as they miss autonomy, or peace, or Cricket, you can never forget how it felt when it was here.

The little things—grass, earthworms, notes under the door—slip by unnoticed.

But besides this grass and their hole in the ground, there is nothing anywhere around. Nothing for miles. Only hills and grass and grass and grass and every few hills, a dandelion.

No food, no water, no other creatures, and no hope. Nothing but the two gnomes on either side of her, and it is the most beautiful thing Beckan has ever seen. No explosions, no screaming. She turns around and cannot see the city and has no idea in what direction it is. Then the three of them are holding each other, running their hands through each other's hair, shaking and whispering how glad they are that the others are alive. And she breathes as if she has just discovered how. Her brain throbs with *ScrapJoshaPiccoloFerrum* but her lungs breathe.

"We should get moving," Tier says.

Beckan says, "Where?"

Tier looks around and lets out something between a laugh and a cry. "I don't know."

"Someone is looking out for us," Rig says, when, just before they are about to faint, they find a stream.

They drink with hands clenched on the banks, faces in the water like animals.

Beckan coughs. "What?"

Tier looks at Rig, his eyes somehow still, steady.

"It's just something the tightropers used to say," she says. "At first we thought they were mocking us—if one of us got a little extra food, they'd tell us, *someone is looking out for you,* but then we started noticing they'd say it to each other. If one of the generals' small sons fell and didn't get hurt—*someone is looking out for you.*"

Beckan is confused. "Who's looking out for you?"

"I think someone you met once or twice who you didn't know was important," she says. "You just passed by them and had no idea they were secretly taking care of you. Maybe they don't know either." She scoots back from the water and lies on her back, her eyes closed. Beckan cannot imagine how she could stop drinking. She thinks she will never stop drinking. Her dry cake of a tongue absorbs all the moisture before she can swallow. She pours water directly down her throat. She burrows in the mud and absorbs water through her skin.

Tier says, "Rig likes to extrapolate."

Rig laughs a little. "I always thought about this woman I once knew. She lived in the deepest tunnel, and she sat with one candle, and she'd knit."

"Rig," Tier says.

"That's all she ever did, knit, and tell stories, with her head down. She only knew a few stories. Maybe three. When I was a kid, I liked to imagine she was knitting the stories. Grabbing the familiar bits from the air and winding them around on the needles and turning them into the story about the girl who learned to sing when her lover left, and the boy who traded places with the girl rabbit and saw how brave she was and how brave he had to be. But she knitted and knitted and no new stories came out. So I started reading to her, and she'd repeat the stories back to me."

Tier isn't drinking anymore. He's watching Rig.

"Except she'd always give the stories I taught her a twist," Rig says. "She'd add in a girl. Not a girl who needed to be rescued, but not instead of her. There would be a whole new girl who didn't have to do anything, who did things when she wanted to and when she thought they were right and nothing else. And someone still got to be rescued, and everyone still got to be in love."

Beckan tucks her chin onto her knees. She feels as if she's in that room now, listening to a story. But she is so aware of the outdoors and how alive she is. The sun is so warm and she is so hot.

"What happened to her?" Beckan says.

Tier drags his sleeve over his mouth. "My father ate her." They're quiet for a minute.

"She was your mother," Tier says.

Maybe it is thanks to Beckan's mother, somehow, that three hills later they find a cabin. Maybe she is looking out for them.

At first they think they've discovered a relic of another world. That there used to be a village here—maybe even a city—and they have uncovered it with the magic of the universe or Beckan's mother. The cabin is certainly old; it sinks into the ground in a way the cottage at home does not, and the windows are sticky and the wood is soft around the edges of the glass.

But it is sturdy and clean, and, upon closer inspection, they find hot water and a wind chime and dust conspicuously absent on top of the stove and the table and a few of the beds.

The cabin is old, but someone has already discovered it.

She feels like she is playing make-believe. She and Josha, sheets over the kitchen table, napkins folded into hats on their heads, used to pretend they were creatures no one had discovered yet and they were living their lives together, apart from everyone, and the rest of the world would never know. This house could be the house they were always imagining.

"Maybe gnomes were here," Rig says.

"Gnomes live underground," Beckan says, before she stops and reminds herself that they would rather not.

Tier hopefully checks the fridge, but there's nothing.

"Gnomes hate underground," Rig says, and laughs a little. "And they wouldn't leave food."

"Maybe it was tightropers."

"No ropes," Tier says. "Maybe nymphs."

"Tigerladies," Beckan says. "Or backpackers. They carry their babies in their backs, have to cut themselves open to get them out, it kills most of them. Scrap's mother was a backpacker. He has a mark on his back. That's how he looks like her."

"What about Josha?" Tier says, gently.

"Nymph. He likes water and he's tall, fingers are longer. . . . I have a gnome nose. But I'm no good at digging."

"You don't know that," Rig says, and Beckan realizes that, no, she does not know that.

"What about Cricket?" Tier says.

She can't remember.

Did she ever know?

She does not know what else Cricket was.

But then she thinks about his long, thin feet, his eyebrows always smiling even when the rest of his face was not, the way he wrapped himself around Josha like he was born to twist himself into Josha's every nook, the time he balanced on the top of the headboard and walked all the way from one end to the other. . . .

"I think he was half tightroper," Beckan says.

They give her small smiles.

She goes to the living room and finds a half-gnawed piece of taffy, a hair bow that a child would wear, a used but empty glass.

And then the sun shifts from behind a cloud and the entire cottage drowns in sunlight, and they all start to laugh, first with wonder and then with everything in them, because every surface of every room is covered with glitter. Glitter of fairies who were here, together, recently. Glitter of fairies who were alone and who sparkled and who were not ashamed.

Beckan drops to the carpet and rolls around in it, and she is stunned by how little time it takes before the other two join her, and they roll back and forth until Tier starts to sneeze, like Scrap, and suddenly she is crying so hard she can't breathe.

Beckan is surprised to find out how little Tier and Rig knew about Scrap and what he had to do.

"It didn't sound like there was a chance he was going to take the job," Tier says. "He was . . . resigned to being eaten."

Beckan shakes her head. "He told us he was going to take it."

"He did?"

Now she can't remember. "I told him to."

"Oh."

She hears Scrap's voice now, saying *No*. She shakes her head hard. "I don't want to talk about this."

He had to take it.

He had to.

"Did you see what happened to Josha?" Tier says.

She is dizzy. "No. No, no."

Because the whole city was dust and smoke and blood, and the last thing she can imagine surviving in all of that is a fairy. Especially when one is unruly and one is a little scrap.

"He's . . . he's got to be dead," Beckan says. "They've got to both be dead."

The gnomes don't say anything.

She had heard someone call him King Scrap.

She does not know whether or not to cling to that.

Beckan looks around at the furniture, at the piles of glitter in the corners she'd thought were dust. "Maybe I'm the only one left," she says.

"Then you're a gnome now," Rig says.

"I love you guys," she says. "But I don't know what I am."

She tucks her chin on top of her knees and squeezes her eyes shut for a minute. She wraps her arms around herself and holds herself still and together. Hours ago, just hours ago, she was in her cottage. She hadn't made her bed yet. There were dishes in the sink. And now it could all be gone, it could all be dust and rubble and just the tiniest bits of glitter and *maybe she'll just never know.* Maybe she'll make like a fairy and never go back, and it scares her that, for the first time, she really understands why someone might. She understands why those fairies at that meeting, so long ago, laughed at her and her pack because it was their first war.

How do you go again?

Beckan sleeps alone in one room and hears, through the walls, the sound of Rig and Tier doing the same in the other.

She scoots herself against the shared wall and presses her cheek against it. She hears one of them roll over in bed and nothing else.

"Do it," she whispers. "Clothes off. Do it. Come on."

After a while she can no longer stand it. She gets out of bed and wraps the sheet around herself because suddenly she is cold. She tries not to care that she is getting glitter all over it.

She pads through the house in bare feet and opens all the cupboards as if she is looking for something. But it isn't until she cracks open a low one in the living room before she realizes that she has been, and here they are, three shabby books. She chooses the shabbiest.

It is too dark to read in her room, and she's afraid that if she lights a candle the gnomes will smell the match and worry about her. So she sits on the bed and pretends she can read the words with her fingers, but these were printed like real books so she can't feel anything. Not like Scrap's notebook, with his bumpy left-handed writing that bleeds from page to page. Not like those stories that she already knows.

She has known them all. Even the ones that aren't real. She has known them for a very long time.

She has known Scrap's love story.

The next morning, hunger hits them at full force, and they whine their way around the house, checking all the cupboards Beckan opened last night for anything digestible. Beckan briefly considers eating her book.

They need more water, so they decide—or the gnomes decide, and Beckan exhaustedly agrees—to take a wide path back to their stream to see if they can track down anything alive. This phrasing worries Beckan.

Tier leads the charge through the fields, while Rig wanders off every so often in search of a flower to match one she has just found or because she thinks she's seen something in the distance. Beckan stays with her, but then feels like she should be making conversation, and the truth is she still isn't fully comfortable with Rig.

"I don't think they're dead," Rig says, suddenly.

"What?"

"Any of them. Scrap almost certainly. With all the gnomes up on the ground like that, fighting again, he'd be an idiot not to pick a side. That side."

"There was all that glitter. . . ."

"What?"

"You didn't see it?"

Rig shakes her head. "But I was underground, so maybe . . ."

"I think they tore someone apart," Beckan says. "I think . . . I think the glitter was someone being torn apart."

Rig doesn't say anything for a minute, then: "Scrap is fine. And Josha, almost as likely. Scrap would keep him safe."

"And Piccolo?"

"Well . . . chances are the worst for him, because he's a tightroper, and I heard all those teeth. . . ."

"Tightropers were getting eaten."

"I think so. And he's the son of a general . . . but maybe the tightropers are surviving okay. Or maybe they ran away. He could be safe."

"Maybe."

"And if he's in the city, Scrap would look out for him too."

"Scrap hates him."

"There's a big difference between hating someone in peace and hating someone during war."

That is the truest thing Beckan can ever remember hearing.

It's the same reason Josha and Scrap's fighting has nothing to do with whether they will keep each other safe. Josha held Scrap when he cried over the dishes. They are in the same pack.

"Still," Beckan says. "Even if they did all survive initially, there's no guarantee. There could be bombs going off, one of them could be crushed, shot, torn up. . . ."

"I don't hear anything, do you?"

She doesn't. She isn't sure if that means anything—how could she be, when she has only the vaguest idea of how far they are from Ferrum?—but she lets it comfort her just the same. The truth is, now that the immediate shock of yesterday has sunk back below the surface, something in her feels that her pack is alive.

It is stupid and she can't explain it, but she feels as though she would know if they weren't.

She would feel as though she has lost an arm.

Beckan says, "Why aren't you sleeping with Tier?"

Rig looks almost as surprised at the question as Beckan is.

"Oh," she says.

"I'm sorry." Beckan shakes her head. "It's really not my business."

But Rig sits down and looks at her, and Beckan can tell that she's meant to sit too. She feels, very suddenly and deeply, like a prostitute, for the first time in months. Like Rig has hired her to sit down.

It's so, so sad.

The feeling is gone as soon as Rig offers her hand. Beckan sits next to her, and Rig does not wipe the glitter off her hand, and Beckan notices immediately. Of course she does.

She realizes, really, that she did not like being a prostitute.

"It was just a sudden question," Rig says. "We can talk about it."

"I said I'd help you and I guess I haven't really."

"You have, though." She rubs her feet in the dirt. "You're so lovable, Beckan, and seeing you with Scrap . . . I want what you guys have."

"No." She shakes her head. "No. You don't."

"I do."

"We don't have anything. I don't know what we have."

"You are wrapped around each other," Rig says. "When one of you moves, the other does too."

"We strangle each other."

"You keep each other warm. That's what I mean. I want it to be ugly and complicated. I want to . . . not see Tier, and know that I have to spend the rest of my life with him, that this is my partner forever, that everything is . . . set."

"Break up with him."

"No, no! I want to spend the rest of my life with him. But it's scary, too . . . I don't know. I don't know how to be okay with being a person who just wants what she's supposed to want. It's hard to be in love with the boy I was betrothed to and not feel like it's just because someone told me I should be. Doesn't that make me . . . boring?"

Beckan laughs a little. "Love should be more boring."

Rig smiles at her. "I love him. I really do."

Beckan smiles back.

"But I'm afraid I won't be good enough to keep this future that I want. That I'll mess it up, and I'm not good enough. It's . . . hard, looking at you, Beckan. Imagining you sleeping with him."

"It was a job."

"But you're cute and loud and funny and . . . and you kept him going through the war, and now I have to take your place, and I have to do that forever if I'm going to stay with him."

"You don't have to take my place. You have to be you."

Rig doesn't say anything.

"Rig," Beckan says. "Don't ever let a whore make you feel like you're not good enough."

Tier comes running back to them with a lamb, no more than a few weeks old, cradled in his arms. "Look!" he says. Beckan wonders if she has ever really seen him smile.

He says, "Look who's lost too!"

To Beckan's relief, they decide not to eat the lamb.

"She's too small," Tier says. "She wouldn't last us a meal. Maybe for Beckan."

"Please, no," Beckan says.

"She's not enough to be worth it. Animal meat doesn't do much to sustain us," Tier says. "Not as much as . . . you know. Other things." He clears his throat, but this isn't anything Beckan didn't already know. Tier used to grumble, whenever she pissed him off, that he could eat one of her fingers and live longer than he could if he went

A sheep.

rogue and devoured ten of his own kind. It was a comforting kind of teasing. If he was ever going to do it, after all, it wouldn't be because they'd calmly discussed it.

"So we'll raise her and milk her," Tier says. "Find her a mate."

"That will take weeks," Rig says. "At least."

And so they develop a routine. Tier goes out during the cooler parts of the day, looking for more animals. Rig tends to the lamb. Beckan digs up things from the ground that she thinks she can cook and makes them all soup that none of them can tolerate beyond a few spoonfuls. She hates herself for occasionally visually butchering the lamb.

They save energy where they can, which, for Tier and Rig, means that they still do not sleep together, and for Beckan means that she spends a lot of time on the porch, in the rotting rocking chair, reading through the old books.

She reads a poem that says *nobody, not even the rain, has such small hands,* and she thinks that she probably knows someone with hands even smaller, and she drifts off and remembers finally that the day she realized how small Scrap's hands are was the same day Cricket died.

She'd teased him for it. He'd smiled back, not embarrassed, not amused, only full of expectation, because they both knew what was going to happen and it was inevitable enough to be unbearable, and his hair was wet from the shower and she had only half her makeup on so there was something entirely perfect about them, half finished and half naked, but they had to go to work so it would have to wait, and Cricket was already out the door, yelling for them, but he could already taste I mean she could already taste his skin and how his lips would feel and how hard it was going to be to wait just a few hours but they had to, and it would only be a few hours. That was the day.

She is tired and hungry and hot, and she should want desperately to go home, but what she wishes now is not that she was with him but that he was with her, and that they could stay here forever, and also that he would bring food with him, and she laughs.

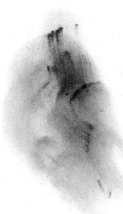

14

SOON, THOUGH, REALITY creeps in on them. After a few
more days, Tier is too weak to go out searching, their lamb is no bigger,
and Beckan has dug so many holes around their cottage that they trip
whenever they step outside, but there are no more vegetables or weeds
that look as though they may be persuaded into becoming vegetables.

They are dizzy. They lie on the floor in heaps, alternately drawn
together for comfort and pushed away in frustration.

"We have to eat something," Tier says.

Beckan feels their eyes on her.

"We have to eat something," Rig repeats.

Beckan sits up. "I'm going for a walk," she says.

Tier says, "It's after dark."

"I'll be fine." She totters on her feet when she stands up. "I'll
take it slow."

But she doesn't. She runs.

With every bit of energy left in her, she runs.

She was so stupid. She was happy to be here. She thought she
was living in some kind of dream. She thought they would find food
and it would be fine.

Tier and Rig would rather not eat her, but this is what they were made to do. The two of them can survive on her body for a long time. She could never eat one of them. She wouldn't. She would die first.

Will Scrap have to eat fairies now that he is king?

What is she thinking? There are no fairies.

She can't run far before she has to stop and pant. She's just so hungry.

She never thought she would die like this. Deep down, she assumed she would someday be eaten; that's how most of them go, eventually. But she'd pictured it in a struggle. She would die fighting for her life. The bits of her left over would kick, bite, hurt however they could. She would not give up, not down to her last speck of glitter.

Bits of her would stay conscious forever, and why did that ever sound like a blessing?

She will someday be lost.

She watches the pieces of glitter on the ground behind her. If she concentrates so, so hard, she can make them move.

She's left pieces of herself everywhere already.

She never thought she would die like this.

She straightens up and looks out into the distance. It is hill after hill after hill, but the stars—

The stars never looked like this at home.

Away from the lights of the city, away even from the dim lights of the cottage, there is nothing glowing but Beckan's glitter and the stars. She feels small and safe in the mouth of the universe.

Her body is hers, and it is hers to give away. And giving a bit of herself to someone she loves will be the exact opposite of being a prostitute.

"A little," she tells Tier and Rig, panting from the run back. "You can have a little."

"I wish we had alcohol or something to give you," Rig says. She is in charge of holding Beckan still, but right now she is only sitting at the table, stroking her hair. Beckan is on her back on the table, her eyes already closed and her shoe already off.

"Do it fast?" Beckan says.

Tier nods. He is concentrating on Beckan's foot.

"Are you sure a knife wouldn't be better?" Beckan says. Weakly.

"Our teeth are much stronger than that."

She tries not to think about how strong their teeth are. About how easily Cricket was devoured. About how quickly the two of them could crush her down to glitter and powdered bone.

She holds Rig's hand.

"It'll just take a second," Rig says.

"But then it will keep hurting." Beckan does not want to cry, but she thinks she probably already is. "It's not going to stop hurting as soon as the toe's off. It'll keep burning for so long."

"Scrap managed," Tier says.

And Beckan stops crying. "Okay."

Rig leans over her and holds her tight, and Tier's teeth come down quickly and precisely, and he bites off her biggest toe.

She screams. She feels it shoot all the way up her leg and into her hip bone, she feels fire as if Tier has cauterized her, she feels her throat sore from crying when she has hardly started.

Tier spits her toe on the table and comes around with Rig and holds her for a while. They have plenty of time to share the little thing. It isn't going anywhere.

Her foot is wet with blood and somehow this soothes her. Tier takes a wet washcloth and very carefully rinses her foot with cold water, guiding all the glitter away from the wound. "We really do not need you to get an infection," he says.

"I won't die," she says, faintly, with the glorious thought that Tier does not want her to die. Her heart drums and the pain energizes her as if she has eaten something too.

When she's feeling a little better, she finds it doesn't take much concentration for her to be able to make the toe move, walk around the table, dance a little, and they all laugh together, so weakly. They discuss whether to cook the toe before realizing she will feel it, and they shake their heads hard and turn off the stove and put Beckan to bed. She thinks the pain will keep her up, but she sleeps for three hours with dreams of monsters and infections and severed arms, and she screams in her sleep when they eat her toe, feeling every bit of broken skin and crushed bone as cleanly as if it were still attached. They are blissfully quick. They love her; they were just so hungry.

A clean cold washcloth against her face, and she opens her eyes and Rig is there.

Beckan doesn't feel her toe inside Rig's stomach, she doesn't think, but she doesn't really know how that would feel.

"Hey," Rig says, gently. She sits on the side of the bed and mops Beckan's face. "How are you feeling?"

She feels young and sick, and like her father has kept her home from playgroup until her fever goes down.

Rig has lit one small candle on the nightstand. The rest of the room is a very soft kind of dark. Beckan's vision is blurry, but she can make out the stars through the window, like a hundred thousand slits of light. They are the same stars she saw when she had ten toes.

"Sip," Rig says, and hands her a glass of water. "And try sitting? I'll prop you up."

Beckan drinks and lets Rig ease her back into a stack of pillows. Something sweaty and foggy drains from her head down to her sore foot. "I'm better," she says.

Rig laughs a little, and Beckan smiles.

"Okay," Beckan says. "But I do feel better."

"Good." Rig tucks Beckan's hair behind her ear. "You're a mess."

"Mmm. How was my toe?"

Rig gives a nervous laugh. "How should I answer that?"

"Honestly."

"Honestly, it was tough but sweet. Kind of like its owner."

Beckan rolls her eyes, but she smiles. "Glitter tastes horrible, I know."

"No. Like electricity. But you must be so hungry." Her hand remains on Beckan's face, cupping her chin now.

Beckan says, "Now there's a little less of me to feed."

Rig laughs again and says, "Oh, Beckan," and she leans into her and puts her arms around her. "I'm sorry," she says. "I'm sorry. I'd let you eat my toes."

Beckan rests her forehead against Rig's. "I'll get by. Eat grass. I'm so tired."

"We should get you home," she says.

"We don't know where home is. Maybe I'll never go home."

It starts to rain, hard, and when Rig gets up to close the window, Beckan wraps herself up in her own arms. "I'm scared," she says.

Rig sits back down on the bed. "That's okay," she says. "I'm scared of everything."

They sit looking at each other for a long minute, until Beckan leans in and kisses her.

This part is going to sound like some sort of irritating fantasy on my part, but I swear this really happened.

They start quietly, seriously, undressing each other with nervous precision, but as they go, they start to smile and laugh, touch hair, fingers, lips. Rig picks Beckan up and pushes her against the wall. They kiss down to their bones.

Rig is soft and smells like earth, and she kisses Beckan like she is special instead of like she is a nine-toed prostitute. They tangle their hair and lie down, side by side. They silently decide not to care whose body is whose. They touch each other and themselves, they make sounds without apology, they hold all their flaws between their bodies and cradle them with each kiss.

Which is not to say that it is entirely gentle, painless, unremarkable. They gasp, they claw, Beckan begs Rig to rest her teeth against her neck. They knock elbows and hip bones.

It isn't love, exactly. It's that they are dear to each other, and that they have been careful with each other in a way the rest of the world has not. Rig has been under the ground and high above their heads but she has never been here, on the land, steady, and Beckan has been a dirty little secret and a kiss in an elevator but never anything but an empty everyone wants to fill.

It is somehow a kind of sex that brings them closer to everyone else as well. It is shared, it is equal, and it is not the powerless thing Rig thought she wanted, but something so much more. It is power shared between them, stretched from one to the other like a tightrope, like a power line, like electricity. And to Beckan, it feels like a promise. That her life is not over, it is just over in the way that it was. That she will get out alive. That there is a whole world out there with stories and sweet kisses and someone with small hands and poetry about those small hands.

Kisses, fingers, nineteen toes, they remind each other, teach each other for the first time maybe, how to feel safe.

Beckan wakes up in the morning to sunlight, a dull pain in her foot, and mattress-squeaking, mouth-breathing, voice-breaking sex next door. She expects to feel jealous, at least momentarily, but all she feels is panic that she won't get her pillow over her mouth before she starts squealing and laughing. She does, barely. She kicks her nine-toed feet in the air and laughs and feels every bit of herself. For a few hours, she isn't hungry. She rolls in her own glitter.

(I wanted to write Rig's point of view here, something about the conversation she must have had with Tier, something even about how their room looked, how they lay when they slept, how it feels to be this woman in this story. I tried. But I can't do it. There are things I don't know, and I'm not going to take those from her. I can pretend to be a lot of things, but I cannot pretend to be this girl. This woman. I hope you write a book someday, Rig.)

Tier digs up what seems to be an onion and simmers it on the stove for Beckan, and she nibbles on it in her rocking chair. She has finished all the books, so she watches their lamb, who gallops around, gnawing greedily at the grass and lapping up every drop of water Rig pours into the hole Tier dug for her.

Beckan heals well, and soon she can walk around with nothing more than a vague limp. It helps that any time she wobbles close to Rig or Tier, they gather her into their arms like she is the most precious thing.

"Do you need more?" she asks, weakly.

"No," they say. "Absolutely not."

It's midday, and she is chewing on a blade of grass and downing cup after cup of water when she hears something. A voice.

Calling, *"Miss Beckan! Miss Beckan!"*

"Tier!" she yells.

He comes running. Rig clambers onto Tier's shoulders to see better. And there it is, a puffy white shape coming over their hill. "It's a *sheep!*" Rig says.

They're so excited, it takes Beckan a minute to remember that she heard a voice.

"Is there someone with it?" she says. "Anyone?"

Rig narrows her eyes, and a few seconds later she breathes out. "Oh, Tier. It's Shug."

Beckan uses Tier's elbow to pull herself to her feet. "Who's Shug?"

"A gnome," Tier says. "This kid."

He isn't just any kid, Beckan realizes when he's a few feet closer. He's the boy she wouldn't give meat to, the one who bit Scrap's leg down in the mines the day Scrap decided to harden up.

The look on his face makes her believe he doesn't recognize her, which is silly, because with four—three—fairies in the city, who could forget them? "Are you Miss Beckan?" he calls.

Beckan and Tier yell at him to come up and he does, his sheep at his heel. Rig jumps off Tier's back and hugs Shug hard, like a mother. Beckan hates herself for being surprised that the two of them have a relationship she never knew about, as if a few visits to the mines and a few days alone with Rig and Tier makes her privy to everything that happens underground.

"What are you doing out of the city?" Rig says. "Oh, baby, do you have food?"

"Of course," Shug says, and he takes a parcel of jerky out of his pocket. Rig and Tier take one small piece each and give the rest to Beckan. It is dry and tastes like bugs and Beckan devours every bit of it.

Tier brings Shug a glass of water, and Shug says, "So glad I found you, Miss Beckan. Mr. Scrap would be so mad at me if I hadn't—"

"Scrap?"

Scrap is alive.

Scrap is alive. (Of course I am, Beckan, who the fuck do you think is writing this?)

"Yes ma'am. I'm his messenger, see."

She bites her lip when she smiles. Of course Scrap would pick this boy. Not because Shug owed him something to make up for the hole in his leg, but because Scrap needed someone he knew would not let go.

Shug says, "It was so hard even getting out of the city for the day! Everything's crazy. Had to sign a pass to get out and I'm not even in trouble for anything! If they knew I was working for Mr. Scrap, though—"

Beckan can't find the word *what*, but Rig can.

"What do you mean, sign a pass?" Rig says.

"They've gone crazy," he says. "Everyone's crazy. All these rules, everyone doing blood tests and filling out paperwork and registering. All these records being pulled, everyone giving . . . what's it called? Talking about everyone else. Having someone write it down. *Here's this thing I did and who else was there.*"

"Statements," Tier says.

"Yes. Statements." he says to Beckan. "I'm very glad to meet you," he says to Beckan. "You're a fairy!"

He really doesn't remember. She forgives him. He looks different, too.

"They've got the rest of you," he says. "The ones who were in the city. Gathered them up. The big tall one, he got off okay. He has to pick up rubble and sweep or something for a while. He and that dark, scary tightroper."

"So Scrap took care of them."

"Scrap? Scrap can't take care of anyone! Scrap can't take care of himself! He's the one in trouble in the big trial today, that's why I had to come get you! He sent me a message. They have him all tied up, see, but I went to see him and he told me to go out and see if I could find you! I've been leaving every day looking for you. Just in time!"

"Scrap's in trouble?"

"For killing Crate!"

Tier grabs Beckan's hand.

Beckan figures out a few things very quickly.

Scrap is not the king of anything.

Some group now has enough power to grab Scrap, try him, and convince everyone to come and see.

That group is not her pack.

If it is the tightropers, everything is going to be okay. If they decide to punish Scrap, they will lock him away. And a fairy can only be locked away for so long. Everyone who has jailed him will die or forget or give up, and he will sit in his cage until it rots away, and she will read him books through the bars. It will be tragic and romantic and he will write about it.

If it is the gnomes, they will eat him.

Every last scrap.

"Who?" Beckan says. "Who's putting him on trial?"

Shug looks at her like he's crazy.

"The fairies," he says. "You didn't know the fairies were back?"

See, the tightropers didn't plan for the fairies to come back. They thought there wasn't a chance that they would.

Beckan won't ever be sure why they did. Maybe they realized that they wouldn't have to do much of anything to get the city back. The numbers were on their side. There just weren't that many tightropers. There just weren't that many gnomes.

Her theory, as you'll see later, is that the fairies were planning to come back all along. That they left so that the tightropers could take out some gnomes for them, and the whole time they were waiting for everyone to thin each other out and let their guard down and then they were going to fly in (so to speak) and the rest of the tightropers would move on like they were supposed to and the fairies would have a safer city, at the end of all of it, without having to do any of the dirty work themselves. And sometimes, when Beckan's in a particularly conspiratorial mood, she'll decide that the fairies planned the whole thing, that they intentionally got the tightropers to come by leaking some information that they were oppressed and so weak and so afraid, and oh yes, have you *seen how* beautiful *our city is,* let's throw in a line about our accessible waterways and diamond mines and steel production, wouldn't you like to come save us?

But there's another theory, and it's that none of it, nothing a single one of those fucking flighty fairies did, was planned. They left because they wanted to and came back because they wanted to, because fairies are impulsive, fairies are spoiled, and fairies have eternities to learn to be better and they never do. The fairies felt like coming back, so they did. And they felt like winning without fighting. So they did.

So that's another theory. Who knows, really. This isn't a textbook.

Anyway. The fairies came back.

Shug agrees to bring Beckan back to the city. He also agrees to leave Tier and Rig his sheep.

Tier kisses Beckan's cheek and Rig hugs her tightly. Tier says, "Be careful on that foot, okay?"

"What about you guys?"

"We'll be fine."

They will be. She knows that. She can picture them with a whole family of sheep, a field of flowers, sex, and stories they remember, and stories they make up. She knows that they would have kept her safe for a long time, but she also knows that those sheep are not ready for slaughter, so eventually they would have eaten her, and it is strange to know both of these things at once, but she is getting used to it.

And with each careful step behind Shug, she thinks less and less about them and more and more of the glint of glitter, the hiss of yellow smoke, the smell of her city.

This city that is hers to protect and hers to mold. She can do it. She and her pack can save everything.

It's their job. It's their burden.

They approach Ferrum from the North End, where the farms are still recovering from their long abandonment. And here they are, at what should be their usual stone walls.

But no, these walls are new; these walls are blocking their old walls. Smooth metal with dark, sharp wire, warnings of alarms, fairy guards (fairies, fairies) stationed on either side of a solid, locked gate.

A year of a sprawling war has made her forget how quickly things can happen.

"Shug," the gnome boy tells one of the guards. "And this is Beckan Moloy."

"She isn't in uniform."

"She's been away."

The guard puts a stamp of one color on Shug's hand and another on Beckan's. "Bring her straight to the hospital. Don't delay."

"Won't. Thank you, sir."

The fairies put keys in the locks and turn heavy wheels on the ground. Beckan leans into Shug and says, "Where did these walls come from?"

"They've put the gnomes to work," he says. "Put everyone to work."

"I can't go to the hospital," she says. "I'm not sick, I don't need . . . I have to get to the courthouse."

Shug says, "No, you can't go anywhere looking like that."

"Like what?"

The gates open, so slowly, and Beckan steps through and sees her city. She sees glitter, pounds of it, clinging to hundreds of fairies.

Each fairy in a gray uniform. Each gnome in blue. Each tightroper in white.

And everyone is on the streets. The tunnels are still open at the tops, and guards man the sides to stop anyone from jumping in. The gnomes all look so uncomfortable above the ground, their bare feet on the cobblestone.

There are no tightropes, just long, lean boys and men and women and children in white uniforms slouching against the buildings, snapping to attention when the fairies walk by, sweeping. A whole race of messboys (and if Beckan hadn't recently been part of a three-member race, she's not sure she would even count these tightropers as their own. There are *so few left.* And so many gnomes who just look so not-starving. The math is not hard.)

There is no one she recognizes.

There are uniforms and streets she knows and buildings that have been rebuilt since she left, but rebuilt shinier and newer and brighter than they once were, and the sun shines on everything and hurts her eyes, and she recognizes no one.

A whole city of uniforms and clean slates and blank faces.

"You won't get anywhere unsorted," Shug says.

This isn't her city.

How could this have happened so quickly?

How could she have let this happen?

Ferrum (an artistic rendition)
around 7/31/546

15

BECKAN MAKES SHUG LEAVE HER and walks to the hospital herself. She knows where it is. It's where she kissed Scrap and his fever all those years ago.

The last time she saw it was the day Josha was burned. They were going to pick up Cricket together and a bomb—from aboveground or below ground or somewhere, did it really matter?—went off at the next block and destroyed the hospital. Josha, like an idiot, like a boy who had stayed inside the whole war, ran toward it to see if anyone was hurt. No one was, besides him, and that was just a shrapnel burn on the side of his face, but it was enough to make him terrified and angry and desperate to join the fight, to end it, to get hurt for a reason.

She passes a gnome pushing a broom behind a fairy. "How's Tier?" he mumbles as she passes.

"Safe."

He nods to himself and continues. She realizes that a part of her was afraid of him.

Everyone is watching her, the dirty little fairy girl without a uniform. Everyone is watching her except the ones she most wants to see her.

Where is her pack?

She realizes that, as far as she knows, Ferrum does not have a courthouse.

"Excuse me," she asks a fairy woman. "Where's the courthouse?"

"Go to the hospital," the woman says, without looking at her.

"I don't care about a fucking uniform!" she yells, but she's jostled as she walks and soon the hospital is right in front of her, and through the window she sees a boy on a bench with an ice pack over his eye. A boy getting prodded by a fairy in gray uniform.

A boy in a white uniform.

"Piccolo!"

Immediately, she's through the doors, and she hears a load of doctors or nurses or someones yelling at her to go to the front desk, to sign in, but Piccolo sees her and drops the ice pack and they hug like they haven't seen each other in years.

"No," Piccolo says. "No, don't cry."

"Are you okay?"

"Just hit in the eye. They wouldn't let me in the courtroom, I kind of freaked out."

"Why not?"

"No tightropers 'cept the ones on the jury. I can't believe you . . . fuck, we thought you were dead."

She shakes her head. "Josha . . . ?"

"Josha's fine. In the courtroom."

"With Scrap."

He nods.

Then, behind her, a skinny throat gives a thick *ahem,* and she turns around to see a tall fairy with her hair put up on top of her head, her red glitter somehow perfect, her gray uniform sharp and clean.

It's the woman from the meeting before the war. Jenemah. The one who told Scrap that no city was worth losing a limb.

So what is it worth losing, is the thing.

"Name?" she says.

"Beckan Moloy?"

"Come with me."

Beckan looks at Piccolo.

"I'll wait for you," he says. "I'll be able to get in once you're with me."

"What?"

"You're a fairy."

She forgot that ever meant anything.

Fairies could go anywhere, could do anything, ruled their little world.

That's what the history books said. (That was history.)

Jenemah leads her through the hall to a bed surrounded by curtains, where she rolls up Beckan's sleeve and takes a vial of blood. While it fills, she swabs off glitter from Beckan's cheek and wipes it onto a small piece of glass.

She flips through pages on her clipboard. "You're not on my list. Were you in Calman's traveling party?"

"I wasn't in anyone's traveling party. I took a walk for a few weeks. Before that I was in this city. Every day. For my entire life."

She chuckles and tucks her hair behind her one remaining ear. "Right. Your name has come up in the trial, I believe." She runs Beckan's blood through a machine. "Good. Fairy."

"What else would I be?"

Jenemah gives her a look. "You never know who might be pretending these days. You could be a gnome covered in glitter. The first step toward reorganizing this city is to have each creature in its proper place. We cannot make any progress in chaos."

"Why did you come back?"

"We will always come back when we are needed."

"Bullshit."

"Scrap's predicament is delicate. The outcome of his trial will determine a great deal for the city and for our race relations as a whole. Scrap involved himself in a conflict between all three races."

She says, "It doesn't matter anyway. Scrap's a fairy. He'll get off."

"We'll see."

Beckan is cold. "Where is the courthouse?"

The fairy woman throws an armful of cloth at her. "Put on your uniform."

She does, shaking. "You said my name came up. As a witness? I'll be a witness. Everything that Scrap did was self-defense. Piccolo was a witness too. The tightroper. That boy out there."

"Miss Moloy," Jenemah says, "might I be frank?"

"Scrap never did anything he didn't have to do, and he's the only one in the whole war who can say that."

"At this point," she says. "Our main focus is on fostering suitable species-to-species relationships. The necessary opinions in the matter are those of a carefully selected council consisting of two gnomes, two tightropers, and two fairies."

"And a fairy judge," Beckan guesses.

"Naturally."

"None of whom were here when it happened."

"Oh, the gnomes were," she says. "Rest assured, the gnomes remember quite well. And bringing a fairy to justice might be all they need to stay content underground for a long, long time."

They have plenty of time, Beckan thinks.

What she says is, "This is bullshit. Tell me where the courthouse is."

JUDGE PEONY LACHTURN: Mr. Oregna, you stand trial today for the murder of the late gnome king Crate. How do you plead?

SCRAP OREGNA: I don't know.

JUDGE PEONY LACHTURN: Do you understand the charges brought against you?

Whereupon the door opens and two latecomers slip through the cracks. The defendant does not turn around.

SCRAP OREGNA: Yes.

JUDGE PEONY LACHTURN: And how do you plead?

SCRAP OREGNA: I don't know.

FAIRY COUNCILMAN CALMAN CREED: He's stalling, Your Honor.

JUDGE PEONY LACHTURN: Mr. Oregna. You've had nearly three weeks in confinement to contemplate your trial. What more could you possibly ask for to help you make the decision of whether you are guilty or not guilty?

SCRAP OREGNA: A lawyer.

Whereupon there is a disturbance near the back of the courtroom as one of the aforementioned newcomers rises and charges toward the front of the courtroom.

JUDGE PEONY LACHTURN: Young lady, if you please!

RUDE NEWCOMER: Scrap requested a lawyer. I've decided that I'm up for the job.

Whereupon Scrap Oregna stares at the rude newcomer as if he has just seen a ghost.

Rude newcomer, in accordance with her title, does not look at him.

JUDGE PEONY LACHTURN: You decided, in the two and half seconds between Mr. Oregna's request for a lawyer and your own charge toward the bench, that you are adequate to stand as a lawyer in this trial?

RUDE NEWCOMER: Yes.

JUDGE PEONY LACHTURN: And your name?

RUDE NEWCOMER: Beckan Moloy.

A FAIRY BOY, HIGH IN THE STANDS: Fuck yeah, Beckan!

Beckan knows now why she didn't know there was a courthouse. This isn't what used to be here.

This building used to be a library.

These spectator seats used to be shelves.

The judge's bench is stuck in the middle of the children's section.

She came here a few times for her lessons with Scrap, but largely her memories of the place are from her childhood, with her father, with Josha, snuggled into a chair in the corner with a picture book, trying to read.

GNOME COUNCILMAN PLUG: Your honor, I must object to this. The fairy girl has not been sworn in and she hasn't shown us any credentials.

Whereupon everyone ignores this objection and Beckan Moloy whispers back and forth with her new client.

JUDGE PEONY LACHTURN: Well, Miss Moloy? How does your client plead?

BECKAN MOLOY: We plead bullshit.

SCRAP OREGNA: We plead not guilty. She says I'm not guilty.

"Where's Josha?" Beckan whispers to him.

Scrap jerks his head toward the side of the courtroom. He's there, up in the stands, still smiling after cheering her name. Piccolo has climbed up beside him, and they beam down at her and Scrap like they have all gotten along this whole time. There is a difference between hating someone and hating someone during a trial. She grabs Scrap's hand and squeezes it hard before she lets it go.

"I'm sorry," he says. "For the book."

"Are you still writing it?"

He nods, a little.

"Then don't apologize. Keep the hope alive, kid."

His smile stretches to his ears.

She notices his hand, the metal one, has its fingers bent into the tightest fist. He must have used his other hand to fold it that way. It must have been hard.

She'll ask about that later.

JUDGE PEONY LACHTURN: Plug, you've gathered up reports of the alleged murder from various sources, have you not?

GNOME COUNCILMAN PLUG: I have, your honor.

BECKAN MOLOY: Objection! I'm afraid I have to insist that these sources be disclosed to my client and I—

SCRAP OREGNA: Me. Client and me.

BECKAN MOLOY: Prior to Plug delivering his report.

Whereupon the judge appears already exhausted of playing house with the children.

JUDGE PEONY LACHTURN: Sustained, I suppose.

GNOME COUNCILMAN PLUG: The testimonies are those of various gnomes who witnessed the incident and were not so horribly traumatized that they couldn't stand to speak of Crate's murder.

BECKAN MOLOY: Excellent, so we can all agree ahead of time that these testimonies are biased and likely false, as the murder—*alleged* murder—took place aboveground, where very few gnomes would have witnessed it. Thank you. You may continue.

GNOME COUNCILMAN PLUG: On the morning of Fairy Date 4/16/546, the defendant, his lawyer, and a fairy by the name of Cricket Oregna, the defendant's first cousin, were leaving the mines where they had been performing another night of prostitution to the gnome forces. They had just come out of the elevator when Cricket Oregna began to fraternize with a pair of tightropers hanging relatively close to the ground. Several gnomes report that he was speaking suggestively to them and offering them the services of himself and his friends. While this was occurring, King Crate had ascended the elevator to view tightroper carcasses. They were, at this point, nearly starving, as most of their food was going toward paying said fairies for said ... services.

Whereupon Beckan Moloy makes a crude gesture to her defendant, who rolls his eyes and smiles.

GNOME COUNCILMAN PLUG: Both of Crate's attendants had recently been killed, so he was uncharacteristically alone. When one of the tightropers stated that he thought the gnomes had an exclusive right to the fairies' services, Cricket Oregna began to mock the gnomes. He said, "We have them wrapped around our finger. We're the ones in charge here. They are starving and won't even eat us." At this point, Crate lunged toward Cricket and promptly ate him.

Crate next targeted Beckan, but she was armed with a small knife that was enough to make him hesitate. The defendant took advantage of this opportunity, leapt on the king, and proceeded to strangle him. The king, weak with hunger, was able to rip off only one of the defendant's arms before he perished.

BECKAN MOLOY: My client, therefore, suffered heaps and piles of pain and suffering, and his arm was never returned to him.

JUDGE PEONY LACHTURN: So a murderous part of your client is still loose in the city.

BECKAN MOLOY: It's in gnome custody, I believe. Largely destroyed.

Whereupon a few gnomes mutter in the affirmative and the defendant looks at his false hand.

FAIRY JUROR CALMAN CREED: Further evidence that the defendant is a danger to society, Your Honor. Why else would the arm need to be destroyed?

BECKAN MOLOY: Truly bulletproof logic, thank you.

JUDGE PEONY LACHTURN: Thank you, Mr. Creed. Miss Moloy, do you have any objection as to how the incident was presented? Was any of it factually incorrect? Is there anything you'd like to add?

Whereupon the defendant and Beckan Moloy look at each other in silence.

BECKAN MOLOY: No, Your Honor.

JUDGE PEONY LACHTURN: We will now hear a statement from the prosecution followed by the recommended sentence. Miss Moloy, you will then have a chance to respond.

Whereupon the defendant mumbles something to his lawyer about improper courtroom procedure and misreads of historical documents, and it is his lawyer's turn to roll her eyes.

GNOME COUNCILMAN RAP: Your Honor, we've just heard the story of Crate's cruel murder at the hands of his employee, but what we haven't yet heard is how much a betrayal this was to the relationship Crate had forged with Mr. Scrap Oregna. Scrap was the only one of the three prostitutes ever allowed to fraternize with Crate himself, and he did, frequently. In addition, Crate would often recommend Scrap to his close associates. He protected Scrap from some of his seedier clients, passing them instead to Mr. Oregna's cousin. Many gnomes noticed that there was a tenderness in their relationship. Perhaps Crate believed that Mr. Oregna looked upon him as a father figure, as the defendant's father left Ferrum, never to return, very early in the defendant's life.

So the question arises: Why murder Crate, if they were so close? Was it truly a heated argument leading to the consumption of a cousin Scrap dragged into prostitution (and left with the aforementioned seedier clients)? Was his relationship with his cousin really strong enough to be grounds for murder?

What we believe—what we hope the entire council will come to believe by the end of this trial—is that Crate's murder was not a crime of passion. It was a power play.

As a confidant of Crate, Mr. Oregna would no doubt have known that Crate, in order to ascend to the throne, had to kill the previous king, the late Sir Hoole. No doubt this planted a seed in Scrap's mind, and his cousin's transgression provided the perfect opportunity for his own coup. This was interrupted by the aforementioned arrival of the fairies.

What appears to be one unfortunate murder was, therefore, the beginning of an attempt to deconstruct gnome power. And let us not forget that, by instigating a rebellion, Mr. Oregna put both his fellow fairies and the tightropers in danger.

He is a hazard to society, and we recommend that he pay the gnomes the flesh debt he so sorely owes. We recommend he be jailed, divided into parts, and eaten.

BECKAN MOLOY: Objection.

JUDGE PEONY LACHTURN: On what grounds?

Whereupon the defense has no words.

JUDGE PEONY LACHTURN: Miss Moloy, are you ready to deliver your statement?

BECKAN MOLOY: Tomorrow.

JUDGE PEONY LACHTURN: I'm sorry?

BECKAN MOLOY: Give me until tomorrow. I need time to speak with my client.

JUDGE PEONY LACHTURN: Unfortunately, that won't be possible. Mr. Oregna will be taken back to his underground confinement. But the court will grant you until tomorrow at 10 a.m. sharp to prepare your statement. Court is adjourned.

"I'm going to figure this out," Beckan says, while they drag him away. "You'll be fine."

Scrap nods, his eyes huge, his one arm clutching his notebook, his stupid life flashing in front of him.

"Hey!" Beckan yells after him. "You don't owe anybody anything!"

Josha and Piccolo tackle her into their arms as soon as they're out on the street.

"Shit, Becks," Josha says, lifting her a few inches off the ground. "When I saw you come in with Piccolo . . . I'd thought you were dead."

"I almost was. Shit, what are we going to do?" She turns to Piccolo. "Why aren't your guys on the jury talking? They don't have anything against Scrap. They don't have any reason to protect the fucking city—"

"The tightropers are fucked. They're trying to stay on the fairies' good side so you don't chuck us out. You know they burned down four of our other settlements on their way back home? Killed hundreds."

"What?"

"Yep. So now we're basically all there is left, and we have no idea how far we'd have to go to find more of us. So yeah, you could say they have a reason to protect this city. This is fucking ridiculous. If I don't get out of this uniform, I'm going to shoot something."

Josha says, "Everyone's trying to play big happy family because right now everyone's at the same strength, so no one wants to fight. The fairies could get overthrown again at any second, and everyone knows it. Scrap's a nice symbol of resistance because he pissed off the fairies and the gnomes, and the tightropers don't care enough to save him."

They are talking about these races as though they are not part of them, and maybe they're not.

"Out of this uniform," Piccolo says, "I swear, I don't know what I'll do. . . ."

Josha puts a hand on his arm. "Hey. Try to stay calm, okay?"

On either side of them, gnomes and fairies and tightropers are pouring out of the courtroom, jostling them, ignoring them.

They took Scrap out through a back entrance. She doesn't know where he is underground, because she sees no movement in the torn-up tunnels.

Piccolo sees her looking and says, "Oh, that's bullshit. They've built tons of them back up already, they just have those open so we think we see everything that goes on. Everyone knows it and no one talks about it. Have you seen Tier and Rig?"

"Yes. They're alive. They're fine."

"Oh good, okay, okay."

"Maybe it would help if they were here," she says. "Some gnomes on our side."

Josha says, "A ton of them are on our side. You know a bunch of them loved Scrap. Best little whore and all that."

She hears the words in Cricket's voice and wants to cry, and also scream and rip her hair out and hit somebody because the words she truly remembers in Cricket's mouth are the ones calling Scrap a whore.

"But they're not exactly welcome to speak their minds right now," Josha finishes.

"So what do they expect us to do?" she says.

Josha runs a hand through his hair. "They expect us to sit down and shut up and watch an example made out of our best friend."

Piccolo is watching Beckan. "So what are you going to do?" he says.

She says, "I'm going to . . . write a defending statement."

"And I'm going throw myself off a very high rope," Josha mumbles.

"No ropes," Piccolo says, but Josha slips away and walks back toward the cabin, muttering to himself. "No ropes anymore," Piccolo says again. Quietly.

"Your revolution didn't work," Beckan says to Piccolo as Josha is walking away.

"No shit," he says.

"No," she says. "I mean, it didn't work on Josha. Fix him," she says. "Or I don't know what to do."

He looks at her like she's crazy. "You don't know what to do with a damaged fairy? What the fuck kind of defending statement are you writing? *Use him.*"

She thinks. "I'll need to use you, too."

"I'm your boy."

"Thanks. I . . . I guess I need to think for a while."

"Beckan," he says.

She stops and turns around. "What?"

"You know nothing you can say is going to change anything, right?"

She is quiet.

He says, "You can go in there and make the best fucking statement anyone's ever heard, and it is not going to change what that judge decides."

"I'm not giving up on Scrap."

"I'm not saying give up. I'm saying you've got stuff in your house we can fashion into something . . . explosive."

"And then what."

"And then grab him and run. It'd be pretty chaotic. That's how you got out last time."

"Someone will get hurt."

"Beckan." He takes a step toward her. "The pacifism thing . . . it's beautiful. I mean that. But Scrap is more beautiful than any principle and you've got to know it."

"I can't kill anyone," she says.

"What if you have to?"

"Then I'll end up like Scrap!" she says. "Okay? You got me. Fine." She can't fucking breathe. "Do I wish that Crate were alive? Fuck no, but *shit* I wish that Scrap hadn't been the one to kill him, because of what it did to Scrap. And I live with the fucked-up fact that I don't hate Crate for killing Cricket nearly as much as I hate him for what his death did to my little broken soul of a best friend who's now going to get eaten because I was too smart to slit Crate's throat, because I had an idea of what it would do to me and how being a murderer would destroy me from the inside out. So don't tell me not to bother. I know exactly what the fuck I'm bothering."

Piccolo watches her.

He says, "If anyone can do it, you can, Becks."

"But you don't think anyone can."

"No. I don't."

"I need to think. Go look after Josha?"

"Yeah. But one last thing, okay? There's a lot of gray area between talking and killing. There are a lot of things you can do that you won't like and that will scare the shit out of you but won't leave you believing someone has the right to eat you. You just . . . might have to meet in the middle."

She nods.

"But for now," he says. "Talk."

So she walks. She walks with her head up and her hand shielding her eyes from the sun. She thought seeing dozens of fairies shining like dozens of ugly stars would comfort her. She used to lie awake during the war dreaming about all the glitter pouring back into her world.

But none of these fairies is pink and blue, and none of them has that chapped lip, and none of them is missing an arm (at least none cut from the exact right place, with a metal arm at the end curled into a very tight fist), and none of them is her boy.

She realizes where she's heading only a few steps before she reaches it. She is at 7th and West, where their elevator used to be, but the entrance has been sealed over. It is nothing but concrete now.

Here is where Cricket was eaten. Here is where Crate was killed. She has stood on this spot a hundred times since that day, and she never forgot. She has never tried to hide from Cricket's death. She doesn't need a minute here to think about him and be hit with grief she has suppressed. This is not her breakdown.

She grieved well. She knows that. But she spent so much time judging Scrap and Josha—fuck you, Scrap, how dare you stay up writing the same night your cousin died, the night you killed a man; Josha, it's been a month, get the fuck off the bathroom floor—as if her way, her beautiful, correct way, was doing any more good.

She closes her eyes and lowers her forehead to the street and tries to pretend she sees a bit of Cricket's glitter ground into the pavement, but she closes her eyes and she is right back to pink and blue and the missing arm and that smile.

Because there wasn't anything clinical about it, really. The gnome had the actions, the semantics of that day all right, but the whole thing wrong.

There are things you can't say out loud.

What always got to me was how incredibly quick it was. That one minute Becks and Cricket and I were standing there and Cricket was being stupid and not shutting up when he should've because Cricket thought he was invincible, but what kind of thing is that for me to say about him? Because we all thought we were invincible. Fuck, I still do. I still feel my arm, whatever's left of it, bone and tendon and some piles of ash.

We are invincible, but we can be so lost, and I guess Crate saw Cricket talking to the tightropers and got paranoid. Maybe he thought his little spy was a double agent. Maybe he thought Cricket was getting close to them. I don't know.

But Crate grabbed Cricket and had his whole head in his mouth and it was just so, so fast. His teeth crunched through bone and spinal cord like Cricket was made of twigs.

He was smiling, and then he was gone.

How do you deliver that in a testimony?

How do you write this?

How do you stand on trial and say you're not guilty when you pushed down on that throat with everything in you, when you pressed your thumb across that windpipe just the way you'd learned from those books, just in case you ever were in this exact situation?

He ripped off the one arm and I didn't even feel it, not for minutes afterward. My entire life was that remaining hand, that grip around his neck, that fist.

You can't go back from that.

I wasn't supposed to write about this. There aren't feelings in history books. This is where I should put an anatomical sketch. This is where I should explain how the fuck you kill a man.

That last second, the moment when he flicked his eyes to mine, I knew that was it. That was my last chance to let go.

I felt him die. That was something I hadn't prepared myself for. Crate wasn't as big as everyone thinks, but I felt all of that weight slump against me, and I fell. Crushed by two dead men. The king and the bones of my cousin.

The strangest part was how there were no repercussions. How the gnomes didn't try to stop us as we ran home. How when we came back, shaking, a few days later, starving, hands clasped together in that elevator, ready for anything, they accepted us gently and said nothing of it until they offered me the throne a few months later. Needed to give me time to decompress, they said. To fall in love with the gnomes again. Needed to give themselves time to want another war.

I didn't know that killing him would make me king. Crate would never have told me that.

He wasn't that stupid.

And besides, the gnome said it himself in his testimony. I never took the job, Beckan.

I am that stupid.

What she will never forget isn't the blood and the glitter—so much blood, so much glitter—but Josha's face when they ran through the door. How he was first so worried about Scrap, seeing he had been injured, ushering him into a chair, cupping his face, comforting him. And then Beckan came in and then a pause where he realized that no one else was walking through that door.

And Beckan thought, *Why didn't I slit open Crate's body? Why didn't I dig into him and grab all the bits of Cricket I could find?*

And Josha just kept waiting. Staring out the door like Cricket was at the bottom of the hill. Staying absolutely silent so he would hear Cricket if he called, staying crouched with his hand still around Scrap's cheek.

She sleeps in her own bed that night. No Josha, no Scrap, just her glitter and the stars and the vague sounds of foot traffic down in her city.

And when she wakes up, she starts writing.

Me.

16

THE COURTROOM IS even more full today. The council arrived early. Everyone stands when Judge Peony Lachturn takes her place at the old librarian's desk. Twelve years ago, she sat there and taught a very young Scrap how to read.

They bring him in, chained and colorless underneath the glitter. A patch of it is missing on his cheek where a scrape is red and raw.

They drop him beside Beckan at the bench. She does not look at him.

She cannot get emotional right now.

She will not look at him.

If this is the last time she will see him alive, she does not want to know it. (She is terrified that she will already be able to see the life leaving him.)

"What are you wearing?" he says. She doesn't answer.

He is so tired. He puts his head down on the desk and waits for it all to be over.

"Don't you dare give up," she whispers.

He opens his eyes. She still isn't looking at him.

His hand is still in that fist.

"I don't know how," he says.

"You fucking idiot." She grabs his hand.

Court Transcript
The Trial of Scrap Oregna
7/1/546

JUDGE PEONY LACHTURN: Miss Moloy, what are you wearing?

BECKAN MOLOY: A uniform.

However, Miss Moloy is wearing what appears to be a white T-shirt covered in mud and glitter with ropes twisting up the sleeves.

JUDGE PEONY LACHTURN: That is not your correct uniform. That isn't any sanctioned uniform.

BECKAN MOLOY: No, Your Honor, it is not.

JUDGE PEONY LACHTURN: Immediately after the proceedings, you'll be changing back.

BECKAN MOLOLY: Fine.

The minutes from yesterday's trial are read.

JUDGE PEONY LACHTURN: Now that the minutes from yesterday's meeting have been presented, today should go fairly smoothly. We'll proceed with the defense's argument, then go right into our ruling. Nothing should take much time. Miss Moloy, are you planning on taking a lot of time?

BECKAN MOLOY: I don't know. What you've just said changes everything, doesn't it?

JUDGE PEONY LACHTURN: Miss?

BECKAN MOLOY: If I talk forever, you can't kill him, right?

Whereupon the judge looks quite pained.

JUDGE PEONY LACHTURN: You have five minutes, Miss Moloy.

BECKAN MOLOY: Five. Okay.

Look.

The issue isn't whether or not Scrap killed Crate. He did. We know that. For the crime of killing Crate, I have come up with a much more appropriate sentence that I hope the court will find acceptable. I suggest that he perform fifty hours of community service and consent to the destruction of the arm currently held in gnome custody to ensure that it can be responsible for no more murders.

JUDGE PEONY LACHTURN: That is the extent of the punishment you find fitting?

BECKAN MOLOY: Yes.

Whereupon there is much snorting and eye-rolling that Miss Moloy ignores.

BECKAN MOLOY: And here's why. Because the issue isn't that he killed Crate. The issue is whether you can ethically kill him for killing Crate.

It was a war. Everyone was killing everyone.

But that doesn't make it okay. And that's not the defense I'm going to use. Mass murders of tightropers and gnomes and the very un-mass, very murderous-murder of our fairy don't make killing one gnome okay, as much as I wish it did. That's not why you shouldn't kill Scrap.

You shouldn't kill Scrap because it wouldn't make sense to do so.

Whereupon everyone is waiting for the girl to fuck up and get her friend killed.

Look.

Whereupon Beckan takes a deep breath.

Look.

None of you wants to kill Scrap.

Every single one of the gnomes on this council has slept with Scrap, and I know he was an absolute

gentleman about it and you all asked for him again
and again.

The fairies know him. You know this boy. He brings
you soup when you're sick. Soup from a can, because he
can't cook worth shit, and are you really going to kill
someone who's still such a freaking kid that he can't
even figure out how to make soup?

Whereupon she gestures to the tightropers.

And the tightropers—he kept your general's kid, so
fed up with the horrible way you've treated him, from
planning a rebellion that would have brought down
your entire race.

None of you has anything against Scrap and none of you
really cares that he killed Crate, because that isn't
what this is about. This is about all of you wanting
to have and to kill a common enemy. To improve race
relations! And Scrap is convenient.

Killing Scrap to prove a point is ridiculous, because
it's because of Scrap—and me, and Josha, and Cricket, our
Cricket, who you took away—that we can even be here in
this courtroom, that there is even any point to prove.
Because without us, you could not have had your war.

We held your war together. Fairies, we gave you an excuse
to come home. We proved for the first time in who the fuck
knows how long that fairies don't have to be flighty and

irresponsible and heartless. We let you stay in the war from far away and then come in and be the heroes.

And the whole time you were fighting, the whole time you were gone, we gave everyone in this city sex and laughter and reminded you that there were real faces, real actual individuals behind this war. We fed your war like the gnomes fed us. And then it killed us and we killed it, because *that's what happens when you start a fucking war.*

But we did what we could.

Because nobody loves this city like we do. And we are not flighty little fairies who run away. If you keep Scrap alive, if you give us the slightest reason to stick around this city, we will stay and keep this place safe for a very, very long time.

Or you kill him.

Because why not, right? He's just one kid. He's worth the sacrifice, right?

But killing Scrap won't do it.

Whereupon two boys, one fairy and one tightroper, stand up behind the bench and cross their arms. They are wearing the same "uniform" as Miss Moloy.

Whereupon the defendant pulls at his own dirty fairy uniform in annoyance until Moloy puts a jacket

around his shoulder that matches their T-shirts, and
he smiles.

JUDGE PEONY LACHTURN: Order!

Whereupon the two boys do not come to order.

BECKAN MOLOY: Killing Scrap won't do it. You will have
to kill me. And Josha. And Piccolo. And you will have to
find Rig and Tier and kill them, too. And at some point,
everyone will *stop listening to you.* They will stop
killing. I have to believe that at some point you will
realize that you have to stop killing.

But if you don't, and you try to kill every single
creature who's stepped out of line, we will fight you
and we will win.

Because we are young and we are tough and pissed off
and we are missing *very few limbs,* and that, Your Honor,
is what we call *good race relations.*

THE COURT REQUESTS A BRIEF RECESS.

I can't remember what we did while we were waiting.
    I don't want to make something up.
    I don't want to remember.

JUDGE PEONY LACHTURN: Council, have you prepared
your verdict?

GNOME COUNCILMAN PLUG: We have, Your Honor.

JUDGE PEONY LACHTURN: What is the verdict?

GNOME COUNCILMAN PLUG: While the court was impressed by Miss Moloy's statement, for the charge of the murder of the gnome king Crate, the court finds the defendant . . . guilty.

Whereupon there is silence.

Absolute silence.

GNOME COUNCILMAN PLUG: We therefore sentence the defendant to be divided and eaten by the gnomes.

JUDGE PEONY LACHTURN: The court approves the verdict. Thank you, ladies and gentlemen of the council. Court is adjourned.

Scrap stays calm at first.

They knock the new uniform off his back and drag him out the back door, away from Beckan and Josha and Piccolo screaming his name, away from the fairies covering Beckan's mouth to make her shut up, down through a hole, back underground. There are an inexcusable number of hands on him. They jeer at him and gnaw on his ears and drag him back to his cell. And he is calm.

And then it hits, at once.

He thrashes and yells and does the one thing he can think to do; he throws himself against every wall they pass and leaves as much glitter everywhere as he can. He scrapes himself against the corners and falls to make them drag him across the ground. He leaves a trail.

And they lock him up, just him, his metal hand in that fist, and his notebook, and he throws his head back and screams.

17

BECKAN, PICCOLO, AND JOSHA sit at the cottage's kitchen table, their glitter and mud uniforms on their backs, their heads in their hands.

They are sore and heavy from crying, and their throats hurt from shouting, and they just do not know what to do.

"I'll put on some tea," Piccolo says.

Beckan and Josha nod without lifting their heads, and Josha says, again, a version of what they have been saying to each other for the past hour since the trial ended.

"We've got to get him out. We have to save him. It can't end like this. We have to get him out tonight."

And they launch into the same frustrated protests.

"We don't know where he is."

"The city is crawling with guards."

"They'll capture us and eat us, too."

"If Scrap knew we were risking our lives for him—"

"How would we even keep him safe after we got him?"

"We don't know where he is."

"The tunnels are huge, torn open, anyone could see us—"

"—not to mention how the fuck would we get down there in the first place?" But they come, again and again, to the same conclusion. *"We've got to get him out."*

Beckan stands at the window drinking tea. She looks out at the guards standing around the hill, the same ones who rounded them up and dragged them here immediately following Scrap's sentencing. She's sure in the morning there will be someone knocking, someone ready to put the three of them on trial. Obstruction of justice. Refusal to conform to race guidelines. Camaraderie. Something.

She says, "There's no way we'll be able to get to him from here," she says. "We have to get out and strike from somewhere else."

Josha looks at Piccolo. "Maybe you could string ropes?"

Piccolo says, "The highest point is the chimney. Hardly high, and I don't even know where I'd string the other end. There's nothing around. And no way the guards wouldn't see."

"What about the power lines?" Josha says.

"Yeah, that's definitely better than the chimney." Piccolo smiles at him. "But still the problem of the guards. We'd definitely be seen, and even if we got out of the city that way, we'd still have to get into the tunnels."

They keep thinking.

Beckan goes to the bathroom and draws thick stripes of war paint under her eyes and cries them off.

And draws them again.

Below them, in a final and accidental act of kindness, Leak is the one guarding Scrap.

"Not that it's really necessary," Leak says. "How the fuck wouldya escape from this one?"

Scrap gives a small laugh from the corner.

"Anything I can get you, son?" he says.

"I'm glad you're here."

"I'm not gonna eat any bit of you," Leak says. "Already decided."

Scrap leans his head against the wall. "Could you get the transcripts from my trial? I can put them in my book. Someone can glue them in for me. Maybe someone will edit them up and make them more interesting. Add commentary or something."

"What're you writing about?"

He looks at the notebook and the pen in his hand as if he has forgotten. His metal hand and real hand are bound to each other, so writing goes slowly, but he continues. "Right now what it looked like when you guys broke out of the ground and the fairies came back. How panicked it was."

"A whole book about that?"

"Oh, no. The book is about a girl."

"I'll get you those transcripts."

"You're allowed to leave me here?" Scrap says.

"Supposed to do rounds. Circulate the tunnels, make sure we don't see signs of a break-in. Fairies delegated me and me alone to stand guard while the other gnomes go back to work. Must make the most of my one self."

"Would have thought I'd be higher priority than that."

"Heh, maybe there's hope for you yet."

Scrap ducks his head.

"I'll be back," Leak says. "You going to be lonely?"

"I'll be okay."

As soon as he's gone, Scrap, naturally, throws himself against the bars, looks for weaknesses around the edges, tries to pry them with his teeth. Anything.

He looks at the only other living thing in this cage with him—the twisted, bloody remains of his arm that they've thrown in here to keep him company—and feels his stomach heave. But he pries his metal fingers just a little bit out of their fist and remembers there is maybe one thing, maybe there is a bit of something left, and between that and the words on his pages he is able to survive the loneliness for a while.

Josha says, "If we're talking about coming from outside the city, it's stupid not to think about our main resource out there."

They look at him.

"Rig and Tier," he says. "Of course. You know they'd want to help. And they know the tunnels better than you do, Becks."

"But how do we get to them?" Beckan says.

"Okay, so maybe that should be the first part of the plan."

"But what about after we find them? How are they going to help?"

Josha breathes out, slowly. "That's the second part."

Scrap keeps writing.

"Beckan," Piccolo says, carefully.

She is on her fourth cup of tea. "Yeah?"

"Can you dig? Like a gnome, I mean."

"I don't think so."

"But a little? Better than average?"

"I don't know." But she is biting her lip. "Maybe."

"She was the best in the sandbox," Josha says. "And she's so good with her hands. Her welding."

"What's the floor in your basement?" Piccolo says.

"Nothing, it's just dirt."

"Well," Piccolo says. "That's something."

Ten minutes later, they have gathered supplies. Josha brings a compass that used to be Cricket's. Beckan stuffs her welding torch and mask into her tote bag. Piccolo brings a knife.

"No," Beckan says. "Not that one."

"It's the biggest."

"And I'm going to cut my hand reaching into my bag. Bring the switchblade if you have to."

Piccolo grumbles and brings the switchblade.

In the basement, Beckan puts on her thick welding gloves and gives the dirt floor an experimental scrape. The ground gives under her as if it were sand rather than the hard-packed dirt they press down every day.

How did she not know she could do this?

"Look," she says.

They were, of course, already looking.

"You guys try," she says, but when they do, the ground stays firm and hard, which gives her confidence that a tunnel wouldn't cave and suffocate them.

So she starts to dig.

She is not full gnome, which becomes clearer and clearer as she goes on. It is difficult and rather slow. She keeps reminding herself that she does not need to go very far. But again and again, she's tempted to take a hard turn north and dig right into the gnome tunnels, to let the already-formed passageways do the work for her.

"They'll see you," Josha reminds her every time her hand drifts too far to the left. "Chances are way too good that they'll see you. Just make it to the wall."

"I know. I know."

So she digs. Josha and Piccolo stand behind her with flashlights, clearing dirt out of the way, coughing, but if they are ever scared that the tunnel will collapse and kill them here, or that Beckan will tire or hurt herself or give up, they don't say it. Both of them are slouching quite desperately to fit into a tunnel Beckan's height, but neither complains.

Her hands are bleeding under the gloves where her nails are bent back. She grits her teeth to stop herself from groaning every time she digs out another clod of dirt. "Stop and rest, Becks," one of the boys says, she doesn't even care which.

Their tunnel is too narrow for her to sit down. She leans against the wall and pants and does not know how the gnomes do it.

"How far have we gone?" she asks, when she can breathe.

Josha looks behind them. "Fifty feet, maybe?"

She moans. "How much more?"

"Thirtyish? We should have measured or something. . . ."

She takes off the gloves and looks at her hands. "Shit, look at this."

Piccolo winces.

She says, "I can't wait for my part in this to be over, let me tell you."

"Except your part is all we have planned out. . . ."

She shuts her eyes. "Shut up, Piccolo."

It's only twenty excruciating feet later that they hear footsteps above them. The heavy pounding of boots. With each step, a bit of dirt falls from the roof of their tunnel onto their heads.

"How far are we from the surface?" Beckan whispers.

"No idea," Piccolo whispers back. "Ten feet, maybe?"

"That's enough. They can't hear us." She holds her breath and waits for whistles, screaming, alarms. "I think."

They laugh nervously.

"If those are guards," Josha says, "then we must be right at the wall."

Sure enough, three feet later, Beckan's hand hits metal.

"Shit," Piccolo says, because they had been seriously hoping the walls did not extend underground.

"We were prepared for this," Beckan says. She digs around in her tote bag. "You guys back way up. Cover your eyes."

She turns around to see them ten feet behind her, hiding in each other's shirts.

Well, she thinks, despite herself. Despite everything. *That's pretty cute.*

She secures the mask over her face, throws her bag behind her, and fires up the welding torch. She feels instantly at peace like she is back at her apartment or back in the basement of the cottage, like this is just another project, another piece of metal she's melting down to build something pretty. She has been in a trance since she started digging, wrapped up in what she is doing, not thinking about Scrap, really, just about where they need to go. Now the torch is scorching and heavy in her arms and she has turned back into herself, and everything hits her all at once.

She wishes all of a sudden that they'd brought the big knife, never mind her fingers. She wishes she'd had a gun in that courtroom.

She wishes she had killed Crate and she does not, does not give a shit anymore about the moral implications about it or what it would have done to her heart because they *got her boy.*

She keeps going until she has melted the wall out of their way, then turns off the torch and sets it off and slumps against the wall.

"Good job," Josha says, softly.

There's nothing standing between them and the real world anymore.

"Just give it a minute to cool down," Beckan says.

They huddle together and listen to the footsteps above their heads.

"This is meeting halfway, isn't it?" she asks Piccolo.

"Yeah," he says. "Not so bad, is it?"

"I just burned up a part of our city."

They can't surface immediately or the guards will see them, so Beckan keeps digging for quite a while. Eventually the boys tell her she can stop, that they're far enough away, but she isn't convinced. Even worse, all these long brown ropes are in their path now, tangling with their hands, threatening to strangle her. She reaches for her torch. She does not have time for this shit.

"Becks, Becks, stop," Piccolo says. "They're roots. Trees."

"Oh."

It isn't as if Beckan has never seen a tree, or that she didn't know that they had roots, but even when she was in the cabin with Rig and Tier, she'd forgotten to think about how things grow.

"The city we were in before was full of trees," Piccolo says. "It wasn't much of a city, really. Houses and grass and big steam plants. And ropes slung between the trees." He clears his throat. "Dig up. I'll stick my head out and make sure we're safe. If you hear yelling or anything, you guys run back to the cottage and plug the hole."

"Bullshit," Josha says.

"Shh."

They lift Beckan up so she can dig into their ceiling. She stops periodically to cough up the dirt that falls down her throat.

She breaks through the surface, and Josha kisses her cheek. "You did it."

She coughs for a while and takes off the gloves.

"Are you all right?"

"Just exhausted."

"It'll be over soon."

Something will, she thinks. What if they've already eaten him?

Piccolo sticks his head up and immediately they hear him spit up a rope and throw it high above their heads. He holds out his arms for them, and they latch on and climb with him up to the tree branch where he's fastened the other end of his rope. They sit in the tree and pant. Beckan can't believe the smell—so alive it feels almost like a creature, like she could curl up and sleep and it would tell her stories. It makes her miss her cabin and her gnomes. She takes a bottle of water out of her bag and they drink like it will wash the dirt off their bodies.

"I can't even see our cottage," Beckan says.

"There, I think, look," Josha says, and they squint for a while and think that perhaps they can make it out. They can see the wall, but not the guards; maybe they have gone in for the night, or they were never on this side. Or maybe they are really that far away.

"You are a champion digger, Beckan," Piccolo says.

"You should see the full gnomes. They're incredible."

"We'll see them soon," he says.

Josha says, "How?"

"Yeah, that's a good question."

Because they are outside the city, yes, but they are all the way at the south side, where the cottage is. And the cabin where she stayed with the gnomes, judging from the route she took back to the city with Shug, is miles from the north side of the city. Far enough away that they couldn't see the—admittedly meager, nowadays—skyline. Far enough that the journey back with Shug seemed to take a lifetime.

"We should get down and start walking," Josha says, but Piccolo laughs.

"You know what's a lot faster than walking?" Piccolo says.

They look at him.

"Flying."

Beckan startles. "Flying?"

"I mean, in a manner of speaking."

"Oh."

Piccolo climbs farther up the tree. They follow, shakily, after him.

"See that tree?" Piccolo says, pointing, and they shrug and say "Yes," though he could mean any number of trees, truly, because they continue like skyscrapers as far as Beckan can see. How did she never truly process that they were here?

She looks at Piccolo and is glad the tightropers came, and she almost laughs.

"That tree," Piccolo says, and he spits out a new rope and throws it, hard. It goes so much farther than she was expecting, but Piccolo tugs a little and smiles and she knows it stuck.

"No low branches," Piccolo says. "We have a really clear path. Shit, I was made for this jailbreak."

And then he winds the other end of the rope around his wrist, grabs Josha under one arm and Beckan under the other, and jumps.

It takes everything in her not to scream.

Their rope goes taut and they stop falling down and swing, hard, toward the faraway tree, and Beckan feels the wind on her cheek and she opens her eyes. Piccolo is right. There was no way they could have walked this fast.

They are flying.

They clear the city in a matter of minutes. From there, everything rests on Beckan's direction and some extremely blind hope.

"Shit," Beckan says, when they're taking a break.

"What?" they say.

"I just wish we could have brought them a sheep."

Piccolo looks at her like she's crazy, but Josha laughs.

And shit, is that boy great when he laughs.

Before she can hug him, Piccolo does, and she can tell he's thinking the same thing.

Beckan drops to the ground in front of the cabin and runs at the front door. She is almost, but not quite, too anxious to notice that there are now three other sheep besides their lamb grazing out in front of the house.

She pounds on the door and hears immediate panic inside, shuffling, whispering.

"No," she says. "It's Beckan. It's just Beckan. It's okay."

The door swings open. Tier reaches her first, and he grabs her and spins her around. "Hey," he says. "Fed up with Ferrum so soon?"

Rig points behind Beckan as Josha and Piccolo jump to the ground. "Tier, look."

The boys shake hands with Tier and kiss Rig's cheeks. They tell each other they're looking well when it's only the gnomes who are. "Tightroper soldier washed up in the river," Tier says. "Um . . . and well . . . we saved the gun, and it looks like some sheep family came looking for our lamb after all, and Rig can hunt rabbits like . . . where's Scrap?"

"He didn't get off," Beckan says.

Rig says, "What? I thought the fairies were in charge."

So the three of them tell the gnomes everything, overlapping, cutting each other off, arguing—*no, I didn't say that the first day, that was during the closing speech; I was never going to shoot anyone; don't bring Cricket into this any more than you have to.*

Tier and Rig are holding hands, and their grip gets tighter and tighter the more the others talk, until their fingers are white.

Beckan says, "We need your help."

"Okay," Tier says.

"We need to get back into the city, through the tunnels."

"Scrap is underground?"

"Yes."

"Where?"

"We don't know."

Tier takes a deep breath. "Are you sure he's still . . ."

"We don't know."

"Okay," Rig says. "Then we're going to need to dig our own set of tunnels so we don't risk running into one that's open to the rest of the city." She starts sketching a map in the dust with her shoe. "Our tunnels go like this," she says to herself, drawing.

"This one's a little more west," Tier says.

"Are you sure?"

"Yeah."

Rig says, "If we just dig around those, with spots to check at the major intersections . . . Can you guys remember what parts of the tunnels were still covered?"

Piccolo, who they are beginning to realize has a much better visual memory than the fairies do—is that a tightroper quality, or is that just Piccolo?—crouches down by the drawing and helps the best he can. Josha helps out with scaling the map to figure out how close to the tunnels they can get, and he turns his compass around on the drawing to help work out which way they should always be facing.

Beckan waits for someone to admit that this is very nearly impossible. That they can't possibly be expected to try this mission with so little information, for a fairy boy that half of them have only met a handful of times (and for most of those handfuls was not the nicest), on a quest that gives them a very good chance of being caught and tried and killed. If the council likes using Scrap as a good example for what happens when one race attacks another, they'll adore using the five of them to show what happens when you don't toe the line.

But nobody says anything.

Nobody gives up.

It isn't as if being young and stupid has been glamorous or has worked out so well for Beckan. She probably should have left Ferrum with the rest of the fairies. She probably should have given in and turned into a flighty little stereotype, setting cities on fire and running away. Probably her goal should have been to live thousands of years with as much of her body as she could.

Rig smiles at her and holds out her hand. "Come help," she says, and Beckan kneels beside them and doesn't do much more than nod along when they talk, but they love her anyway.

She would choose this.

He sits on the floor of his cell, still writing, listening to the beat of Leak's footsteps as they come closer to him, pass by his cell, fade back away.

He is much too far underground to hear anything else, but he tells himself that the whole world is sleeping, and that Leak's footsteps are all in his head, and there are no reasons left to feel anything. There is no reason to be sad or to be scared. He is alone and ready and brave. He lowers his forehead to his knees.

He is not going to die with dignity, he realizes. He is not ready. He will never be ready.

He is going to die fighting and kicking and screaming and crying, and whether that's good or bad, it's just the reality. It's just Scrap. He doesn't know how to give up.

But he wishes he could almost as much as he wishes he could really die, that he wouldn't be torn apart and bits of him wouldn't rot inside gnome stomachs or lie discarded on the floors of the tunnels. It will get so cold.

And he will miss them, and how much he misses them will rip at every tiny scrap of him, until . . . there is no until. Forever.

He looks at his arm across the cell from him, and he makes it go up on its remaining fingers and crawl its way across the floor to him. For all these weeks, a bit of him has been with this arm, cold and lonely and scared. And it was so hard, but there were enough things happening, enough real life, for him to push it aside.

He strokes the arm with his good hand, and he feels it and his heart shudder and calm. A little.

But no one will take care of the tiny bits of him. No one will find them. There will be too many, and the little scrap fairy will finally just be too small.

Like Beckan's father, and Cricket, and everyone they write off and forget, he will blow around and get buried in the dirt and burn into ash in the fire, but he will never go away. He will be stuck in these tunnels forever.

Please let them find me, he thinks. *Please let them keep a piece of me. Don't let all of me be lost forever.*

"Just a bit of me," he whispers. "Just enough."

He will haunt this city like a ghost.

The exit Beckan and Rig and Tier took when they fled the city, freshly dug, is still open. "They think they know everything," Rig says, laughing.

They enter through there, but they don't continue down the tunnel Rig and Beckan and Tier took from the city. That's much too risky. They veer immediately east, and Piccolo and Josha are, as predicted, stunned by how quickly the gnomes dig.

The others stand back while Beckan blowtorches their way through the wall, and after that they proceed more slowly, always aware that one handful of dirt cleared in the wrong direction could have them in a tunnel with no ceiling for the whole city to see.

"What was that?" Tier says.

They freeze.

There is a sound coming toward them. It sounds like rain, at first, slow, coming down on the roof of their cottage.

"Someone's coming," he says, and they flatten, together, against the wall of the tunnel. Beckan's ears are full of the sounds of them all breathing, hard and fast, at conflicting rhythms. They are a mess of panic. Her chest hurts.

"Breathe," Piccolo whispers, and she takes a deep breath in. She hadn't realized she wasn't.

The footsteps are coming toward them. They stare at the other wall of their tunnel, where it sounds more and more each second like someone is about to break through.

But no, the footsteps turn, go back, and gradually disappear.

"We're close," Tier says. "Must be whoever is guarding Scrap. It's got to be."

"How do you know?" Beckan says.

"I . . . I don't know. I don't."

"It does sound like patrolling," Rig supplies. "The rhythm of the steps."

"We're right up against their tunnels," Josha says. "We should veer off. We're way too close."

"Hmm," Tier says, and then he pushes out the wall separating them from the gnome tunnels. Dirt rains down, and ahead of them are empty granite hallways, dim candles, and silence. Piccolo and Josha quickly click off their flashlights while whisper-cursing at Tier along with the girls.

"What the fuck are you doing?" Beckan says.

"We're not going to find Scrap by circling around. He's somewhere they can get to. He's in their tunnels."

For a while, as far as they can see, the tunnels are covered. Closed.

Besides the footsteps, safe.

"Someone else could be coming!" Beckan says.

"No. We heard the last guy, we would have heard them too." Josha says. "I don't see Scrap. We've got to go." He backs back into their tunnel.

Beckan stops him. "Josha."

She touches the blue and pink glitter smeared across the granite walls.

"He was here," she says.

And before they can think about it any longer, they take off down the hallway.

There is glitter all over the walls and the floor, and it's making Beckan's head ache. Did they rip him to pieces here? There are no bones and no blood, but how did this much glitter get off him without hurting him?

The glitter leads them down hallway after hallway, but there is no Scrap. They keep freezing, thinking they heard feet that weren't theirs, grabbing at each other's hands and whispering *what was that—*

"Maybe he's not on this level," Rig says.

"The elevator," Beckan says.

This is the point where Scrap hears feet coming, multiple feet, and he writes *THE END* in his book over and over and throws it away from him and shakes down to his bones.

Leak is here, and Scrap says, "Is it time?" He thought they'd let him wait in here for longer, make him sweat (fairy sweat tastes good; Crate told him that once).

"I think so," Leak says, and he takes his rifle off his belt.

"Wait. What are you doing?"

He points it at Scrap and slips the nose through the bars and Scrap closes his eyes and nods.

But then the nose is in his hands.

"Make it look real, kiddo."

"What?"

Leak sighs and gets to his knees so his head is level with Scrap's and with the butt of the gun. "If they're breaking you out, then you gotta make it look like I got fought off. I'm not getting in trouble over you. Come on, before I change my mind."

Scrap catches his breath and whispers, "Thank you," and slams the butt of the gun into Leak's skull.

The elevator will not take them to any other floors. It has been sealed up, locked in with steel and cement on all sides, packed in so hard on the top that the ceiling is bowing, the metal grate at its front locked and locked again. Leak is unconscious on the floor.

But they do not need to go to any other floors, because they have found Scrap.

18

"FUCK," SCRAP BREATHES. "Hi. Shit."

Beckan is already digging into her tote bag, testing the bars on the grate with her other hand.

Piccolo scales the side of the elevator to get out of the way. "Let me see your wrists, man," he tells Scrap.

Rig looks at Leak. "Is he dead?"

"Just unconscious. He's not a bad guy. Guys guys guys."

Piccolo says, "Your wrists, Scrap."

Scrap holds them up, both metal and real.

"Good. I know those knots." He talks Scrap through how to untie them and Scrap tries, very hard, but the ropes are too thick and too tight.

"Come here," Tier and Rig say together, and they bite cleanly through the ropes.

Piccolo gives a weak laugh. "Yeah, should have thought of that."

Beckan puts the mask on. "Stand back, guys. Scrap, get to the other end of the elevator."

"What can I do?" Josha says. "How can I help?"

"Josha," Scrap says, and he pushes his hand, hard, against the grate, and Josha is immediately there, his hand pushing back so hard that their palms touch through the cage.

"It's okay," Josha whispers. "It's okay."

On the other side of the elevator, Beckan melts the cage like it's nothing. "Wait," she tells Scrap, "let it cool," but of course he doesn't, he's out of there like he was thrown, and he's touching all of them at once and their hands are all over him, *Ican'tbelieveitareyouokay-didtheyhurtyou?*

"We're going," Tier says. "Now."

They start to take off, but Beckan stops them. "Scrap," she says. "Do you want your arm?"

He looks at it, lying there in the cage. "No."

"Are you sure?"

"It doesn't matter. I don't need it." He is hard and sure. "It's not important." His metal hand is still in that fist.

Josha says, "But what about—" and above their heads there is a rush of movement, and they don't know if it is for them, and they don't know if the vibrating is in their heads or in the tunnels, but Rig orders them to run and they are running, through tunnels they have made and tunnels they have not, and they're stopping so short they're falling when they see tunnels that are open to the ground above. They are grabbing on to each other and they hit one of their new, fragile tunnels, and dirt collapses on top of them and they gasp and choke and duck as a rock falls. And when they look up and count there is one missing. And they do not know how long he has been gone and they do not know where they lost him.

"No no no," Beckan whispers. It is so dark. "No."

"*Josha!*" It's ripped through Scrap's throat, ugly and raw, painful. "*JOSHA!*"

Tier says, "Scrap, hey, we'll find him, we have to be quiet—"

"*JOSHA!*"

Scrap is small and scared no more. Scrap is big, angry, throwing himself against the tunnel walls, looking for a weaker part, looking for anything, anything, that will give and fold and show him where he left the last one of his pack he'd ever thought he needed to worry about.

You drove him so crazy, you stole Cricket, you disobeyed and you rolled your eyes and you made Beckan smile more than he could sometimes and you are his family and you are the one he never thought he needed to think about, you are the one who made him turn cold and hard—

Beckan is quiet, crying, whispering, "Josha Josha Josha okay okay."

"*Josha!*" Scrap yells.

And then there's a rush of air from fifty feet away, and the waterfall rumble of dirt, and coughing, and their fucking fairy. Beckan sprints to him and wraps herself around him, and he wheezes and hugs her and says, "Hey, I'm fine. Fuck, you guys took off. . . ."

Scrap hits him and pulls him down roughly into his neck. "You okay?"

"Mmmhmm. You?"

"The fuck was that, huh?"

"You forgot this." Josha untucks something from underneath his arm.

Scrap's notebook.

Scrap stares at it, swallows, lets Beckan take it and stuff it into her bag. Then he tugs on Josha's sleeve, just once, and pries back the fingers on his metal hand.

Inside is one speck of glitter.

"It was on my arm," he says, and holds it into the light.

It's green. Bright yellow-green, like an insect.

They all look at Josha.

Josha swallows and doesn't speak for a while. When he does, his voice sounds so much more normal than they expect. "It's his."

"It has to be," Scrap says.

Josha nods.

It just has to be.

Piccolo opens the locket around Josha's neck, and Scrap, after just a second of hesitation, gives him the piece of glitter. Piccolo presses it into the inside of the locket, snaps it closed, and then holds it against Josha's chest.

Josha can only feel so happy. He is exhausted, used up. He can only feel so many things anymore.

And looking down at that locket, he feels a few possibilities come back. Like relief. Like love.

Desperately, he can hear Cricket say. *Right, kid?*

"Desperately," Josha whispers.

Right at the exit, as Tier starts to hoist them up, Beckan says, "Just a second."

Piccolo groans. "Seriously, we're almost out of here."

"You guys go ahead," she says, but of course they don't.

She takes Scrap's wrist and pulls back, just a little, only a few feet from the others.

He is watching her.

She says, "I can't believe you kept your hand curled around one piece of glitter this whole time."

He doesn't look away. She feels him, his wrist in her hand, his face close to hers, so warm. He is so warm.

"I can't believe you said no to the gnomes," she says.

So warm.

"I can't believe you left your book behind."

"I . . . was thinking about getting out."

"You chose getting out." She's smiling. "You chose being real."

He rests his forehead against hers. "Giving me too much credit, Becks."

"Never."

He is smiling too.

"You never hardened up, did you?" she says.

"No."

"You fucking idiot," she says, and then she pushes him against the wall and kisses the breath right out of him.

At this point, I need to pause and say how fucking ridiculous it is that I managed to write an entire book without needing to stop and write what I am about to write.

Which is that Beckan is the most incredible anything I have ever met.

And I can't believe I was writing this fucking book when I could have been kissing this girl, touching this girl, grabbing this girl when she's trying to brush the sheep and throwing her down and tickling this girl, or feeling this girl slide into bed next to me when we'd agreed to try to take it slow, to rest, we have plenty of time, and do things to me that this whore has never dreamed of.

There isn't anyone in the world who can make me laugh this much or make me this fucking angry, and every time I look at this girl, no matter what she's doing, I think I could do nothing but watch her do that—wash her hair, sweep the floor, work in her garden, laugh—for the rest of my life, for forever, and never need a thing more.

There is no until.

And we're in bed together, and she is lying on top of me, her arms over my neck, her hands in my hair, and she is sweet and dark like wine . . . shit, how do you write about this stuff? There aren't words. There is blood and glitter and the feel of her cheek cupped in my hand while she kisses my temple, and her hands on my shoulders when she leads me back to bed when I've been sleepwalking. I don't do the dishes when I sleepwalk anymore. I dream I'm dancing with her.

And then she leads me back to bed and kisses me from my stomach to my neck, and I dance down to my last speck of glitter. Back in those tunnels, my arm dances.

This girl. This girl, this girl. And I wake up with a cold, sticky mouth, breathing hard, terrified that something could happen to her, and then I think of Josha and Cricket and all these things that I've done and fuck, if this girl could fix everything, if the amount of life in this girl could somehow bring all of me back, but I can still hear the bombs in that city, I can still feel Crate's throat under my thumb and that cold cell where my arm is curled up and sometimes I cannot make it dance, sometimes it is just too scared, and I can still hear my cousin's voice shouting my name when I run too far ahead and he is worried about me.

So they settle in. Piccolo balances on tree branches. Rig hunts rabbits. Tier tends the sheep. Josha cooks. Beckan starts a garden. Scrap writes.

Beckan and Scrap continue to be unable to keep their hands off each other.

The others laugh because it seems like they are everywhere, that no matter where they go, Beckan and Scrap are there, occasionally wearing some clothing, usually not, always kissing so hard it looks like it must hurt, pushing each other into things, grabbing at each other's ears and hair.

They kiss under the kitchen table while the others are eating. They lie on the stairs and the others have to nudge them with their feet as they go by. They roll in the grass and lie forehead to forehead, nose to nose, and whether or not they can kiss like that is so much less important than that they be touching each other with as much of themselves as possible. Beckan misses Scrap's arm just because it is a part of him that she does not get to hold. "It's fine," he tells her, whenever she asks. "It's keeping watch of the city."

"Arms don't have eyes."

"It's keeping hold."

If I still had that writing book, here I would put an excerpt about the importance of endings! The excerpt would talk about symbolic and narrative symmetry and the importance of crafting an ending that reaches emotional satisfaction for all of its characters! And it would not, absolutely would not, leave room for a sequel. Because stories need to have endings, just like lives! Oh, wait!

—Scrap, being a dick

(Fuck off, Beckan!)

But one night he gives up, spreads his book out on the kitchen table, and begs them to help him. They sit on each other's laps and roll on the floor and tell stories of what actually happened when Scrap wasn't there, embellishing in all the right places, laughing at him while he tears out page after page of stuff that is too far from the truth to make it into his book. (*"I never hated you, Scrap, take out the parts where we hated you."* Sometimes he listens. Sometimes he believes it.)

Beckan gives the court transcripts more pizzazz, and Josha and Tier add illustrations when Scrap indicated them and sometimes when he didn't. Rig refuses to make herself sound more like Rig.

Scrap combs over Beckan's scenes with Piccolo. "I'm keeping this part," he says.

Beckan says, "I never slept with Piccolo. That's kind of an enormous part of your book."

"Poetic license. It works. Everyone loves a good love triangle."

Piccolo says, "Yeah, but it's disgusting."

She hits him.

"It makes sense!" Scrap whines. "What else were you in it for?"

"Um, freedom?" Piccolo says, and very carefully does not look at anyone.

Josha twists the locket around his neck and is mostly quiet, nowadays.

And so all should be mostly well. Tier and Rig are happy, hunting together, holding hands at dinner, having a much more discreet and mature relationship than Scrap and Beckan. Piccolo is so happy to have a family that he'll impulsively stop what he's doing and beam at them. Scrap and Beckan, clothes half on, hands all over each other, lips on each other's lips, should be perfect.

They are content, they are sated, they are so horribly in love, and Beckan is happy, but Scrap is not, and she doesn't know if there is anything she can do.

He sits at the top of the stairs and watches Josha pace, watches Josha's hand on the locket.

"Stop chasing," she tells him, when he is still staying up to all hours, tearing through his book and finding more reasons why Cricket should not have died. "Stop chasing and come to bed."

But he can't. She wakes up in the middle of the night and he is sitting up in bed, his head in his hands, his mouth moving to a million conversations. He relives everything again and again and pretends that there could be a reality where he didn't kill Crate, or where he killed Crate before he killed Cricket. Or he fixed Josha. Or he never hurt anyone. Or he never started writing this book.

"Stop chasing," Beckan says. "Stop writing."

But he can't.

Then one day he starts downstairs early after a night of barely sleeping, and he sees Josha and Piccolo making breakfast. Something causes him to stop and sit on the top step instead of going down.

Josha and Piccolo are next to each other at the stove, not speaking. And Piccolo moves his hand, just to grab a fork, Scrap thinks, but instead his hand stops at Josha's wrist, slowly turns it, and presses itself against Josha's palm.

Josha doesn't look at him, just opens his fingers and slips them between Piccolo's.

And Josha's shoulders relax—*Josha relaxes*—and Scrap feels something inside him give and a hundred things pour out of him with his next exhale, and the next thing he knows he is back in bed with Beckan, forcing her awake, whispering in her ear that there are some things that he has not ruined, that Josha is not a lost cause, that there is still hope, there is still hope, there is still hope. It's all things she already knew, but it feels amazing to be able to tell her them, to be, for once, the one to reassure her. He believes. He truly believes that his pack will survive.

He realizes, for the first time, that it already has.

But it isn't his nature not to fret, and some evenings he sits on the roof with Piccolo and faces the city and watches the flashes he is sure are bombs.

"Idiots," Piccolo mumbles. "Fucking idiots."

"I hope your guys got out."

Piccolo raises an eyebrow and says, "My guys *did* get out."

"I meant the tightropers."

"Eh." Piccolo lies back. "Fuck 'em. How's that book coming along?"

"Almost done."

"About time."

"Scrap!" It's Beckan. Happy. He climbs down from the roof and meets her behind the house. "Look," she says, and tugs him over to the flat rock Josha hauled up for her a few weeks ago. A makeshift workbench. "Look what I made."

It's a mess of twigs and leaves; there isn't much metal to work with now. They are learning to enjoy it, but the truth is that they are still children of iron and stone and it will take many, many more years of soft greens and browns to change that.

Beckan holds it up. It's a long piece of bark with sinew straps splayed in all directions and slit after slit cut into the wood. It has joints that bend and wooden fingers that fan out along the edges.

He looks at her.

"It's a wing," she says.

"For flying?"

"Mmhm. For you. You said maybe fairies did have wings."

"A long time ago."

"And maybe again."

"Becks."

"But I only have one."

"Beckan," he says. So softly.

"I figure you get the first one, since you don't have an arm. Then the next one's for me. Then Josha, Piccolo, Rig, and Tier, whatever the order, it doesn't matter, and then I'll make second ones for all of us and then we'll see what happens."

"Will they work?"

"I hope so. Hard to tell with just one." She touches it. "Can you imagine, though? If I made them for all of us? We could chase each other, play. And then we could fly back to the city and watch it from so high up. No one could stop us. We'd never have to come down."

"Someday."

"Yeah. We have a very long time."

He leans his head against hers. They are so perfectly the right size, his lips right against her cheek, and she looks up at him with a smile that could burn down the whole fucking forest.

He kisses her, softly.

They have plenty of time.

THE END

Beckan closes the book. "What a sappy fucking ending."

"Amazing, thank you. We can put that on the front of the book, like a quote. *My boyfriend wrote this book and I don't even like the ending.* And you realize I'm going to have to write this part down now. Now my shitty book has an epilogue. Do you know how much I hate epilogues?"

She laughs and sits down on my lap. "I liked it. I still don't think you should have ripped all those pages out of Tier's books. That's kind of destructive. You should also put it in order. And take out all the parts where you go a little crazy and start talking to me and stuff. And all the times you made fun of my nose."

"Can you blame me? Look at that thing."

"I like your book," she says. "I like the parts that I'm in." And she laughs because she thinks she is very funny, and I laugh because fuck am I in love with this girl.

But then I look at the book and stop.

"What?" she says.

"I don't know what to write next."

"Scrap," she says.

It takes me too long to look up.

She holds out her hand. "Come to bed."

I do. We curl up and look out the window. We face the city, and I see the lights exploding upward and into the sky.

Our city.

Another bomb goes off. "Like fireworks," Beckan says.

"Yeah."

We stay still for a very long time. She brings my fingers to her lips and kisses them.

It will never be okay that we left.

But it just has to be okay that we're alive.